The Vicious Cycle

by Timmy Ray

DORRANCE
PUBLISHING CO
EST. 1920
PITTSBURGH, PENNSYLVANIA 15238

Dorrance Publishing Co
585 Alpha Drive
Suite 103
Pittsburgh, PA 15238
Visit our website at *www.dorrancebookstore.com*

ISBN: 978-1-6461-0978-4
eISBN: 978-1-6461-0267-9

Contents

Introduction

Sheila Jones was born in Cincinnati, Ohio, to Ronald and Josephine Jones. They were a loving family of three. They lived in a decent neighborhood and gave Sheila the best of everything. She was an only child so she had all of their attention.

The story starts with Sheila about to graduate from high school. She had been accepted to a prestigious college in the South. This was where life was going to start to change for her. It may seem that it was changing for the worse, but it was actually going to make her the woman she was supposed to be.

Sheila was a virgin all the way through high school. On graduation night, she decided to try having sex. It wasn't what she expected so it kind of turned her off. This didn't make her boyfriend too happy; in fact she made him feel ashamed. When he tried to make advances toward her again, she denied him. His reaction would cause permanent damage to their relationship.

Sheila went off to college and met a new set of friends. This was going to forge camaraderie like no other she had before. The girls were going to become as thick as thieves. When tragedy strikes, it would pull them closer together.

College life would give Sheila more of an education than she bargained for. She would learn some real life lessons, real hard and real fast. She would learn about different types of sexual relationships. She would learn about men the hard way. She would learn about drugs. She would learn that if a deal sounded too good to be true, then it probably was.

Sheila graduated from college and moved back to Cincinnati. She had already been hired at Procter & Gamble. She got a decent position with them and things were looking good. She got her a boyfriend, whom she liked pretty well, but things were going to come up that transpired from college to make her question her sexuality.

Her new boyfriend was the son of a preacher. He was a little tamer than Sheila, but yet they were a good match. She was teaching him some things and he was trying to teach her some things. He wasn't into everything that she was into but he loved her anyway. Sheila was very resistant to what he was trying to teach her, this ultimately would almost cost her life.

This story is very graphic in nature. I am sure that someone somewhere has experienced variations of this story. This story is meant to enlighten and inspire. It will show you that no matter what you've done or where you've been, there is still hope. It will show you that an education doesn't make you any better than anyone else. There are situations in life that all the education in the world won't prepare you for. I hope you enjoy it.

Chapter One

The Beginning

Sheila Jones was a very pretty young lady. At the age of 16, she was 5 feet 7 inches tall. She weighed about 140 pounds. She was well put together. All the guys in school were after her. She not only had looks, she was intelligent also, I mean she had real star power.

Josephine worked part time at a department store basically so she could have something to do. It was not like they really needed the money. They lived a pretty simple lifestyle. It was easy to see where Sheila got her looks. Josephine was fine. The only difference was she was brown skinned. She was also tall and lean, real model material. In fact, she did a little modeling for the department store.

Now they also had a good Christian home. They believed in God and went to church occasionally. They tried to follow some spiritual principals, but like many of us they fell short sometimes. Sheila had a pretty close-knit family. Her parents drank a little on the weekends and at family gatherings. They were by no means alcoholics; however, they would go out on weekends and have a couple drinks, and come home.

Sheila had most of the same traits, except she didn't drink at this point. She didn't party like most girls her age. Along with her good looks, she was also very intelligent. She was on the honor roll, a cheerleader, ran track and was also in various school clubs. She was a pretty popular girl. Like most girls, she had a boyfriend while in high school and like most of the pretty girls, they looked for the athletes and the most popular cool guys in school. Sometimes the most popular, best-looking guys in school brought nothing but trouble.

Sheila managed to stay a virgin all the way through high school. On graduation night, Sheila and her boyfriend got a hotel room with some of their friends to celebrate their graduation. They bought some alcohol and some weed and they were passing it around. Troy, Sheila's boyfriend, knew she didn't smoke or drink. He planned to have big fun with her.

Everyone was sitting around partying. When the party was over, Troy asked Sheila if she would stay with him.

Sheila said, "Yes."

They said goodbye to everyone and chilled. Everyone was gone now and Troy made his move, he tried to kiss her. Sheila pushed him away in a playful sort of way. They started wrestling around and then started kissing and petting on each other. It wasn't long before they were laid back on the bed grinding on each other. Troy asked, "Do you want to?" Sheila's mouth said yes, but deep inside she was scared. This was going to be her first time.

They got naked and under the cover. Troy got on top of her and tried to put his penis inside of her. It was very tight and a little painful for her. Troy finally got it inside and in about three or four strokes it was over. This left Sheila very disappointed. Sheila asked Troy, "Is this all there is to it?" Troy felt embarrassed. Sheila and Troy never had sex again.

Sheila was accepted into Spelman. It was really a blessing that she didn't get pregnant when she and Troy had sex. That could have really put a damper on things. The time came for Sheila to leave for college and Troy took her out for a goodbye dinner. They sat and talked while they were eating. They talked about how they were going to always stay boyfriend and girlfriend and always keep in touch. He told her how much he was going to miss her. Sheila told him she was going to miss him also.

Troy took Sheila to the drive-in after dinner. They were watching a movie and then Troy tried to put the moves on her. Sheila told him no. Troy tried again and again, but Sheila resisted. Troy begged and begged.

Sheila still said no. This made Troy pretty upset. After the movie, Troy took Sheila home and let her out and left without even a kiss goodbye.

The next day Sheila was going to be leaving to go to school. Troy called to see if he could come by before she left for school. Sheila told him she didn't want to see him.

Sheila said, "You took me to the drive-in and because I wouldn't have sex with you, you got an attitude. You brought me home and put me out and didn't even give me a kiss goodbye. All you want me for is sex. Maybe I will see you at Christmas break if you want to."

Off Sheila went to school. She was so excited, getting away from home and all. Going to start adulthood and living on her own was so exciting to her. On the way to school, her mom and dad gave her a good long speech. You know, the one the children never listen to. You know, "Don't be down there partying and chasing boys." Sheila assured them that that was the farthest thing from her mind. Sheila had always been very responsible so they had no reason not to trust her. Especially after that experience with Troy.

They finally made it to school. As she was unloading her stuff, she was starting to get a feeling of freedom already. This was going to be her new home for at least the next four years. She was glad she chose an all-girls' school. In the back of her mind she was still upset with Troy.As they unloaded the car and carried her things to her dorm, they noticed the door was open. Her mom and dad said to her, "Your roommate must be here." Sure enough, she was.

Sheila introduced herself. "My name is Sheila Jones," as she extended her hand.

Her roommate said, "My name is Tonya Earlham."

Sheila said, "These are my parents, Ronald and Josephine Jones."

Tonya said, "It's nice to meet you."

Sheila's mom asked Tonya where her parents were. She said they had already gone. They had gotten there around nine A.M. They went to get a hotel.

"They are coming back later," Tonya said. "They have been driving all night."

Sheila's dad asked where they were from.

Tonya said, "Dallas, Texas."

Sheila's dad said, "That is a long drive."

Tonya said, "Yes, sir, it is."

Sheila's dad said, "You have manners, I like that."

Sheila kind of snickered because of Tonya's accent.

Sheila's dad asked Tonya what her parents did for a living. Tonya told him her dad was lawyer and her mom was a professor at Texas Tech. Sheila's mom asked Tonya why she didn't go to Texas Tech. Tonya said she wanted to get as far away from Dallas as she could. Spelman offered her a full ride so she took it.

Tonya said, "There are a lot of benefits in going to a black all-girls' school with such prestige."

Sheila's mom said, "Are you sure it had nothing to do with Morehouse being near here?"

Tonya asked, "What is Morehouse?"

Sheila's mom said, "Oh."

Sheila's mom and dad helped her finish unpacking her stuff. They all sat and talked for a bit, then Sheila's parents left.

Sheila and Tonya started getting their room arranged and getting to know each other. Tonya asked Sheila where she was from. Sheila told her Cincinnati.

Tonya asked, "What is Cincinnati like?"

Sheila told her, "It is nice sometimes. Sometimes it can get kind of rough."

Tonya asked Sheila where she went to school. Sheila told her she went to Hughes High School. Tonya asked Sheila if she had a boyfriend.

Sheila said, "I did. What about you?"

Tonya told her, "Yeah, but I don't know how long it's going to last. I don't trust him."

Sheila told Tonya about Troy. She told her they had sex and she didn't like it. Sheila said it hurt and it was over almost before it got started. Sheila said when she didn't want to do it anymore he got mad.

Tonya said, "Well, you know how boys are."

Sheila asked Tonya if she had the same experience.

Tonya said jokingly, "I don't even know Troy."

They both laughed.

Sheila said, "No, really, how was your first time?"

Tonya said, "I haven't had my first time yet."

Sheila said, "You haven't?"

Tonya said, "Nope."

Sheila jokingly called her Patty Le'pure.

Tonya said, "Ha-ha, very funny. I'm hungry, what about you?"

Sheila said, "I guess I could eat something, but where will we get something, and better yet, how will we get there?"

"You know, you're right, let's go up in the lobby and see what's happening." They got to the lobby. There they met some other girls. Their names were Sharon, Lisa, and Rene. This was their first day also. Sheila and Tonya told them they were going to get something to eat. They said that they were about to do the same thing. Neither one of them had a vehicle so they decided to order pizza and have it delivered.

Sheila and Tonya were both going to be economics majors. Sharon was going into fashion design. Lisa was going to be a doctor. Rene didn't know what she wanted to do yet. She just wanted to go to school. They discovered they were taking some of the same core classes. As they sat and talked, the pizza came. They ate and made some more small talk and went to bed.

The next day class started. Sheila, Tonya and Rene were in the same English class. English was a strong subject for Sheila. Sheila had always gotten good grades in English in high school. Even in grade school, she won all kinds of spelling bees.

Later on in the day they ran into Sharon and Lisa in algebra class. The good thing about this relationship was each of them had a different strong suit. This would allow them to draw off of each other. As we know with life the good always comes with some bad.

They all drank a little. Lisa and Sharon were real party girls. They added weed to the equation. Sheila and Tonya had never really partied a lot. Rene was the wild one. She took things to another level. Along with everything else, she was a little promiscuous. Rene was looking for men from day one. The other girls with the exception of Tonya had their experiences, but they could take it or leave it.

Time went by as it does. One weekend word got around about a party at a Morehouse frat house. They had been studying hard for a few weeks so they decided to let their hair down a little bit. It was Friday afternoon. By now these girls were as thick as thieves. You hardly saw one without the others being somewhere around.

They met at Sheila and Tonya's room. They were doing each other's hair and trying on clothes to get ready for the party. They were so excited because this was their first frat party. Well, at least for four of them. Rene had already been introduced to the college party life.

Rene proceeded to tell them what to expect. She told them that it would be plenty of alcohol and weed, and maybe even a little powder.

Rene said, "As for me, I am horny as hell. I need to find me something to fuck." Then she pulled out a joint and lit it.

The other girls were shocked

She passed the joint and said, "Girl, I am serious. I am going to find one of those Morehouse boys and fuck his brains out."

The girls died laughing.

Tonya said, "Girl, you are a hoe."

Rene said, "I'm a good one, though. Keep it real, girls, keep it real."

The girls get to the party. The music was bang'n and there was the smell of weed in the air. There were people everywhere.

Rene said, "I am in heaven."

Sheila said, “Um, um, um. You need to slow down, missy.”

The girls made their way to the bar. As they were ordering drinks, they were checking out the scene.

Tonya said, “Sheila, look at that guy over there. Damn, he is fine.”

Sheila said, “Slow down, Patty.”

Tonya said, “He is fine.”

Sharon said, “He sure is.”

Lisa said, “It’s a lot of fine ones in here.”

Rene said, “Yeah, and I am going to fuck one.”

Sheila said, “Come on, girl. You sit your ass right over here so we can watch you.”

The girls found a seat over by a window. As they sipped their drinks and talked, one of the guys brought over a couple joints.

He said, “Do you ladies partake?”

Sharon said, “Sure.”

He looked at Sheila and asked her if she would like to dance.

She said, “Not right now.” She wasn’t really interested at all.

Lisa said, “I will dance with you.”

As the girls sat and talked, they were smoking the joints and drinking their drinks.

Rene set her eyes on her victim. She went up to him and said, “Will you dance with me?” Now Rene wasn’t a real beauty queen, but she had this sexiness about her that hardly any man could resist.

So Rene and this guy started dancing. Rene asked him what his name was.

“Mark,” he replied, “and yours?”

She said, “My name is Rene. It’s nice to meet you.”

Mark said, “Likewise.” Mark said, “So what brings you to the party?”

Rene told him they had heard about it at school.

Mark asked, “Where do you go to school?”

Rene said, “Spelman.”

Mark said, “Oh, you go to Spelman.”

She said, "Yeah, I'm right in your neighborhood."

He said, "What are you studying?"

Rene said, "Right now I am studying you."

Mark said, "Really?"

Rene said, "Yeah, really."

Sheila, Tonya, Sharon and Lisa were sitting on the couch watching Rene.

Sheila said, "Look, they must be talking about something serious. They can't take their eyes off each other."

As they were talking, various guys came up and asked them to dance. At one time or another they were all up dancing. Rene and Mark stayed with each other. They were having a great time. Rene was working her plan. They were laughing, talking, and drinking they even smoked a joint or two. Then Mark asked her if she did blow.

Rene said, "Sure."

Mark said, "Come on," and they left the floor and went upstairs.

Once they got upstairs there was a room that was only privy to the upperclassmen.

Mark said, "Isn't this better?"

Rene said, "Yes, I like this a lot." Her plan was starting to come together. That was what she wanted all the time.

They sat down on a couch. Mark pulled out his stash and made a few lines on the table. They each did a line.

Rene said, "This is some good shit. I haven't had any of this in a while."

Mark said, "I only keep the best."

They were sniffing away.

Rene said, "I am feeling real tingly." She slid over closer to him and started kissing him. She put her hand on his thigh and started rubbing it until she worked her way up to his swollen penis. Then she whispered in his ear, "Now I want to give you something."

Back downstairs at the main party, things were starting to really jump. While Mark and Rene were having their own party, people were up dancing everywhere. The other girls had forgotten all about Rene.

It was about one o'clock. Sheila asked Lisa if she had she seen Rene. Lisa said she hadn't. They went and asked Sharon and Tonya. No one had seen her.

They said, "We are about ready to go."

About that time Rene and Mark were coming down the stairs.

Sharon said, "There she is."

Sheila said, "What a hoe," and then they laughed.

Rene came over to where they were. Sheila, Sharon, and Lisa were standing there staring at Rene.

She said, "What, what," with a guilty look on her face.

They laughed and said, "You're a hoe."

Rene laughed and said, "The best." She said, "You girls ready to go?"

They said, "Yeah, let's get Tonya."

Tonya was hugged up in the corner with some guy named Charles.

They went over and said, "We're ready to go."

Tonya said, "Okay."

As they were leaving, Mark ran up behind them and asked Rene if there was a way he could get in touch with her. He said he wanted to see her again.

Rene said, "I don't think so."

Mark stood there with a look on his face like his whole world was crushed.

Tonya said, "Damn, girl, what did you do to him?"

Rene said, "You know."

They all started laughing as they walked across the yard.

Sheila said, "Damn, girl, you are bad."

Rene said, "I told you, the best."

As the girls walked back to campus, they were laughing and talking about their night.

Sheila said, "I have never drunk that much in one night."

Tonya said, "Yeah, I'm kind of tipsy too."

Sharon started singing, "Everybody in the club getting tipsy."

They all started laughing. They were high as hell.

Lisa said, “I have never seen so many dogs in one place. They thought they were going to get some ass.”

Rene said, “One did. I had him screaming like a bitch.”

They were laughing their ass off. They said, “You are crazy, girl.” They got to the dorm and everyone went their separate ways.

Sheila and Tonya said, “We will see you all tomorrow.”

Sheila and Tonya got to their room and got ready for bed.

About an hour and a half later, Sheila was awakened to moans coming from Tonya’s bed.

Sheila said to herself, “I know she is not over there masturbating.”

She laid there and listened for a while. The moans and the rustling of the sheets got to be a little much. Sheila covered her head with her pillow and turned her back, trying to ignore it. Soon she was consumed by an overwhelming urge to touch herself. The next thing you know Sheila was masturbating also. Sheila said to herself, “Damn, this feels good.” As Tonya’s breathing got heavier so did Sheila’s. Then, almost simultaneously they both got off. After that a hush fell over the room and they both fell into a deep sleep.

Chapter Two

The Encounter

Christmas break was quickly approaching and the girls were studying as hard as ever. They were all making pretty good grades, but as usual Sheila was the star of the bunch. She was carrying a 4.0 while all the other girls were carrying a little higher than a 3.5 and 3.8. It seemed like Sheila was a natural. It seemed like studying and taking tests were easy for her. She didn't mind helping the other girls. That was mainly the reason they all had such good grades.

One day, as they were studying together as they often did, Rene said, "We should all get an apartment together."

Sharon said, "How are we going to do that, none of us have a job."

Rene said, "We just have to get one."

Lisa said, "How are you going to get a job? You can't stay off your back long enough to work."

Rene gave her the finger and said, "Hater."

Tonya said, "That's actually not a bad idea. I mean, we are always together anyway."

Sheila said, "That would be something we would have to work on when we get back from Christmas break."

All the other girls were in agreement.

Midterms came and went. It was now time for finals. The girls were studying very hard, it was like they were in competition to see who could get the best grades.

Sheila asked Tonya, "Do you see the way Sharon and Lisa act around each other?"

Tonya said, "Yeah, but I wasn't going to say anything."

Sheila said, "I think they may have a little something going on."

Tonya said, "Could be, but that's not our business. Besides, don't knock it until you have tried it."

Sheila said, "Have you?"

Tonya said, "No, but I have thought about it."

Sheila said, "Me too, but it was just a passing thought."

Tonya said, "I often fantasize about it."

Sheila said, "Who do you fantasize about?"

Tonya said, "That's a little much, don't you think?"

They all took their finals and felt pretty good about their success. They were all in Lisa and Sharon's room drinking and smoking weed.

Rene said, "The Morehouse boys are having another party."

Sharon said, "What's new, they are always having a party. It's a wonder they get any work done."

Rene said, "Oh, yeah, they get work done."

Lisa said, "Hoe."

Rene said, "I'm a good one."

Sheila said, "I know, the best."

Tonya said, "Let's do something special."

The other girls said, "Like what?"

Tonya said, "Let's go somewhere else and go out."

Sheila said, "That sounds good but how will we get there?"

Rene said, "I got that covered."

Lisa said, "We ain't fucking for a ride."

Rene said, "Why you always tripp'n? Don't nobody want your tight ass anyway."

Lisa said, "That's exactly why they want it."

There was such excitement in the air. They were all so giddy they hugged and left to get dressed.

Sheila and Tonya went to their room to get dressed. Tonya took her shower first. While Sheila was getting undressed, it was hard for

Tonya to keep her eyes off of her. Sheila didn't think anything about it because they often held conversations while they were getting dressed. Besides, they saw each other naked all the time. When Sheila got out of the shower Tonya was almost dressed. As Sheila was getting dressed they were talking about the past semester and how proud they were of each other. Sheila asked Tonya to help her with her hair. They were dressed now and Tonya began to help her with her hair. She told Sheila how glad she was that they met and how glad she was that they were roommates.

Sheila said, "I like you a lot also. I don't believe I could have had a better roommate."

They hugged and Tonya kissed Sheila right on the mouth and held it for a second.

Sheila realized what was going on and pushed back. She said, "What was that?"

Tonya said, "Girl, I don't know. I'm sorry. I was a little excited."

Sheila said, "Don't get too excited."

Rene came to the door. When Sheila opened the door, Rene said, "What you girls in here do'n, eat'n each other's pussy?"

Tonya nervously laughed and said, "Girl, you are so crazy."

Sheila asked who was taking them to the club.

Rene said, "I have a friend that can get us in Club 112."

Tonya said, "Really? I am impressed."

Sheila asked, "Does he have a vehicle big enough for all of us?"

Rene said, "Do you think a Navigator is big enough?"

Sheila said, "I think that will do." Sheila asked what his name was.

Rene said, "Sucker, I mean Tony."

Sheila said, "You better be careful always trying to play people. You're gonna get played one day and it's not going to be nice."

Rene said, "I will cross that bridge when I get there."

Tony showed up with one of his boys named Ralph. They all introduced themselves and off to the club they went.

It was a nice little ride, so Tony said, "You girls ready to get this party started?"

Tonya said, "What did you have in mind?"

Tony said, "A little Cîroc and hydro."

Tonya said, "You don't have any hydro."

Tony said, "Sure I do."

Sheila said, "Then blaze it up, my nigga."

The girls looked at Sheila and got weak laughing. They wondered where that came from. They didn't know she was still reeling from the shock of Tonya kissing her.

They got to the club and they were already high as hell. They smoked three joints and bashed a fifth of Cîroc. They got straightened out a little and headed to the door. The doorman was turning people away.

Sharon said to the other girls, "How are we going to get in here?"

Rene said, "Just watch."

As they got to the door the doorman said, "What's up, T, what up, Rene? How many?"

Tony said six and they cruised right on in.

Once inside, Lisa said, "Damn, Rene, you are the shit."

Rene said, "I told you, the best."

They found a table and the waitress came and they ordered some drinks. Ralph found his way to a seat next to Sheila. He said, "You sure smell nice."

Sheila said, "Are you sure it's not the hydro?"

He said, "Maybe, but the scent of your perfume makes it that much better. What is that you're wearing?"

Sheila said, "I'm not telling you so you can buy it for your other women."

Ralph said, "What makes you think I have other women?"

Sheila said, "Are you gay?"

Ralph said, "Do I look gay?"

Sheila said, "This is Atlanta, what does a gay man look like?"

Ralph said, "You have a point, but no, I'm not gay. In fact, I am seeing one young lady but it's not that serious."

Sheila said, "Is that how she feels?"

Ralph said, "I am sure she would like it to be more. But then what woman wouldn't want one of the most prominent young lawyers in Atlanta?"

Sheila said, "Oh."

As they were sitting having their drinks and talking, Jay-Z and his crew walked in and Sharon almost lost it.

Lisa said, "Girl, you need to quit tripp'n."

Sharon said, "I am going to get his autograph."

Before they could say anything Sharon jumped up and almost started running toward Jay-Z but that didn't last long. His bodyguards all but tackled her and told her not tonight.

She came back to the seat and said, "Fuck him. He ain't shit anyway."

Everyone just laughed at her and said, "We tried to tell you."

Sharon said, "Fuck you all too."

They said, "Poor baby."

They all got up and started dancing, they were having the time of their lives. Sheila was kind of preoccupied with how Tonya kissed her. This really tripped her out, but she got past it and had a good time anyway. It helped having Ralph in her ear, though.

A slow song came on and Tony and Rene get up to dance. Ralph asked Sheila if she would like to dance, she said sure. They got up to dance and Ralph took her in his arms. They were dancing and talking. As Ralph pulled her in tighter she started to feel more relaxed.

All of a sudden, she felt a bulge in his pants and said, "Settle down, big boy."

Ralph said, "It's hard," and paused, then he said to settle down.

They looked at each other and laughed.

She said, "You are something else."

He said, "I know, don't you love it?"

She said, "You're alright."

As they danced and partied through the night more celebrities came through. Andre 3000, Big Boi, Jermaine Dupree, Anthony Hamilton and some others. This was a night that they would remember the rest of their lives. They danced and danced. They all were up having the time of their life. It came time to go so it was off to the Waffle House.

Even after eating they were still high as hell. It may have had something to do with smoking that hydro on the way home. They hugged and thanked Tony and Ralph for a good time. Ralph gave Sheila his number and told her to call him some time. She said okay.

Sheila and Tonya get to their room. Tonya took a shower to get the sweat from the night off of her. When she came out Sheila got in. Her mind was just racing a mile a minute. She was thinking about Ralph, Tonya's kiss, going home for Christmas—a lot of stuff. So she got out of the shower and dried off. When she came out of the shower, the first thing out of her mouth was, "Tonya, why did you kiss me like that?"

Tonya said, "I knew that's what was on your mind tonight. I apologize. I got caught up in the heat of the moment."

Sheila said, "You know I'm not like that."

Tonya said, "I'm not either, but I told you I fantasize about how it would be. You know when you asked who I fantasize about. It's you."

Sheila said, "Hell no. Why me?"

Tonya said, "Through our closeness I have developed a love for you and I wanted us to experience something together for the first time."

Sheila said, "Wow."

Sheila and Tonya get in their beds. Sheila was just about to fall asleep, when she heard Tonya at it again. She didn't turn away this time. She started masturbating herself. As the feeling got more intense, all of a sudden, Sheila and Tonya made eye contact.

The next thing you know Tonya said, "Can I help you with that?"

Sheila nodded and it was on.

Tonya came over to Sheila's bed and sat down. She put her hand on Sheila's thigh and rubbed it gently until she worked her way up to her love mound. It was as wet as the spring rain. Then Tonya leaned forward and started kissing her and fondling her breast. Sheila's body was on fire by now. Her body was flexing and gyrating.

Tonya said, "Do you like that?"

Sheila said, "Yes."

Tonya started sucking on her nipples and finally made her way down to her vagina. Sheila's body started trembling and then she pulled Tonya up and started kissing on her. Then they were finally up and down each other's body, finding all those sensual spots. They ended up in Tonya's bed in the sixty-nine position. Both of their bodies were just thrashing around all over the place as they licked and sucked each other's clits.

Then finally Sheila let out a scream and said, "What's happening?" She said, "Damn, this feels so good."

Then she started sucking on Tonya again. She made her way to her clit and locked in on it. Sucking and licking, licking and sucking. Then all at once both their bodies started shuttering uncontrollably. And they kept it up until neither one could stand it anymore. They came so much they just collapsed.

When they woke up the next morning Sheila said, "What did we do?"

Tonya said, "I think we made love."

Sheila said, "Hell no. That was just sex. Two women can't make love. It's not natural."

Tonya said, "Whatever it was it felt good as hell."

Now this messed Sheila up. She had never done anything like this before. She didn't know how to process it. She knew that she liked boys, but could she be gay? She said to herself, "No, I can't be," but she just wasn't sure. Why did it feel so good and the fact is she kind of liked it. The encounter she had with Troy was nothing like that. Sheila couldn't wrap her mind around being with another woman. She knew in her heart that it was just unnatural. This would not be the last time, though.

Chapter Three

Home Again

It was now Christmas break and the girls were leaving to go home. They exchanged numbers, hugged each other, and said goodbye. Sheila caught a taxi to the airport. The other girls were leaving at various times. Rene was from Charlotte so Tony took her home. She really had his nose open.

Sheila landed at Cincinnati Airport and guess who was there to pick her up. That's right, Troy.

Sheila asked, "What are you doing here?"

Troy told her he had told her father and mother he would pick her up.

"What about asking me?"

Troy said, "Would you please slow down a little? I needed this time to talk to you. I know I was wrong for acting the way I did before you left and I am sorry. I realize I should have taken my time with you. I wasn't experienced at this sex thing either."

Sheila said, "I noticed."

"Very funny," said Troy. Troy said, "While you were away I missed you so much. I never knew how much you meant to me until you were gone."

Sheila said, "That's the way it always is. You don't miss your water until your well runs dry." Sheila said, "So what's up with you?"

Troy said, "I went to U.C. I walked on the football team."

She said, "Really, congrats."

Troy said, "It wasn't all that. I did a lot of riding the bench, but with some hard work I am going to take someone's position next year."

Sheila said, "That's going to take a lot of hard work."

"I know," said Troy. "So tell me about Spelman."

Sheila said, "It is a lot of hard work, but it's worth it. I mean, I really have to do a lot of studying."

Troy said, "Not you."

Sheila said, "Yeah. It's a lot different than high school. It's a whole 'nother level of learning process."

Troy said, "I know. U.C. is a lot more intense itself."

They pulled up in front of Sheila's house and she said to Troy, "You can't just leave me this time because my bags are in the car."

Troy said, "Sheila, can we please just start over?"

She said, "I'll think about it."

They got out of the car and Troy got her bags out of the trunk. As they went to the house, Sheila's dad came out to meet them. He gave Sheila a big hug and offered to help with the bags.

Troy said, "There is more in the trunk."

Her dad said, "I knew that."

They got in the house and put the bags down in the living room. Her mom was in the kitchen cooking dinner. Sheila snuck up behind her mother and grabbed her. Josephine almost dropped the mixing bowl.

She put the bowl down and hugged Sheila and said, "How is my baby doing? You look thin."

Sheila said, "I'm fine, Momma."

Josephine asked her if she was hungry.

"Not right now."

"What about Troy?"

Sheila said, "He is getting ready to leave."

Sheila's mom hollered in the other room and said, "Hi, Troy, are you hungry?"

Sheila said, "No!" in a loud voice. "He's leaving."

Troy said, "No, Mrs. Jones, I have to go."

Sheila went in the other room and said, "Bye, Troy, thanks for coming to pick me up."

Troy said, "Not a problem. Goodbye, Mr. and Mrs. Jones. Bye, Sheila, I will call you later."

Sheila said, "Okay, bye."

Ronald asked, "Why are you treating Troy so cold?"

Sheila said, "Dad, just leave it alone."

Sheila and her dad took her bags upstairs to her room. They opened the door and Sheila screamed with excitement. They had completely renovated her room. They had gotten her the most beautiful bedroom suit she had ever seen. She went and dove on the bed and ran back to her dad and gave him a big hug and kiss and said, "Thank you."

Ronald said, "That's why I didn't come and pick you up, I had to finish this."

She said, "Okay, I forgive you."

Her dad asked, "What do you have against Troy?"

"Let it go, Dad," she replied.

They went back downstairs and went in the kitchen, where her mom was, and sat down.

Josephine said, "So tell me about Spelman, young lady."

Sheila said, "Wow, it's nice but it's tough. It's a lot harder than I ever imagined, but I'm making it. I made the Dean's List!"

Her mom said, "Really? Congrats. How's Tonya?" her mom asked.

Sheila said, "She's fine."

Her mom said, "Are you sure? You sounded kind of funny when I asked that."

Sheila said, "No, Mom, she's cool."

Josephine said, "Okay, I don't want you down there getting into any mess. Have you met any other girls?"

Sheila said, "Yes. There is a group of us that study together. We talked about getting our own apartment."

Her mom said, "Do you think you all are ready for that?"

Sheila said, "As soon as we get jobs."

Josephine asked, "Who are these girls?"

Sheila said, "Sharon, Lisa, and Rene."

"What do you know about them?" her mom asked.

Sheila said, "They are all good girls. They work hard at their studies and they are not all boy crazy. Well, at least most of them."

Her mom said, "What do you mean by that?"

Sheila said, "Well, Rene is a mess. She makes men do anything she wants."

Josephine said, "Yeah, but what is she doing?"

Sheila said, "Well. Her mom said she better be careful."

Sheila was now getting ready for bed and the phone rang.

Her dad said, "Sheila, telephone."

Sheila said, "Okay. Hello?"

"Hey, Sheila."

"What up, Stephanie, how are you?"

"I'm good, girl, what about you?"

"I'm great now that school's out."

"How is Spelman?"

"It's school, you know. I know it has to be a lot different than U.C. The biggest difference is there are no boys."

Stephanie said, "That has to suck."

Sheila said, "It took some getting used to but it's okay. It's a lot easier to stay focused. There is Morehouse near there, though."

Stephanie said, "Wow, a whole school full of boys."

Sheila said, "More boys, more dogs."

Stephanie said, "You know Troy is at U.C."

Sheila said, "I know."

Stephanie said, "All the girls are sweating him all the time but he just ignores them. Girl, all he talks about is you. What did you do to him?"

Sheila said, "I didn't do anything. Hold on, let me see who this is. Hello?"

"Hi, Sheila, it's Troy. May I please talk to you?"

"Wait a minute, hold on."

"Girl, you talked his ass up. Okay, I will talk to you later, Sheila."

"Okay, Stephanie. Okay, Troy, what is it?"

"Why are you treating me so cold? I said I was sorry."

"Just because you said 'I am sorry' doesn't mean that everything is alright."

"Sheila, I realize that what I did wasn't right. I should have never got an attitude with you just because you didn't want to have sex with me. That was my own selfishness and I am truly sorry."

"Troy, you know how I feel about being pressured."

"Yes, Sheila, I know. I just wanted you so bad. Sheila, I love you and you are all I can think about. These other girls at school keep trying to throw me rhythm and I just ignore them. Baby, all I want is you. Please, baby, please, can we start over?"

"I don't know, Troy."

"Sheila, tell me you don't want me and I will leave you alone."

"Don't ask me that right now, Troy. I have a lot of things going on in my head right now."

"Okay, Sheila, I will call you tomorrow."

"Alright."

As Sheila was lying in bed trying to go to sleep, she had a million thoughts going through her head. She thought about what Troy had said to her and their first sexual encounter. Then she started thinking about Tonya. That couldn't have been Tonya's first time doing that because it felt too much like she knew what she was doing. Then she thought, *It was my first time and she seemed like she liked what I was doing to her.*

As Sheila lay there with all these thoughts going through her mind, she started getting horny. It wasn't long before she was touching herself. She got up and turned on the music and laid back down. She started rubbing her breasts and pinching her nipples. Her breathing started getting heavier. She slid her right hand down into her panties and started rubbing on her clit while pinching on her nipple. Her breathing started getting heavier and her vagina started getting wetter. She said, "Shit." Then her leg came up and off came the panties, and with one swoop she kicked the covers on the floor. She continued pinching her nipples and rubbing her clit. As her body started to flex, she was getting more and more excited. Then she slipped one finger inside her vagina. She said, "Damn, girl, you are wet." By this time she was moaning and sighing. She started getting a little more aggressive with the fingering. She slid another finger inside and said, "Oh, shit, this feels good." She fingered herself a little more. Then she pulled them out and started rubbing her clit very briskly. Then her body flexed so hard she could have almost snapped. "Oh, fuck," she said and started having an orgasm. She rubbed her clit until she couldn't take it anymore. It was so sensitive; every time she would touch it she would start cumming again until she was drained. Then she fell into a deep sleep.

The next morning her mom knocked on her door and said, "Hey, babe, you ready for breakfast?"

She said, "Okay, Mom." When she woke up and seen one leg out of her panties she chuckled and said, "Wow." She got up, grabbed some pjs, and washed up, then went downstairs for breakfast.

Her dad said, "Did you sleep good, honey?"

Sheila said, "Like a rock."

Her mom asked, "How do you like your new bedroom? Is the bed comfortable?"

Sheila said, "Oh, yes."

"So what do you have planned for the day, Sheila?" her mom asked.

"Nothing," Sheila replied.

"Good. You want to hang out with me and do some shopping?"

"Sure, Mom."

Sheila got out of the shower and started putting her clothes on and the phone rang.

Her dad called up and said, "Sheila, telephone."

"Okay, Dad. Hello?"

"What's up, girl?"

"Hey, Tonya, what's happening?"

"Nothing, just got back to Dallas last night."

"How was your flight?" Sheila asked.

"It was cool, and yours?"

"Mine was cool too, until I got here and Troy was at the airport to pick me up."

"Girl, that boy ain't gonna let you go."

"It seems that way. I am going to make his ass sweat first, though."

"Okay, Rene. Whatever, speaking of Rene. Have you talked to her or any of the other girls?"

"No, not yet."

"Well, I was just thinking about you."

"Yeah, I thought about you too."

"You didn't call."

"It was too late to call your parents' house. You know we're an hour behind y'all."

"Oh, okay. So what were you thinking about, Sheila?"

"Whatever. Bye, Tonya."

"Later."

Sheila and her mom got to the mall. Josephine asked her where she wanted to go first.

Sheila asked, "Whose gift are we going to get first?"

"Let's look for something for your dad."

Sheila asked, "What do you want to get him?"

Her mom said, "You know how funny your dad is."

Sheila said, "I know."

Meanwhile in Charlotte, Rene was up to her old tricks. She went shopping with her girls and ran into an old acquaintance at the mall. His name was Charles.

She said, "What's up, boy."

"Hey, girl, what's going on?"

"Just out doing some shopping."

"Really? The way you played me, I hoped I would never see you again and here you are, Ms. Rene. What do you have planned for Christmas Eve?"

"Nothing, I don't guess."

"Would you like to go to a party with me?"

"I thought that you hoped you would never see me again."

"Girl, I was just tripp'n."

"Sure, give me a call."

"Is your number still the same?"

"Yeah, give me a call."

Christmas Eve came and Charles called.

"Hey, Rene, are you ready?"

She said, "I didn't think you were going to call."

"Why, because you treated me so shitty?"

Rene said, "Look, Charles, are we going to this party or what?"

"Yeah, we're going. It's going to be a blast."

Rene said, "Do you have something for me?"

Charles said, "Yeah, I got just what you need."

Charles pulled up and called and told Rene he was outside. She came out to the car.

When she got in she said, "Damn, Charles, that smells like some of that good sticky icky."

Charles said, "You know what it is," as he coughed.

Rene said, "Easy, big boy."

"Here, you want some?"

Rene said, "Let's get this party started."

Charles said, "Sure, you're right."

As Rene hit the blunt she asked, "What are you sipping on?"

Charles said, "You know what it is."

Rene said, "Where is my cup?"

He said, "We have to stop and get some cups and ice."

He pulled up to the store and gave Rene some money to go in and get the cups and ice. When she got out of the car, Charles made a call and told his boys, "It's on. Meet me at the spot."

Rene got in and poured a drink.

Charles pulled out some powder and said, "You want a bump?"

Rene said, "You're the 'everything man' tonight."

Charles said, "Sure, you're right."

Rene said, "Where is this party at anyway?"

Charles said, "It's at the Marriot."

Rene said, "Yeah, that's what's up."

Charles said, "Yeah. You want another drink? Here, smoke this. This is a special joint. I just cooked this up."

Rene said, "Hell yeah. You are trying to get some pussy tonight, huh?"

Charles said, "This is going to be a special night."

They got to the room. Rene saw all the liquor, but no one else was there. She said, "Where is everyone?"

Charles said, "They're coming."

He turned on the music. And there was a knock on the door.

He said, "Get the door."

Rene opened the door and four of his boys came in. Rene felt a little uneasy at first, but they were getting so high she dismissed the thought.

After a bit, Rene said, "Where are the other girls?"

Charles said, "You're it, bitch."

Rene stood up and said, "Hell no."

Charles slapped her and said, "Bitch, get those clothes off."

Rene said, "I ain't taking off shit."

POW, he slapped her again.

Charles said, "Bitch, I am going to teach you about fucking with people's emotions. Get her ass."

His boys grabbed her. She put up a fight, but they overpowered her. They beat her almost unconscious. Then they took turns on her.

They passed her around like a ragdoll. They made her suck dicks. They fucked her in the ass until it started bleeding. Then they took a break. They drank and smoked some more. She was lying there pleading with them. She was so weak she could barely speak, let alone scream.

Charles said, "Shut up, bitch," and stuck his dick in her mouth. He pulled out his gun and put it to her head. He told her if her teeth so much as scratched his dick he would blow her brains out.

Then they started fucking her again, until she finally passed out.

When they were finished with her, they wrapped her in a blanket and put her in the back of one his boys' SUV and threw her in the Catawba River off the 85 bridge.

Christmas morning a knock came at Rene's mother's door, it was the police. They told Rene's mother they had found her body in the river. Some passersby saw two people throwing something big over the rail of the bridge into the river and called the police. They found her wrapped up in a blanket with her clothes, and her ID was in her pocket. Her mother passed out at the door.

Around one o'clock, Sheila's family was sitting around opening gifts and the phone rang. Sheila answered the phone. The voice on the phone was so frantic, she could hardly make it out.

She said, "May I speak to Sheila?"

"This is she. Who is this?"

She said, "This is Lisa," frantically.

Sheila said, "What's wrong, Lisa? What's wrong?"

"They found Rene dead this morning."

When she told Sheila what happened, Sheila threw up and broke down crying. Her dad ran in to see what was wrong.

Sheila's mom was screaming, "Baby, what's wrong? What's wrong?"

Sheila could barely get it out.

When she did her mother said, "Oh my God," and held Sheila close as she cried her heart out.

By this time Troy called. Sheila's mother told him what was going on. He asked if he could come and see her. Her mother told him to come on over.

When he got over, Sheila's mom said, "She is upstairs."

Her dad said, "Leave the door open."

Josephine said, "Ron."

Her dad said, "What?"

Troy sat there on the bed with her and held her and stroked her hair. He said, "Baby, I am here with you as long as you need me."

Over the next few days, Troy and Sheila started spending more time together. They went to movies, out to dinner, and just sat around talking and holding hands. He asked if he could spend New Year's Eve with her. She said yes. He was so happy. He told her he was going to plan something special. She said, "Oh, really?" He said, "You will see."

New Year's Eve came and Troy came to pick her up. They went out to dinner, then they went to the club. Even though they were too young to get in, he knew the bouncer. They danced and had a great time. They were out on the floor slow dancing.

Sheila said, "This is nice."

Troy said, "Are you having a good time?"

Sheila said, "Yes."

Troy looked deep into her eyes and gave her a deep, sensuous kiss.

She said, "Wow, that's different."

He said, "Sheila, will you make love to me tonight? I promise that will be different also."

She said, "Yes."

They went and got a room when they left the club. When they got in the room, Troy held her gently and started kissing her. Sheila noticed his kiss was different. The thought crossed her mind, *Where did he learn this?* She was actually getting turned on. Then they got undressed and got in bed. He slid up close and kissed her. He got over top of her and started kissing her on her lips. Then he worked his way down to her neck. She started panting. He worked his way down to her breasts and started sucking on her nipples. She started moaning. Then he slid his tongue down her stomach. He got down to her pelvis and gave her a little nibble. He made it to her clit and started sucking on it very gently.

Sheila said, "Oh, Troy."

He said, "Wat?"

She said, "What are you doing to me?"

He said, "Do you like it?"

She said, "Hell yeah."

They made love for about an hour and then they collapsed in each other's arms. All kinds of thoughts were running through her mind at this point. This wasn't the same Troy she had left. He had learned a few things.

Chapter Four

Back to School

It was a new semester, and it was time to get back to business. The girls were trying to get back in the swing of things. After being away from school, they had to get used to all the studying, taking tests, and dealing with the death of their friend.

Tonya was already there when Sheila came to the room.

"Hi, Tonya, how are you? How was your vacation?"

"I am good. My vacation was great. I got a bunch of stuff that I needed, like clothes. What about you?"

"My vacation was going good until I got that call from Lisa."

"I know, girl, wasn't that a trip?"

"Yeah, girl, did they ever find out what really happened?"

"Yes, it was bad. They caught the guys that killed her."

"What happened?" Sheila asked.

"Rene had gone to the mall with some of her girls to do some Christmas shopping. She ran into this guy she knew named Charles. He invited her to a party Christmas Eve. Girl, he set her up."

"Really?" Sheila said.

"Yeah, girl. He had his boys there. They did her so bad." At this time Tonya was starting to tear up. She said, "They beat her and raped her. I mean, they screwed her in her ass until it was all torn up. Her vagina was all ripped up and everything."

By the time she got finished with the story they were both in tears. They were holding each other, and all of a sudden Sheila pulled away from her. Sheila dried her eyes and asked if Lisa and Sharon were back yet.

Tonya said, "I don't know, let's go find out."

They got to Lisa and Sharon's room and knocked on the door. Lisa came to the door and her eyes were red like she had been crying.

Sheila and Tonya came in. Sharon was in the bathroom. When she came out, they all looked at each other and just started crying all over again. They hugged each other and were saying how much they were going to miss Rene.

Sheila said, "Girls, we've got to go on and do what we're supposed to do. We have to stick together. We can't go to any parties unless we go together."

Sheila went to class Monday. It seemed like almost everyone had found out what happened to Renee. Lots of people were asking her about it. When she told them they were amazed that a person could do someone like that.

Her professor came in and said, "Okay, let's get started. Ms. Jones, are you okay?"

"Yes, Professor Smith," Sheila said.

He said, "I would like to see you before you leave."

She wondered what he wanted. He always looked at her kind of different.

After class was over, Sheila hung around to see what he wanted. He told her he had heard about what had happened and was very sorry. He said, "Sheila, I know this is kind of hard for you, but you have got to stay focused. You are a good student. I would hate to see your grades drop. If you need anything let me know," as he grabbed her hand.

Sheila said, "Thank you, Professor."

As Sheila left the room, he watched her every movement. He watched that slim brown frame as she sashayed to the door. He was admiring her nice round ass and long firm legs. Sheila was only 19 and already had a womanly appearance. From the way she talked to the way she walked. She was a real prize.

Sheila noticed the way he was holding her hand. She said to herself, *He doesn't mean anything by it.* She said to herself, *He is kind of cute, though.* The professor was about 6 feet 3 inches tall. Light brown-skinned, bald, with an athletic build. He was almost 30 years old. Sheila thought that was too old for her.

Sheila met up with the other girls in the cafeteria at lunchtime.

Sharon said, "Everyone has been asking about Renee."

Tonya said, "They have been asking you too?"

Lisa said, "I guess it made national news."

Sheila said, "Okay, girls, remember, we said we were going to see about getting an apartment together. The end of the school year will be here before we know it. We need to start thinking about jobs."

Lisa said, "The malls would probably be a good place to start."

Sheila said, "That's a good idea."

Sharon said, "Let's go after class today. What time does everyone get out?"

Sheila said, "We're all out by at least four, aren't we?"

They all chimed in and said yes.

After school off to the Greenbriar Mall they went.

Tonya said, "I'm just going to hang out."

Sheila said, "Okay, when we get ready to move if you don't have your part you're not going to be able to move with us."

Tonya said, "My daddy's got me."

Sharon said, "Brat."

Tonya said, "Hater."

Lisa said, "I wish my parents were rich."

Tonya said, "My parents aren't rich, they are just very comfortable."

Lisa snickered and said, "Rich."

Sheila said, "We need to split up. It won't look good us going in the stores in a pack looking for jobs."

So the girls split up to put in applications.

They were going from store to store putting in applications. A couple of them would cross paths and ask how the other was doing. As Sheila came out of one store, she ran into Ralph.

Sheila said, "Hey, Ralph."

He said, "Hey, Sheila, how are you?"

"Fine," she said. "How are you?"

Ralph said, "I'm good. I'm out doing some shopping. What are you up to?"

Sheila said, "The girls and I are out putting in some applications."

Ralph asked, "Are you having any luck?"

Sheila said, "I don't know. You put in a bunch of applications and hope someone calls you."

Ralph said, "I have a friend that owns a men's clothing store in here. In fact, that's where I was headed. Come on," he said. "I will see if I can get you hooked up."

Sheila said, "Okay."

Sheila and Ralph got to the store.

Ralph walked in and said, "What's up, Lucky?" Lucky was his friend.

Lucky turned and said, "What's up, Ralph? Who's the pretty young thing you have with you?"

Ralph said, "This is a friend of mine, Sheila."

Lucky said, "Hello, Sheila."

Sheila said, "Hi."

Ralph said, "Her and her girlfriends are out looking for jobs, so I brought her here to see what you had."

Lucky said, "What can you do besides look good?"

Sheila laughed and said, "This will be my first job. I learn quick, though."

Lucky asked, "What have you been doing?"

Sheila said, "School. This is my first year at Spelman."

Lucky said, "Oh." Lucky said, "Most of your pay is going to come from commission. You think you can handle that?"

Sheila said, "I think so."

Lucky asked her when she wanted to start.

Sheila said, "How about Saturday?"

Lucky said, "Bet see you then."

By that time Ralph had picked out a few items and brought them to the counter. He checked out and then they left.

As Sheila and Ralph left the store, Sheila spotted Sharon and Lisa. She said, "Hey, girls."

"Hey, Sheila," they said.

Sheila said, "Do you girls remember Ralph?"

Lisa said, "Yeah, from the club."

Ralph said, "Yeah, that's right." He said, "Are you girls hungry?"

Sheila said, "I am a little but we have to find Tonya and get the bus home."

Ralph said, "How about you all find Tonya and meet me at the front door and I will take you all out to dinner."

Lisa said, "Bet," and off they went to find Tonya.

Sharon and Lisa didn't have to look far. She was sitting on a bench talking to some guy eating ice cream.

Sharon and Lisa said, "Come on, Tonya. We got to go."

Tonya said, "Sharon and Lisa, this is Larry."

Larry said, "Hello, ladies, good to meet you."

Larry gave Tonya his card and told her to call him and think about what he said. Larry managed a strip club. That was his M.O. He would cruise the mall looking for fine young ladies to bring into the business. He hooked them with how much money they could make and told them it would be the easiest money they'd ever make. What he didn't tell them was how it was normally filled with some seedy characters and weirdoes.

The girls got to the front. They came outside and heard Sheila calling to them but they didn't see her right away. Then she stepped out of his car and said, "Come on, girls."

As they walked toward the car, Sharon said, "Damn, that's a nice-ass Benz."

Lisa and Tonya said, "It sure is." They got in and said, "Damn, it smells good also."

Ralph said, "Yeah, it's that new car smell, don't you love it? What do you girls want to eat?"

Sheila said, "I don't care."

Ralph said, "Do you want a Big Mac or a Whopper?"

Sheila looked at him like what the hell.

Ralph laughed and said, "I was just playing."

So they pulled into an Applebee's. They had dinner and Ralph took them back to campus. He gave Sheila his card and told her to call him if she needed anything. Sheila said, "Okay," and went to get out.

Ralph said, "Can I have a kiss goodnight?"

Sheila said, "Not on the first date."

Ralph said, "This isn't a date."

Sheila said, "Exactly," and laughed. She went to get out and leaned over and gave him a peck on the cheek and said, "Thanks for everything." Sheila said, "I will call you sometime."

Ralph said, "Cool."

"Oh, thanks for the hookup on the job."

"Not a problem." Then Ralph left.

When Sheila got inside the girls were waiting on her and said, "You better wrap that up."

Sheila said, "Why, because he has money?"

Sharon said, "Yeah, and he is fine."

Sheila said, "Yeah, and he probably has a lot of women to go along with it. Besides, Troy and I hooked back up."

Tonya said, "Troy is way in Cincinnati and you don't know what he is doing."

Sheila said, "I am not going to do that."

Lisa said, "Shit, I will."

Sheila said, "Just because he is cute and has money, that doesn't mean anything."

Sharon said. "Yeah, but it helps."

Sheila said, "Goodnight, girls. I will see you all tomorrow."

They said goodnight. Tonya and Sheila went to their room and Sharon and Lisa went their way.

Saturday came and Sheila went for her first day at work. Lucky showed her around the store to let her know where everything was. Then he asked her where she knew Ralph from. She said she met him when Tony came to pick Renee up to take them out one night.

Lucky said, "I know Tony. That's Ralph's partner at the law firm." Lucky said, "Ralph is a good guy. He is part owner in my store. He gave me the money to get it started."

Sheila said, "Really?"

"Yeah."

Sheila asked him why they called him Lucky.

He said that's what they had always called him from back in the day.

Sheila said, "Back in the day?"

He said, "Yeah. That was my street name and it stuck to me. I haven't always been a law-abiding citizen, if you know what I mean."

Sheila asked, "Where do you know Ralph from?"

Lucky said, "We grew up together. We just chose different paths. We have always been cool. He never once judged me."

She said, "Why do they call you Lucky?"

He said, "That is short for Lucius."

Sheila snickered and said, "Okay, Lucky."

Later the phone rang. Sheila answered and said, "Lucky's Clothing. May I help you?"

The voice on the other end said, "Yeah, you can give me a big kiss."

Sheila said, "Who is this?"

"It's Ralph, how is your first day?"

Sheila said, "It is going good so far."

He said, "That's great. Can I take you out tonight to celebrate?"

Sheila said, "That would be nice but I don't go out without my girls, especially after what happened to Renee."

Ralph said, "That's cool, I will take you all out."

Sheila said, "Are you sure?"

He said, "That's no problem. What time do you get off?"

She said, "At seven."

He said, "I will pick you up."

Sheila said, "That's cool. I will call the girls and let them know."

Seven o'clock came and Sheila was walking out the door. Ralph met her at the door with a dozen roses.

"Are those for me?"

Ralph said, "No, I just like carrying roses around for the hell of it. Of course they are for you."

Sheila said, "Thank you."

Ralph said, "You're welcome. I wanted to get you something as beautiful as you are, so this is what I came up with."

Sheila said, "You are so smooth. I bet you tell that to all the women."

Ralph said, "Not at all of them. You seem special so I wanted to do something special for you."

Sheila smiled and said, "Thanks." They got to campus and Ralph said, "Don't take all day getting ready."

Sheila said, "I am going to take a quick shower and throw something on and I will be right back."

Ralph said, "I will be waiting; make sure the other girls are ready also."

Sheila said, "Okay."

While Ralph was waiting, he rolled a couple joints. He fired one up to smoke while he was waiting. As he was waiting, his mind was going a mile a minute. He had plans for them but didn't quite know how to bring them about, so he called Tony. Tony would always give him a different spin on things. These were some good girls, and he didn't know just how to play it.

After about an hour, the girls came out. They got in the car and Ralph said, "I must be the luckiest man in the world. I get to go out with four beautiful women."

Sheila said, "Yes, you are."

Ralph said, "I talked to Tony, he is going to meet us at Friday's for dinner. Then we're going to 112. Is that cool with you ladies?"

They said, "Yes, that's fine."

Sheila said, ",How is Tony?"

Ralph said, "He is fine. He took it pretty hard when he heard what happened to Renee."

Sheila said, "That was terrible, wasn't it?"

Ralph said, "Yes, it was. What would drive a man to do something so horrible? I just don't know."

Sheila said, "You know how some of those D boys are. They think they own the world. I told Renee she was going to get in trouble treating men like that. I just didn't think it was going to be like that or that soon."

Ralph said, "You never know when your past is going to catch up with you."

They got to Friday's and Tony was waiting at the door for them. The girls got out and gave him a hug.

Sharon said, "How are you, Tony?"

He said, "I'm good. You ladies ready for the evening? It's pretty crowded in here so I put my name down on the list already."

Sheila said, "That was smart."

Sharon was checking him out pretty hard. Tony asked if something was wrong.

Sharon said, "No, it's all good," with a smile.

He gave her a big smile. Just then they called his name.

Once inside they got seated.

Tony said, "You girls get anything you want. I got this."

Lisa said, "Bet."

Sharon said, "You all, don't get greedy. You may have to pay for it later."

Ralph said, "Ease up. It's not that kind of party. We just want to show you girls a good time."

Tonya said, "I bet you all show all the girls a good time."

Tony laughed and said, "Just the special ones." Tony said, "No, really, anytime you girls get ready to go we will take you home."

Tonya said, "I'm sorry, we just can't be too careful."

Ralph said, "Trust me, you couldn't be in better hands. We have too much to lose to be trying some bullshit, okay? Let's order so we can eat and get to the club."

Lisa said, "I wonder who is going to be there tonight."

Ralph said, "I don't know but it is always someone there."

They left Friday's and Sharon and Lisa got in the car with Tony.

Sharon said, "This is a nice Lexus. You and Ralph both have new cars?"

Tony said, "Mine is a year old. Ralph just got his. My turn isn't until next year. We take turns getting cars because we put them in the company name."

Sharon said, "There must be a lot of criminals here."

Tony said, "We have our share." Tony said, "If you girls want we can go by the crib after the club and I will fix breakfast."

Sharon said, "We will see."

Tony said, "Okay."

They got to the club and got parked and started for the door. Sheila stumbled a little.

The girls laughed a little and said, "Your drinks are cut off already."

Sheila said, "I don't think so."

They get to the door.

The doorman said, "What up, T? How many you got with you?"

Tony said, "I've got five."

"You want V.I.P.?"

"Cool, if it's available."

"Let me see what I can do, come on."

They got seated and ordered drinks. While they were sitting there making small talk, the drinks came.

Ralph said, "You all get what you want, but I am not carrying your drunk asses out of here so you better be careful."

Sharon said, "You better be careful or we are going to be rolling that Benz tonight."

Ralph said, "They don't have enough liquor in Texas to get me drunk."

Sheila laughed and said, "Yeah, right."

Sharon said, "Tony wants us to go over his house after we leave the club for breakfast."

Sheila said, "We will see. It depends on how long we stay here."

Ralph said, "That sounds good but I am not cooking."

Tony said, "Man, we have got to have your pancakes."

Ralph said, "We will see."

They were having a good time laughing and dancing the night away. A slow record came on and Ralph took Sheila's hand and pulled her closer.

Ralph said, "I have been waiting for this moment since you left for Christmas break. You feel so good in my arms."

Sheila said, "You know I have a boyfriend."

Ralph looked around and said, "Where is he?"

Sheila laughed and said, "You are so silly. He is in Cincinnati."

Ralph said, "He's not here right now, so let's just enjoy this."

Sheila said, "Okay, but I am not going to enjoy it too much."

Ralph said, "Well, let's just relax and see where it goes." Ralph looked into Sheila's eyes and said, "You have the most beautiful eyes." Then he gave her a peck on the lips.

For a moment she forgot about Troy and kissed him back.

Ralph said, "What was that?"

Sheila said, "I'm sorry; I got caught up in the moment."

Ralph said, "That's okay, I enjoyed it."

They got back to their seats and everyone else was on the floor. Ralph started asking Sheila about Troy. She said they were high school sweethearts.

Ralph said, "What is he doing for himself?"

Sheila said, "He goes to U.C."

Ralph said, "You need a man in your life, not a boy."

Sheila said, "I am not even twenty yet."

Ralph said, "So what? I am only thirty-one. I am just what you need, someone with some maturity that can teach you something."

"What is it that you want to teach me?"

Ralph said, "I want to teach you about life and guide you through it." Ralph said, "I think I could really like you."

Sheila said, "You think so?"

Ralph said, "Yes, I think so."

By this time it was getting to be about one o'clock.

Tony said, "You girls about ready for breakfast?"

Tonya said, "I want another drink before we go."

Tony said, "I have a full bar at the crib."

Sharon said, "Oh, snap! Let's go."

Sheila said, "You all sure you want to go?"

Lisa said, "What's going to happen with all of us together?"

Sheila said, "I guess you're right."

So they got up and headed for the cars.

Once at Tony's house, when they walked in the girls said, "Wow."

Ralph said, "This is a long way from Mom's basement, hah." He whispered in Sheila's ear, "Now isn't this better than seeing someone still in his mom's basement?"

Sheila said, "This isn't your house."

Ralph said, "Mine is just as nice. These are the things I can offer you."

Sheila said, "I don't care about things. I want to know what's in your heart and mind."

Ralph said, "Don't you think it would take some kind of mental capacity to achieve something like this? I have a giving heart and I want to share it with you."

Sheila said, "Time will tell."

Tony said, "You girls make yourselves comfortable. If you know how to roll, there is some bud and papers in the bowl on the coffee table."

Sharon said, "Bet." She opened the bowl and said, "Damn, that looks like some serious bud."

Tony said, "Yeah, that's that sticky icky." Tony said, "Alright, Ralph, get in here and get started on your pancakes."

Tony and Ralph were in the kitchen cooking and they heard mass coughing coming from in the living room.

Ralph said, "Why doesn't somebody bring us some in here?"

Sheila took a blunt in to Ralph and Tony.

Tony said, "Thanks."

When Sheila turned to walk away Ralph grabbed her and kissed her. Sheila just smiled and walked away.

Ralph said to himself, "Damn, she has some nice lips."

Tony said, "She is nice. I am going to talk to Sharon and see where it goes. There is nothing to turning out young tender college girls."

Ralph said, "You know it."

"Okay, girls, breakfast is served."

Sharon said, "Good, I am starving. You know us college girls never get enough to eat."

Lisa said, "Let me put this blunt out."

Tony said, "Someone come help grab some of this stuff."

Tonya said, "Okay, I will help you."

After they ate breakfast, they cleaned up the kitchen, sat down and had some drinks and were smoking some weed.

Then Tony said, "Does anyone want to do some lines?"

Sheila said, "I have never done that before."

Ralph said, "Don't worry, I will show you how to do it. See, this is already one thing I can teach you."

Sharon said, "I don't know, I don't want to get hooked."

Tony said, "You aren't going to get hooked doing it one time."

Lisa said, "I've done it once or twice and I didn't get hooked."

Tonya said, "Me too."

Sheila said, "Not Patty Le'pure."

Tonya said, "I guess I'm not so pure after all, huh."

Ralph said, "What's that all about?"

Sheila said, "It's an inside joke."

They passed the plate around and when it got to Sheila, Ralph said, "Let me help you. Inhale real deep through one nostril, then the other. Okay, now just sit back and relax. You are going to be okay."

Sheila sat back and said, "This is kind of nice."

Then Ralph did a line and passed it on.

Tony said, "Man, is that all you are going to do?"

Ralph said, "Yes, you know how I like to do mine."

Tony said, "Yeah, I know."

Ralph said, "T, where are your cooking tools?"

Sheila said, "Cooking tools?"

Ralph said, "Yeah. I am going to cook some up so we can smoke it."

Tony brought out a test tube, water, and baking soda.

Sharon said, "What do you do with that?"

Ralph said, "I will show you."

So he took some powder and baking soda and put it in the test tube with some water and proceeded to heat it. It started bubbling and got kind of milky looking and then it cleared up. There was an oily blob at the bottom of the tube.

As Ralph spun it around, he said, "T, get the pipe."

The rock got hard. Then Ralph poured it out on the plate. He took the pipe and cut a piece off and put it in the pipe. He put the heat to it and proceeded to pull on it. The bowl filled with smoke.

He passed it to Sheila and said, "Pull real easy."

She did and fell back on the couch and said, "Damn, that felt good." She liked it instantly.

They passed it all around until it was gone. This was all the girls' first time smoking cocaine. They said, "Wow, that was different." It was now about five A.M.

Sheila said, "It's about time for us to go."

Ralph said, "I will drop them off."

Everyone said goodbye Tony and left.

On the way back to campus, Sheila said, "Wow, I have never felt anything like that before. It made me tingle all over."

Tonya said, "Yeah, that was kind of strange. I heard bells ringing, then they went away."

Sharon said, "I could feel my heart racing, it kind of scared me."

Lisa said, "I don't need any more of that."

Ralph said, "That's not something you want to make a habit of, that's for sure."

Sheila asked, "Well, why do you do it?"

Ralph said, "I like it and I can afford it. Besides, I haven't been doing it that long."

Sheila asked, "Was that crack?"

Ralph said, "Kind of. It's not like what you get on the street. You don't know what they are putting in that. It's a lot cleaner when you make it yourself."

Sheila said, "I liked it. I think it made my panties wet."

They all started laughing. By this time they made it back to campus and said goodnight.

Chapter Five

The Last Quarter

By now all the girls were working. Sharon and Lisa were working in the mall also. Tonya had gotten a job working in a club as a waitress. Things were going pretty good for the girls. They were all working and still keeping up with their studies.

Ralph and Sheila were getting closer. They were talking more and more. He would come to the mall and take her out to lunch when she was working and dinner on the weekends. Anything else she needed he would get it for her. She was starting to really like him.

One day at lunch they were talking and he asked her if she had been talking to Troy. She told him yes.

He asked, "What are your plans with him?"

She said she hadn't really thought about it. Troy was so far away, she didn't really see the need to do anything about it.

Ralph asked her, "What about us?"

Sheila said, "I really like you and you're a nice guy, but I don't know. Don't know what Ralph said."

Sheila said, "You are so much older than I am and so much more established."

Ralph said, "I don't care about that. I want you to be my woman."

Sheila said, "I don't know. I am going to have to think about that."

Ralph said, "Take all the time you need. I'll be right here."

So time went on. The girls were working and doing their studies. They were doing very well for themselves. They didn't have a lot of time for partying, but they would manage to get it in from time to time. Going to a few frat parties and every now and then they would go out with Ralph and Tony.

It was getting close to midterms and the girls were studying very hard. Sheila got a call from Troy. He was saying how he missed her and couldn't wait to see her. He said some of their friends from school wanted to come down and visit her one weekend. This made Sheila smile. She thought about the last time her and Troy were together. The next thing you know she was touching herself. She got really quiet on the phone. Then Troy noticed her breathing getting heavy.

He said, "Sheila, what's wrong?"

Sheila replied, "Nutt'n." She said, "Okay, Troy, I will call you back and let you know," and hung up the phone and finished what she had started.

The next day they were all sitting around studying.

Sharon said, "The end of the quarter will be here before long. We need to start looking for an apartment. We need to figure out where we want to live."

Tonya said, "I saw some apartment guides in the office, I'll get one tomorrow."

Sheila asked, "What price range should we be looking at? It's probably going to be pretty expensive. We need at least a four-bedroom so we each can have our own room."

Sharon said, "Yeah, that would be nice, I might want to rock somebody's world."

Lisa said, "Right."

About that time Ralph called.

Sheila answered the phone and said, "Hello?"

"Hi, sexy," Ralph said.

Sheila smiled and said, "Oh, hi, Ralph."

He said, "What are you doing?"

"Me and the girls are sitting here talking about apartments."

"Were you? I have some property near there. You know where Cheshire Bridge Rd. is?"

Sheila said, "I've seen it before. That's not far from here."

"No, it's not. I'll come by and get you all so you can see it."

Sheila asked the girls if they wanted to go see it. They said sure.

Sheila said, "Okay, when do you want to come and get us?"

Ralph said, "Whenever you get ready."

Sheila said, "Okay, we will let you know."

The next day Troy called and said they were planning to come down this weekend.

Sheila said, "Okay. When are you all leaving?"

Troy said, "Friday night. We should get there early Saturday morning."

Sheila said, "I have to work Saturday but we can hang out when I get off."

Troy said, "Cool. I can't wait to see you."

Sheila said, "Me too."

It was now Friday. Ralph called and asked if they wanted to go look at the apartment.

Sheila said, "I guess. We won't be out of class until five. I think Sharon and Lisa have to work this evening. Tonya has to be at work at eight."

"Okay, I can take you and Tonya and the other girls can see it later. I can drop Tonya off at work when we get finished."

About six o'clock Ralph showed up to get Sheila and Tonya. They got in the car.

Ralph said, "You girls look nice this evening."

"Thanks, Ralph," they said. "So how far are your apartments from here?"

"Actually it's a four-bedroom townhouse."

"Wow, okay," the girls said. "So how much is this going to cost us?"

"Don't worry, it will be affordable."

They pulled up in front of the townhouse.

Ralph said, "I think this will be perfect for you all. It's got four bedrooms, two full baths and a half, and it's on the bus line."

Sheila said, "That's not a problem. I get to bring my car down here when school is out."

They went inside and looked around.

Tonya said, "Wow, this is nice. It's got a fireplace and everything."

Sheila said, "Okay, how much is it?"

Ralph said, "I normally get $1200.00 a month but I will let you all have it for $900."

Sheila said, "Why would you do that?"

"Because I like you all and I want to help you out."

"Are you sure that's it?"

"Yeah, what kind of a guy do you think I am?"

"I don't know but I am sure I'm going to find out. Let me talk to Sharon and Lisa and we will let you know."

"Fair enough."

They dropped Tonya off at work.

Ralph said, "Sheila, do you know what kind of club that is?"

"No, why?"

"That's a strip club."

"No! For real? I thought she made an awful lot of money for waiting tables."

"She's waiting tables, alright, lap dances."

"I hope she's careful."

"Are you hungry?"

"I'm a college girl, I'm always hungry."

"I've got some steaks out at the house if you want."

"I don't know about going to your house with you by myself."

"Sheila, I promise I won't do anything you don't want me to."

"You promise?"

"Scout's honor."

"Okay, let's go."

So they got to the house and pulled in the garage.

Sheila said, "I wondered what happened to your Navigator."

"I don't drive it a lot anymore since I got my Benz. I need to pull it out, though. Come on in and make yourself comfortable. The stereo is over there. You can put on whatever you want to listen to. The bar is over there so fix us a drink and roll us a blunt. I'll put the steaks on."

"Wow, you got a nice place."

"Thanks. You could be here if you play your cards right."

"Yeah, okay."

So they got finished eating. Ralph asked her if she wanted to watch a movie.

"Sure."

"Go over there and pick one out. You want to do a line or two?"

"I don't care."

"Do you want to or not?"

"You know, Ralph, I would really like to try some of what we did the other night."

"What? Some rock?"

"Yeah, whatever you call it."

"Are you sure?"

"Yeah, I'm a big girl."

"Okay."

Ralph got out his cooking tools.

Sheila said, "That's amazing how you do that."

"It's nothing to it."

"I guess you have been doing it for a while."

"A little bit. Here. Put this on there, I'll work the flame for you. Here, now pull it easy and hold it in."

As she did, her body started shaking as she passed him the pipe.

He said, "What's wrong?"

She said, "I think I am cumming."

He started laughing and said, "Hell no."

Sheila said, "Damn, that is good."

He said, "Here, you want some more?"

She said, "Wait a minute. I'm getting hot."

Ralph said, "Me too. Let's take our clothes off."

They took off their clothes and sat back on the couch.

Ralph said, "Let me show you something."

"What?" she said.

He started the pipe and gave it to her and said, "Pull on that and hold it in."

As she did, Ralph started rubbing on her clit.

Sheila said, "Oh, shit, I am cumming again."

Ralph said, "You like that?"

She said, "Hell yeah. Don't stop."

About that time Ralph got on his knees, put the pipe down, and started eating her vagina. Sheila started scratching and clawing at the couch. All of a sudden, she screamed and grabbed the back of his head and pulled it into her vagina harder. She was so wet. She was squirting cum everywhere.

Ralph asked, "Do you want some dick?"

She said, "Ooh, yeah, give it to me."

Ralph slid it inside her vagina with ease, it was so wet. It was so tight.

He said, "You haven't had sex much."

She said, "No, but don't stop."

He pulled her over on top of him and let her ride until they both collapsed in a pool of cum.

When it was over she said, "Damn, what was that? That shit was good. I can't do this shit anymore. That was too good. I see why people get hooked on it."

Ralph said, "Please don't you be the one."

The next day Sheila went to work. When she got there she was still kind of tired from the night before.

Lucky looked at her and said, "Damn, girl, you look tired. A little too much partying last night?"

Sheila said, "Something like that."

He said, "Why don't you go get some coffee? I got this for a minute."

Sheila said, "Thanks, I will. Do you want something?"

Lucky said, "No thanks. I already have some."

Sheila got back to the store and said, "Okay, I am back. Thanks for letting me go get some coffee."

Lucky said, "It's cool. I have been there before. What did you do last night?"

She said, "Ralph and I were hanging out last night."

Lucky said, "Oh."

Sheila asked, "Why did you say it like that?"

Lucky said, "You are so young. Don't try to go too fast."

"What do you mean by that?" Sheila asked.

"Ralph is a great guy. He already has his career and you are trying to get yours. Ralph likes to party and that may be a little too much for you right now. You need to stay focused on school."

Sheila said, "Okay, thanks," and began her work.

About 10:30, Troy called and said that they had made it to Atlanta.

Sheila said, "Okay. Where are you all staying?"

He said, "We are at the Holiday Inn Express."

She said, "Okay. I don't get off work until six."

Troy asked, "Do you want us to come and pick you up?"

Sheila said, "Okay, that would be nice."

Troy said, "We will see you at six."

Sheila said, "Okay, bye."

About noon Ralph came in the store.

"What up, Lucky? Hey, Sheila."

"Hey, Ralph," they said.

"How are two of my favorite people in the world doing today?"

Lucky said, "I'm cool but your girl is a little tired."

Ralph asked, "Are you okay, Sheila?"

She said, "I am a little tired but I will be okay."

Ralph said, "Lucky, do you want to get something to eat? We can have our business meeting over lunch."

"Okay, let me finish this and I will be right with you. Do you want something, Sheila?"

"Sure, whatever you bring me."

Ralph said, "I got you."

On the way to the food court Lucky asked, "Man, what did you do to her last night?"

Ralph said, "I just showed her the time of her life."

Lucky said, "That girl is just a freshman in college."

Ralph said, "I know but I really like her."

Lucky said, "Really? Well, if you do, don't fuck her up. Give her a chance to grow up and get her life together. I know what you did; it was all over her when she came in today. If you like her, keep that shit away from her."

Ralph said, "Okay, man, you're right."

They got back to the store.

Ralph said, "Sheila, let me holler at you for a minute."

She said, "Okay."

Ralph said, "Here is your food. I want to apologize for last night. I never should have done you like that. I don't want you to mess with that stuff. And I feel bad for turning you on to it."

Sheila said, "That's okay, I enjoyed it, everything. Besides, I am a grown woman. I know how to say no."

Ralph said, "This is true, but still I have seen what this shit can do to people, and I turned someone I care about on to it."

Sheila said, "Oh, okay, I accept your apology."

Ralph asked, "Can I take you out to dinner when you get off?"

Sheila said, "Not tonight. Some of my friends are in town from Cincinnati."

Ralph said, "Who, Troy?"

Sheila said, "Yeah, he's one of them."

Ralph said, "Okay, call me whenever you get a chance," and gave her a kiss and left. Sheila got off work at six and Troy and her other friends were there to pick her up. Troy was so happy to see Sheila. When he saw her, he hurried toward her and gave her a hug and a kiss.

Sheila said, "Wow, you have never kissed me like that."

Troy said, "You just don't know how bad I have missed you."

Sheila said, "I guess."

Troy asked, "Don't you miss me?"

Sheila replied, "Sure I do. Let's go."

On the way to campus, Sheila noticed that she was feeling extra tired. She had no idea that she was still coming down from the drugs.

They got to campus.

Sheila said, "Come on in for a minute while I get dressed. I am going to introduce you all to my friends so they can keep you company while I get ready."

While Sheila was up getting ready, the girls kept Troy, Charles, and Thomas company. Charles and Thomas were the two guys that came to Atlanta with Troy.

They were sitting around making small talk.

Sharon said, "This should be a nice party."

Troy asked, "Do they have a lot of parties?"

Lisa said, "They are always having a party somewhere."

Charles asked, "Do you all go to a lot of them?"

Tonya said, "No, we don't have time with working and studying."

Thomas asked, "What are you all doing for the summer?"

Tonya said, "We should be getting our apartment soon."

Troy said, "You all are getting an apartment?"

Tonya said, "Yeah, didn't Sheila tell you?"

Troy said, "No, she didn't."

Tonya said, "Oh."

About that time Sheila came into the lobby.

Troy said, "You look nice."

Sheila said, "Thank you, Troy. You all ready to go?"

As they were walking across campus heading over to the party, Troy said, "So you all are getting an apartment?"

"Yes," Sheila said.

Troy said, "Why didn't you tell me?"

Sheila snapped at him, saying, "I didn't know I had to. What part are you going to pay anyway?"

Troy said, "Damn, girl, what's wrong with you?"

Sheila said, "I'm sorry, I didn't mean to snap at you. I guess I am kind of tired. I was going to tell you but some big mouth told you before I could."

"Sorry," Tonya said.

Charles said, "I hope these aren't some funny-style niggas."

Thomas said, "I know I didn't come all the way down here to have to whip somebody."

Sheila said, "That's what's wrong with you young boys. You always want to fight."

Troy said, "You aren't any older."

Sheila said, "Maybe not in age."

Thomas said, "Right."

They got to the party and it was jumping already. It was the last party of the year and it had the makings of being a hot one. The music was going, there were a lot of people there already walking around with drinks and blunts in their hands.

Charles said, "Okay, this is alright."

Troy said, "You all behave yourselves."

Thomas said, "We're cool."

Troy asked Sheila if she would like to dance.

She said, "Let me get a drink first."

Troy said, "I guess I will get one too." Troy said, "Sheila, what's wrong?"

She said, "I guess I got a lot on my mind."

And she did. She was thinking about Ralph and what happened the night before. She was thinking about how they were getting high and he ate her vagina. She had never done that before and she really liked it. She thought, *Damn, I am getting wet just thinking about it.*

They finished their drinks and got out on the dance floor.

As they were dancing, Troy asked, "What's wrong, Sheila, you seem so different."

"I guess I am just growing up, Troy. We haven't seen each other in a while. I guess we are changing."

Troy said, "I guess. Are you seeing someone else?"

She said, "Troy, don't start."

"I just asked."

"Can we talk later? I just want to enjoy myself."

Troy said, "Okay."

The party was jumping and everyone was having a good time. Charles and Thomas were dancing with Sharon and Lisa, Tonya was hooked up with some other guy. They were all dancing and partying the night away. A slow song came on while Troy and Sheila were on the floor dancing. He pulled her close and kissed her.

He said, "Damn, you don't even kiss me the same."

"Stop, Troy. Just stop." Then she left the floor and went and sat down.

Troy came over and said, "Did I do something wrong?"

Sheila said, "I am just tired and don't feel like a bunch of questions."

"Fine," Troy said.

About 1:00 the door came open. Sheila heard someone say, "What up, Ralph?"

She looked up and sure enough it was Ralph. *Oh, shit* was the first thought that went through her mind. She couldn't keep her eyes off of him. He spotted her also.

Troy noticed them looking at each other. He said, "Who the fuck is that?"

By that time Ralph had made his way over.

Sheila said, "Troy, this is Ralph, Ralph, this is Troy."

"What's up, Troy?" said Ralph.

"What's happening?" said Troy. He checked Ralph out from head to toe. He was dead sharp as usual. From his tailored suit to his fresh gators.

Ralph said, "Are you all having a good time?"

Sheila said, "Yes," in a reluctant tone.

Ralph said, "Good. I'll get at you all later."

Sheila was stuck as he walked away.

Troy said, "Is that your new friend?"

Sheila said, "Are you all ready to go?"

Troy said, "Yeah, let's go."

On the way back to campus it was kind of quiet for a minute. Then Troy asked Sheila if she wanted to come back to the hotel with him.

She said, "Not tonight, I'm too tired."

He said, "You know we are leaving tomorrow."

"I know," she said.

By that time they were at campus.

Troy said, "That's okay," and he and his boys left in the car.

The end of the quarter came and each of the girls had done great. They went home for a few days to get their vehicles and bring them back to Atlanta.While Sheila was at home, she talked to Troy briefly. She called him and apologized to him for the way she treated him when he came to see her. She said she was very tired and was very irritable. She told him she had met someone else and that they should go their own ways.

Troy didn't like it too much but he said, "Okay. Take care of yourself."

Chapter Six

Moving In

The girls all got back to campus and got their things to move into the apartment. While Sheila and Tonya were in their dorm, Sheila told Tonya that she told Troy about Ralph.

Tonya said, "How did he take it?"

She said, "He didn't like it but he took it pretty good. He probably has someone anyway and didn't want to tell me."

Tonya said, "Yeah, you know how boys are."

Sheila said, "I wonder if Sharon and Lisa are back with the truck. I am not putting this stuff in my car. I don't have enough room anyway."

Tonya said, "I don't either."

They both had little convertibles. Sheila's mom and dad bought her a new Mustang and Tonya's mom and dad bought her a BMW 318i. They both were a little spoiled but they were both pretty good girls. But time can change everything.

So they got down to the lobby and Sharon and Lisa were just getting back with the truck.

Sheila said, "What took you all so long?"

Sharon said, "Traffic was something else."

Tonya said, "I bet it was."

Sharon said, "What do you mean by that?"

Tonya said, "Nothing; I know traffic can be pretty bad around here." In the back of her mind she always thought something was going on between those two.

Soon after the girls got there Ralph and Tony pulled up. Ralph came in and asked if they needed some help.

The girls said, "Sure we do."

"Are you all ready? I have a surprise for you."

Sheila said, "What is it?"

Ralph said, "If I told you it wouldn't be a surprise, would it? Come on, let's get this stuff loaded."

After they got to the townhouse Ralph came over to Sheila and said, "Before we start unloading your things I want to show you something."

As they were walking up to the front door, Sheila asked what the big surprise was.

Ralph said, "If I told you it wouldn't be a surprise, now would it?"

"I guess not," Sheila said ".Come on, girls. Let's see what's up."

Ralph went up to the door and put the key in and said, "Now you girls, close your eyes."

Sheila laughed and said, "How are we going to walk with our eyes closed?"

Ralph said, "Yeah right." He opened the door and said, "Come on in."

When they came in they screamed with excitement. Ralph had furnished the whole house. He said, "Go ahead and look around."

The girls ran through the house. He had bought everything, bedroom suits and all.

Sheila ran down and gave him a big hug and kiss. "Why did you do all this?"

He said, "I wanted to give you all a housewarming gift."

Tonya said, "Housewarming, this is hot."

Sharon said, "What is this going to cost us?"

Ralph said, "Tony and I didn't want you all to have anything to worry about."

The girls said, "Thank you all so much. How can we ever repay you all?"

Ralph said, "Just remember who your friends are."

They got the truck unloaded and returned it to the rental office. Sheila and Ralph were in her room, putting her things away.

She turned to Ralph and said, "I don't want you to think I don't appreciate all you have done for us, but why?"

Ralph said, "We just wanted you all to be comfortable. We know you all don't make a lot of money. We knew it would take you all forever to furnish this place, so we wanted give you all a jumpstart."

Sheila said, "This is a hell of a start. What is your woman going to say about this?"

Ralph said, "I hoped you would like it."

Sheila said, "Oh, so I'm your woman now."

Ralph said, "I hope so. I like you a lot, Sheila, and I want nothing but the best for you. If you will be my woman, I will make sure you have everything you ever need, and most of the things you want. You look out for me and I will look out for you."

Sheila said, "I guess we can see how this works," and gave him a deep, sensuous kiss."

Ralph said, "Okay, we better get out of here. Let's go get something to eat."

They got out in the living room and Sheila called for the other girls. Sharon and Tony came out of her room, they were straightening out their clothes.

Tonya said, "I thought you all were putting her things away, not yours."

Everyone busted out laughing.

Tonya said, "Where are we going to eat?"

She said, "I want to go to Pappadeux, it's my treat."

Lisa said, "Bet, I like Pappadeux."

Tony said, "That sounds like a winner, but you don't have to pay for it."

Tonya said, "That's the least I can do."

Ralph said, "Okay, let's go."

Sharon said, "I know one of you all have some weed. Let's have an appetizer before we go. We need to christen our new place."

Sheila said, "That's not how you bless your new house. We should pray first and then smoke a blunt."

Sharon said, "Works for me."

Lisa said, "There is something wrong with that, I just can't figure out what it is right now."

They got to the restaurant and got seated.

Tonya said, "You all get whatever you want. I got you."

Ralph said, "Are you sure?"

Tonya said, "Yep, I'm sure."

They said, "Okay."

As they sat there drinking and eating, the girls expressed how they really appreciated what Ralph and Tony had done for them. They said if there was anything they needed, all they had to do was ask.

Ralph and Tony looked at each other and said, "Not a problem."

So they sat there having a great time, drinking and eating.

Ralph said, "You all want to continue this party at the house?"

Sheila said, "That sounds good."

Tony said, "We can stop by the liquor store and pick up a bottle or two."

Tonya said, "That's cool, I can stock our bar."

Sheila said, "Girl, where are you getting all this money from?"

Tonya said, "Saving."

Sharon said, "Saving, okay."

The bill came and it was $260.00. Tonya paid it and didn't even flinch. The girls looked at each other with the most puzzling look. Tonya pulled out a stack of money that looked to be about $1,000.00 or more. A few hundreds, some fifties, twenties, tens, fives, and a bunch of ones.

They left the restaurant and on the way to the liquor store.

Ralph asked, "What's up with your friend?"

Sheila said, "Who, Tonya?"

He said, "No, Troy."

She said, "I was wondering when you were going to get around to that. I haven't talked to him in a while. He got mad at me when he was here. He wanted me to go to the hotel with him and I wouldn't."

"Why not?" Ralph said.

She said, "You know why not. After the night you and I had, I just couldn't bring myself to do it."

Ralph just snickered and said, "Yeah, okay."

Sheila said, "Is that funny or something?"

He said, "No, not at all, but I did kind of put on a show, didn't I?"

Sheila said, "You are so full of yourself."

Ralph said, "It is what it is."

They got back to the house and brought in the bags. Tonya had bought all kinds of liquor. Most of it was top shelf. She must have spent about $400.00. Now they were really tripping. Where was she getting all this money? So as they were sitting around listening to music they were all getting kind of tight. Out it came.

"Tonya, where are you getting all this money?" Sharon asked.

"I'm a stripper," Tonya said plainly.

Sheila almost choked on her drink. Ralph and Tony looked at each other and busted out laughing.

Tonya said, "What? I am."

About that time she got up and started dancing around. She got up on the coffee table and started taking her clothes off.

Just then Lisa grabbed her and got her down and said, "Okay, you've had enough. It's time for you to go to bed."

Tonya said, "No, I'm fine. I'll chill out and she sat down on the couch."

Tony laughed and said, "Why did you stop her? There is nothing like live entertainment."

Sharon said, "I got all you need to see."

He said, "Is that right?"

"Yeah, come on and let me show you."

They got to Sharon's room.

She said, "I have been wanting to do this ever since I met you."

She pushed him back on her bed. She bent over him and started unzipping his pants.

He said, "Is that right?"

By that time she had his penis out and in her mouth. She was working it like a pro. "Oh, shit" was the only words he could muster up at the time. She was working him while she was slipping her clothes off. She got her clothes off and got down on her knees and started working him over. Tony gripped the sheets and with a loud sigh he let it go. He said to himself, *Damn, she is swallowing it.* She didn't stop. It got so intense that he had to get away.

She laughed at him and said, "You are acting like a little bitch."

He said, "Oh, yeah, it's my turn now."

He took his clothes off the rest of the way. He started kissing her as he laid her back on the bed. Her nipples were sticking out like bullets. He was working his way down between her breasts. He put his hand on her inner thigh. As he rubbed it, he moved his hand up to her pussy. It was as wet as the pouring rain and as hot and soft as fresh baked bread, and felt as fluffy. As he kissed her stomach she started to shiver. He got on his knees and lifted her foot to his mouth. As he gently sucked on her toes she started squirming and trying to get away. Then he started working his tongue up her toned calf to her inner thigh. He got to her pussy and licked on her clit. She said, "Oh, shit," and squirted instantly. He stayed right there sucking and licking until she said, "I'm cumming." He got up and put his throbbing dick inside her. She started thrashing like a fish out of water. He made love to her until he got to the point that he was about to cum and pulled out and started licking and sucking again. She came even harder. Then he turned her over and started doing it doggy style. Thrusting and thrusting.

She said, "Oh, no, I'm cumming again. Come with me, Tony," she said, "come with me, please. Here I come, baby, here I come." Then they collapsed on the bed and fell into a deep sleep.

Meanwhile, the other girls had gone to bed and Ralph and Sheila were in the living room hugging and kissing. She got up and led him to the room. They both took their clothes off without a word. Ralph sat down on the bed. She said no; sit in that chair over there. Ralph got up and sat in the chair. She sat on him gyrating with smooth even strokes. Around and around up and down until her pussy started to pop.

"Are you cumming?" Ralph asked.

"Yes, yes, oooh, yes. Damn, this feels good."

Ralph put his arms under her legs and stood up. He gripped her ass with his hands and pulled her into him harder and harder. He said, "Are you pissing on me?"

"No, I am cumming so hard."

He laid her down on the bed and started eating her pussy.

She screamed, "Please stop, I can't take it anymore."

He kept on until she almost jumped out of the bed. Then he put his dick inside her.

She said, "Come on, baby, come on."

Their bodies were thrusting together like a well-oiled machine. Then, all at once, they exploded together and fell into each other's arms and held each other until they went to sleep.

The next morning Sheila woke up early and started cooking breakfast for everyone. She was in an exceptionally good mood. When she got breakfast ready, she went to wake everyone up. She knocked on Sharon's door and said, "Time for breakfast."

She went to Lisa's door and knocked and got no reply. She opened the door and noticed she wasn't in there. She went to Tonya's door and was opening to wake her up and ask if she knew where Lisa went. She said, "Aaaw, never mind," and busted out laughing.

The girls jumped up and said, "Oh, shit."

Sheila said, "It's cool, don't worry about it."

They all finally got up to eat breakfast. It was kind of quiet at first. Then Sheila said, "This is really nice. It seems like things are going to work out just fine. We have a nice place, good friends. As long as we keep doing the right things, everything is going to be fine."

Ralph said, "You girls are going to be just fine; I am going to make sure of it."

"Tonya, are you really a stripper?" Sheila asked."

"Yep, I have been doing it since spring break."

"Damn. You are my roommate and I didn't even know. I wondered why you always worked late, though."

"I guess there goes my Patty Le'pure image."

"Shit, girl, that's been gone."

Ralph said, "I am going to try and find something else for you to do. That can be kind of dangerous for a girl your age."

Tonya said, "But it is so much fun and I am making a lot of money."

"Just be careful until I find something else for you to do."

It was getting to be about 11:00.

Sheila said, "I have to get ready to go to work. I will holler at you later, Ralph."

"I will call you later, Sheila."

"Okay, Ralph," by Tony.

Everything seemed to be working out fine. Sheila had no idea of the plans Ralph had for them. He rented the townhouse to them dirt cheap and then furnished it. Being so young the girls were about to learn a valuable lesson. If it sounds too good to be true it probably is. He intended to get every bit of his money back. It was going to be a long, hot summer.

Chapter Seven

The Long, Hot Summer

Everything was going good for the girls. They had a nice place to live. The bills were paid. Everything was good. No one knew the turn of events that were about to occur. They were about to start learning some valuable life lessons. The first is if it seems too good to be true it probably is. The next is anything worth having is worth working for. The next is there is no free lunch.

Tonya had been dancing at this club for a while. She was enjoying it at first but she was growing weary of the owner propositioning her. Almost every night it was something. Finally he was getting tired of the rejection and started putting pressure on her to bring him more money. He was getting a cut off her table dances and he wanted her to do more. One night he came to her and told her she needed to start doing some private dances. Tonya told him that she wasn't a whore and she wasn't going to do private dances for anyone. He told her if she wanted to keep working there she would. He told her if she would be his woman she wouldn't have to.

She said, "Why, so I can be one of your hoes, no thanks."

Tonya kept working in spite of the advances and demands he was putting on her. One night they got into a heated argument. He was mad because Tonya was ignoring him and not doing private dances either.

One night he called her into his office. He said, "Sit down, Tonya."

"What is it, Mack?"

"Tonya, you have been working here for two and a half months now. All the guys are crazy about you. They love the way you look and dance. You just drive them crazy. You could make big money doing private dances."

Tonya said, "I know what goes on in the back room and I ain't sucking or fucking nobody that I don't know."

"What, are you worried about catching diseases or something?"

"No, Mack," she said. "I know I can use protection, I'm just not going to do it. Most of these guys are freaks."

"So you're one of those bitches that think you are too good for anyone."

"First of all, I ain't no bitch, and I don't appreciate you calling me one."

"Fuck you, Tonya, you ain't shit," Mack said. "I gave you an opportunity to be my woman and you turned me down so you get what your hand calls for."

Tonya goes out to start her shift. There was a guy that was there a lot. He would only get Tonya to do his table dances. He looked like a business man. You know, nice dressed, clean cut. He seemed like he had it together. Tonya figured there had to be something strange about someone that was in a strip club as much as he was.

One night she saw him talking to Mack before she started her shift. When she came off the runway he called her over. He said, "Tonya, I have been giving you a lot of money over the last few weeks. I will give you a hundred dollars to go to the private room with me."

Tonya said, "Hell no. I don't care how much you have been giving me or how much you will give me. I ain't going nowhere with you."

"What is it? You think you are too good for me."

"No. I don't do that for anyone."

"What's wrong, you don't like dick?"

"Yeah, that's it, I'm gay."

"He said, "Okay, we will see."

When Tonya got off work little did she know the events that were about to occur that would change her life forever.

It was two o'clock in the morning. She got in the car and headed home as many times before. It was about a fifteen minute ride home. She reached in the ashtray and pulled out a piece of blunt she had left.

She popped in her Beyoncé CD and fired up her blunt. She was so busy puffing on her blunt, and jamming to her music, she didn't notice that she was being followed. She got to the apartment and pulled in. As she was parking the guy that was following her and sped past and went to the next drive way and whipped in. When she opened her door he was on her before she knew it. He put a knife to her throat and said, "Bitch, if you make a sound I am going to slit your throat."

She said, "Why are you doing this to me?"

He punched her in the mouth and knocked her back into the car and climbed on top of her. With the knife to her throat with one hand he was pulling her pants down with the other. He said, "Bitch, you ain't shit. You think you're all that. I asked you nicely now I'm going to take what I want."

By this time he had her pants down and his unzipped and he put his dick inside her. She was trying to fight him off but she just wasn't strong enough. As he thrust harder and harder she was crying. She managed to get hold of the steering wheel and blow the horn. This startled him so bad that he dropped the knife and got up and ran away. Tonya was so shook. It took her a minute to get herself together to go in the house.

Tonya finally made it to the door. She made such a commotion coming in the house that she woke the other girls up. She was crying uncontrollably. Tonya just collapsed to the floor. Sheila was frantic.

"Tonya, Tonya, what's wrong?"

Sharon and Lisa had come out by then. They said, "Oh my God, what has happened?"

Sheila said, "Call 911. Tonya, what happened?" Sheila asked

"I got raped," Tonya screamed.

Sheila said, "Oh my God, girl, come here."

Sheila told Sharon to get her a washcloth so she could wipe Tonya's face. By this time the ambulance and police came. The paramedics came in and put Tonya on the gurney to put her in the ambulance. The police were trying to ask her questions. This was such a traumatic experience, Tonya could hardly speak. They started asking the girls what they knew about it. Sheila told the police they were all in the bed when she came in. The police asked if she was able to give then any information.

Sheila said, "All she said was that she had been raped."

"Okay," the officer said, "we will go to the hospital and try to get some information from her."

Sheila called Ralph and told him she was on her way to the hospital.

"What's wrong?" he asked.

"Tonya got raped and beat up."

"No shit," Ralph said.

"Yeah. Me and the other girls are on our way to see about her."

"What hospital are they taking her to?"

"Grady."

"Okay, I will be there in a minute."

They get to the hospital emergency room. As they are sitting around waiting Ralph shows up. "What's going on, ladies?"

Sheila runs over and gives him a hug, she is in tears. "Thanks for coming."

"What happened?" he asked.

Sheila said, "I don't know. We were asleep when Tonya came in from work all beat up. She was so hysterical she collapsed on the floor. She said someone raped her."

"I tried to tell her about that club. I will find out what's going on."

Tonya comes home from the hospital in the next couple days. Ralph and Tony come over. Ralph tells Tonya to tell him what happened. She said when she got out of her car this guy rushed her and put a knife to her neck. "He punched me in my face and pushed me back in my car and raped me."

"Had you ever seen him before?"

"I have danced for him a few times at the club. I think he knows Mack. I saw him and Mack talking before I went on stage. When I came off stage he offered me one hundred dollars to go to the VIP room with him. When I turned him down he got mad at me."

"Is that Mack Jones that owns that club?"

"Yeah, that's his name."

"I know him," said Ralph. "I will get to the bottom of this. In the meantime you need to think about another job. I've got something that may help you all out if you are game for it."

Ralph and Tony went to see Mack at the club. They told him what happened. He gladly gave them the info they wanted. He said, "I don't want any problems from you, Ralph."

"I am not trying to cause any for you, Mack, but that was foul. Tonya is a good friend of mine and I am going to make this right. I haven't been here right. I got you."

Ralph and Tony left the club and headed to the address that Mack told them about. Tony said, "There his car is." Ralph made a phone call to some of his boys. He had connections to get things done that he didn't want to touch.

"What up, Chuck?" Ralph said.

"What's good, Ralph?"

"Are you busy?" Ralph said.

"Never too busy for you, my brother."

"Good, I got some work for you."

"Is that right?"

"Yeah, and bring Tuffy with you."

"Oh, it's like that."

"Yeah, it's like that. Meet me at the churches over on Moreland and Custer right now so I can give you the key."

"Okay. Be there in fifteen minutes."

"Alright, come on now."

They get there and get in the car with Ralph and Tony. Ralph tells him, "This cat around the corner raped a friend of mine. I need him taken care of."

"What do you want done?"

"Whatever you're in the mood for."

"I could use five grand really bad."

"You got it, do your thing. Call me when you're done so I can get your cheese. It's done, baby. Follow me around the corner so I can show you where his house is and what he drives."

They follow Ralph and Tony around the corner and their mark is coming out of his house. Ralph points at him and drives on. Chuck and Tuffy wait for him to back out of his drive way and take off. He pulls up to the stop sign Chuck speeds up beside him. He looks over and Tuffy blasts him right in the face. They drive off and give each other dap. "Now that's how you do it, baby, that's how you do it."

Ralph is back at the townhouse when he gets the call. "Hello."

"What up, Ralph?"

"What up, Chuck?"

"I just called to let you know I finished the work for you."

"Oh, yeah, how does it look?"

"It looks good; you know I always do good work."

"Okay, I will call you in a bit so I can pay you."

"Okay, Ralph. I'll holla at you later. Peace."

"Peace."

"That was my cat. He took care of our rapist."

Sheila and Tonya looked at each other and said, "Oh, yeah."

"Ralph said, "Yeah."

Sheila said, "I thought you were a lawyer."

"I wear a lot of hats. I know a lot of different people. I know folks to get anything I need done."

Sheila said, "Is that right?"

"Yeah, that's right. I got some nice, easy work that you all can do."

"What is that?" Sheila asked.

Ralph said, "Every so often I have some clients come to town and I could use you all to entertain them."

Sheila said, "Really, entertain how? We're not hookers."

"I know that, silly."

"I'm not silly either."

"Okay, check it out though. All you have to do is go out with them some time or you can entertain here. I got the place all laid out for you all."

"How much does it pay?"

"I will give you all one grand to split however you want every time you all do a job."

"I'll talk to the girls about it and see what they say."

"Okay, let me know as soon as possible. I have some folks coming in this weekend."

It was now almost the end of July. Summer was quickly coming to an end. The girls had been through a pretty traumatic event with Tonya getting raped, the girls were getting some experience and they were getting it quick, and about to get more. This was going to be a summer they would never forget.

It was Thursday evening. The girls were sitting around talking. Sheila brought the proposition to them. "Girls, Ralph has some clients coming in this weekend and he wants us to entertain them."

Sharon asked, "Entertain how? I ain't no hooker."

"It's not like that, he just wants us to go out with them and entertain them here. He said he will give us one thousand dollars to split."

Lisa said, "That sounds good but I ain't sleeping with nobody."

Sheila said, "If that was a part of the deal I wouldn't have even brought it to you all. Besides, I don't think that if it was, we would be doing much sleeping."

They laughed and said, "Okay, we'll do it."

It was now Friday. Sheila was at work and Ralph called.

"Hi, Ralph."

"Hey, Sheila. What did you all decide?"

She said, "Yeah, we'll do it."

"Cool. What time do you get off?"

"I get off at six. The other girls are off today."

"Good, I will send a limo to get you all around 8."

"Okay. How should we be dressed?"

"Wear something nice, kind of sexy."

Sheila called Tonya and told her to tell the girls what was going on. She told them to wear something sexy. A limo was going to pick them up at 8.

"A limo?"

"Yeah, a limo."

Tonya said, "Damn, these must be some pretty important people. Where are we going?"

"I don't know. Ralph didn't say. I imagine it's going to be somewhere nice."

Sheila gets home and starts getting dressed. Tonya comes in and says, "I'm kind of nervous. I haven't been out since I went through my episode."

"It will be okay, Tonya. These are some businessmen, and besides Ralph wouldn't send us into anything crazy."

"Is he and Tony going to be there?"

"He didn't say."

"I hope they are, I don't want any shit."

"I'm sure there won't be any problems."

At 8:00 the doorbell rang. Sharon went to the door and it was the limo driver.

He said, "I am here for Sheila, Sharon, Tonya, and Lisa."

"Okay, we will be out in a second."

Sharon went in and told the girls the limo was here, it is nice as hell too. She was so excited. She had never been out like this before, neither had the other girls.

The girls came out and got in the limo. They sat on the opposite side. As Sheila was sitting there looking at these men she said to herself,

Damn, they look old enough to be our fathers. The guys introduced themselves. It was James, Allen, Keith, and Leonard.

"I am Sheila, this is Sharon, Lisa, and Tonya."

James said, "Nice to meet you," and all the other guys said likewise.

The girls said, "Nice to meet you all too. So where are we going?"

"Wherever you girls want. What do you girls like to eat?"

"Just about anything."

"Do you like Pappadeaux?"

"Never been there before," said Sheila.

James said, "I think you'll like it. Would you girls like a little appetizer?" James pulls out a bag of weed and some cocaine.

Sheila said, "That's what I'm talking about."

Sheila's appetite for drugs was growing more and more. She wasn't to the point where she was going out looking for it yet, but whenever it was around she got her fair share. She was turning into a real party animal. From where she was a year ago, barely even drinking to where she is now, was almost a complete transformation.

They got to the restaurant and got seated.

Sheila said, "This is nice. What kind of food do they have here?"

Allen said, "They have Cajun cuisine. I think you all will really like it."

"If the food is as good as the restaurant looks, I believe we will." The waitress comes. "My name is Sarah. May I start you off with some drinks?"

Sheila spoke up first. "I will have a Grey Goose and cranberry."

Everyone else ordered their drinks.

James said, "Ralph told me you all were in school. Spelman is a great school. You all should be able to get great jobs when you graduate. You all are so beautiful; I would like to hire you all."

Lisa asked, "What do you all do?"

Leonard said, "We are investment brokers."

Tonya asked, "What do you all invest in?"

James said, "We're into everything from manufacturing to commodities."

Sharon said, "What kind of commodities?"

"All kinds."

At this point, Allen changed the conversation. "What are you girls studying?"

"Right now we are taking our core college courses. I want to go into law," said Sheila.

Tonya said, "I am going to be a doctor. Sharon and Lisa hadn't made up their minds yet."

Sheila said, "Where are those drinks?"

James said, "They will get here. We have plenty of time."

The drinks came; Sheila seemed to be in a hurry to get hers.

James asked, "Are you nervous?"

Sheila said, "Well, a little."

James said, "Relax. We won't do anything you don't want us to do. You girls are in good hands. We are going to be perfect gentlemen. Besides, Ralph said if anything happened to any one of you that would be our asses."

Then they all laughed.

Sharon asked, "So what's up after this?"

"Ralph has reserved a section in the VIP at Club 112. That's what's up."

They get finished with dinner and head to the club. It's about ten o'clock so it's still a little early. James tells the driver to take his time. In the limo, they are all kind of coupled off. The liquor and the drugs are flowing.

James rubs Sheila's leg and says, "You are so beautiful. Ralph said you were real special."

She said, "Just remember that," as she moved his hand.

Allen, Keith, and Leonard were making their moves also. They were all met with a little opposition.

Allen said, "Loosen up, girls, we're just trying to have a little fun, that's all."

Sheila said, "That's cool but keep your hands to yourself."

The driver pulls up to the door at the club. A bunch of people were standing in line. They were trying to see who it was in the limo. The driver came around to open the door. A big cloud of smoke rolled out as soon as he did. Someone standing there said, "Damn, I wish I was in there." The girls got out first and they were looking very nice. The guys got out next. As they started to the door, Sheila staggered a little. She was already a little tipsy. Ralph met them at the door. "What's up, you all having a good time?"

They said, "Yeah, great."

"Good, come on in, let's get you all seated."

James said, "Ralph, let me talk to you for a minute."

"What's up, James?"

"Man, these girls are sexy as hell, will they fuck?"

"I don't know, man. I told you I would get you all dates. The rest is on you. I will tell you this. They like to party. You break out a pipe, no telling what will happen. We will go to the pad when we leave here."

They had a good time at the club. At about one o'clock they left to go home.

James said, "Are you girls tired?"

Sheila said, "What's up?"

James said, "Ralph is going to bring some party supplies to the house."

"I thought you already had some supplies."

"I do but I don't have any cooking tools."

"Cooking tools, you do that?"

"Sometimes," Sheila said. "Girls, what you think?"

Sharon said, "Shit, let's get it on."

Tonya and Lisa said, "I'm game."

They get to the house, Ralph is already there. They get out of the limo and James asks Ralph if he brought the tools. He said, "You know it, got them right here."

"Cool."

Once inside, Sheila said, "Okay, guys, make yourselves at home. Girls, get the glasses and ice I will turn on the music."

Ralph asked, "Where is the powder, fellas?"

James and Allen put their stuff together. They had almost an ounce between the two of them.

Ralph said, "You gonna cook all that?"

James said, "Why not? We're going to set this party off right."

"Okay, if that's what you want."

"What I want is some of that ass in there."

"That's on them," said Ralph. "I don't have anything to do with that."

"You already paid them, didn't you?"

"Yeah, but that was just to go out with you all for the evening."

"Ralph, you know how we roll."

"Yeah, James, but these are some good girls."

"I understand that, Ralph. You know we spend a lot of money with you. We are one of your biggest clients. Now you're going to go there with me. Go ahead and start the party and I will tell Sheila to talk to the girls after they get good and high. You know how this shit turns good girls bad."

To the living room they went. They were drinking, smoking weed, snorting 'caine, and hitting the pipe. After a while all they were doing his hitting the pipe. The guys had started to get a little frisky with the girls. Even though they were getting high, the girls weren't having it.

After an hour or so, James said, "Ralph, let me holler at you."

"Okay, James, come in here."

They get in the kitchen and James says, "You gonna talk to your girl? You said that you were going to talk to her for us."

Ralph said, "Sheila, come here."

Sheila came in the kitchen. "What's up, Ralph?"

"These guys are some big clients of mine. I know I just paid you all to entertain them, but they want some action."

"Some action," Sheila said. "What, they want some sex?" Sheila wasn't getting it. "Go get them some hoes then."

"Sheila, you don't understand, they want to get with you and the girls."

"Ohh, hell no."

"Sheila, these guys have spent a lot of money on you girls."

"I don't give a fuck. We ain't no hoes."

"I know, but these are one of my biggest clients."

"Yeah, and I thought I was your woman."

"You are my favorite girl, but this is business."

"So you want me to sell my ass for you?"

"It's not like that."

"That's what it sounds like, Ralph. I thought you did all this for us because you loved and cared about me."

"I do care about you. But this is business. I moved you girls in here and got it all set up thinking we could help each other out."

"So you had this in the plans all along? Put us in here so we could be your hoes and fuck your clients. I tell you what! You fuck'em."

Sheila goes into the living room and goes off. "All you motherfuckers get the fuck out of our house. You motherfuckers think just because you got a little money you can do whatever you want."

Tonya said, "Sheila, what's wrong?"

"These motherfuckers have been setting us up all along. Ralph put us up in this house so we could fuck his clients."

James said, "Ralph, what's going on? Sheila, calm down. It's not like that."

Sharon and Lisa couldn't believe what was happening. By now Sheila was in a rage, "Get the fuck out." She was throwing ash trays, glasses, whatever she could get her hands on.

The guys said, "Let's get the fuck out of here before someone calls the police."

"Yeah, get the fuck out. Ralph, I never want to see your black ass again."

"Fine. You bitches get out of my apartment."

All the girls started throwing stuff at them as they ran out.

The girls learned a couple other very valuable lessons. One is, "all that glitters ain't gold." Two is, " pay your own way." You have to be very careful when people that barely know you want to do things for you.

Chapter Eight

After School

It had been a long four years and Sheila had finally graduated. She was a beautiful young woman ready to tackle the world. The lessons she learned in school would prepare her for a successful career. How well she paid attention to the other lessons she learned, would determine how prepared she was to deal with life.

Sheila learned early in life that when people realize they can't get anything out of you, they have no use for you. She saw what could happen first hand when you go through life trying to use people. She also learned to watch out for people and their motives. When people are overly nice to you, there is sometimes an underlying agenda.

Sheila moved back home after school. She had started to miss Cincinnati. All her family and friends were there and she wanted to be close to them. She was going to stay with her parents until she got her own place. She already had a job when she came home.Sheila started a job with P&G instead of going on to law school. She wanted to take a break from school and make some money. Besides she knew that if she wanted to go back to school, they would help her pay for it. She still had dreams of being a corporate lawyer but they made her a manager right out of college and gave her a healthy salary.

Sheila had a pleasing personality. Just about everyone she came in contact with liked her. I say just about because on your way to the top you are going to attract some haters. Some people at work resented the fact that she was their boss. They had been there for years and they brought her in straight off the street and made her their supervisor.

Sheila was always on time, good with the customers, and was fair with the staff. She had one of the highest customer satisfaction ratings ever achieved. Upper management was very pleased with her results. She won more awards for service than any manager that has ever been over her department. Even with all these accomplishments, something was missing.

Sheila had been working there for six months now. One day, she went to lunch at Bootsy's with some of the girls in her department. This was one of the nicest places in downtown Cincinnati. Some of the other employees from P&G were there also. While she and the girls were eating, a guy, named George, came to their table and introduced himself.

"I don't want to disturb you while you are eating. I've seen you around and wanted to get to know you. Here is my card. Will you call me sometime?"

"I'll think about it," said Sheila.

"Cool," he said and turned and walked away.

When he left the girls said, "Damn, he is smooth and good looking too."

Sheila said, "Yeah, you have to watch that type. I met a guy like that once. He acted all nice. He was good looking, had a great job, money, and property and was nothing but a snake inside."

"Sarah, one of the girls with her, said, "You can't judge them all by that one."

"No, but you need to watch them real close especially the ones that every girl would want. All that glitters ain't gold."

"Yeah, but it's good to look at the shine."

They all laughed and said, "Girl, you're silly."

Sheila said, "Yeah, that shine can blind you."

George was a good guy. He was six feet tall, brown skinned, athletic build, and had curly hair. His father was a minister and his mother was a nurse. He was an Ohio State graduate. He had been with P&G for ten years. He was an accounts manager, one of the best in his department. He had seen Sheila around and wanted to meet her.

The next week, Sheila was sitting at her desk when she got a phone call. "Customer service, Sheila speaking, may I help you?"

"Hi, Sheila, this is George."

"Oh, hello, how are you? How did you find out where I worked?"

"I have been here ten years. I know people in high places. I can find out just about anything I want to know about anyone here."

"Is that right?"

"Yeah, that's right. I have had my eyes on you for a while."

"Why didn't you say something?"

"I didn't want to just bum rush you. I wanted to find out a little about you first."

"So what did you find out?"

"Your name and where you worked and that you were a nice person."

"Nobody here really knows me; I am a pretty private person."

"I see."

"So if you want to know about me you have to ask me."

"So when can I see you?"

"I don't know, call me later in the week."

"Can I have your number?"

"You have it."

"Oh, okay, I'll talk to you later."

Friday came and while Sheila was at her desk, her phone rang.

"Customer service, Sheila speaking, may I help you?"

"Hi, Sheila, this is George."

"Hi, George, how are you?"

"I'm good, why haven't you called me?"

"Did I say that I was going to call you?"

"No."

"Then why would you think I would?"

"I guess I hoped you would be as interested in me as I am in you."

"I don't know you."

"Exactly, I had hoped you would want to get to know me."

"Why, because you're good looking and have a good job? That doesn't mean jack."

"Why are you so mean? I'm not him."

"You're right," and she hung up.

Sheila was still kind of bitter about what went on with Ralph. Even after more than three years later, she just couldn't let it go. She dated other guys but never let them get close to her. She would party with them a little and even had sex a time or two, but she wouldn't let anyone in. She had talked to her mom about it and her mom told her that she was going to have to let that go and live her life.

It was almost time to get off work. Sheila felt bad about hanging up on George like that and decided to call him.

"Hello, may I speak to George?"

"Hi, Sheila."

"How did you know it was me?"

"Are you kidding, nobody's voice runs through me like yours."

"That's original; I've never heard that before."

"Will you stop? Everyone isn't out to hurt you."

"Look. I just called to apologize for hanging up on you."

"I accept your apology."

"What are you doing after work?"

"Going to look at some apartments."

"Really? I have a house for rent."

"No thanks, I got this."

"Well, can I take you out to dinner afterward?"

"Okay, give me your number and I will call you when I get home."

"Okay, I'll be waiting."

Sheila remembered what happened with Ralph. She thinks all men have a motive. That experience, while it was bad some good came out of it. It taught her to be self-sufficient. No one was going to ever take advantage of her again, or so she thought.

Sheila got back from looking at apartments and her mom and dad asked her how it went.

"It went good," she said, "I saw some nice places."

Her mom asked, "What areas are you looking at?"

"The Tri-County area mostly."

Her dad asked, "Why are you moving so far away from your job?"

She said, "After living in Atlanta, I'm used to driving long distances to do anything."

Her dad said, "You know you can stay here as long as you want."

"Thanks, Dad, but I need my own."

Mom and Dad didn't know that she had things she liked to do that she couldn't do at home.

Sheila called George after she got finished talking to her parents. "Hi, George."

"Hello, Sheila, how are you?"

"I'm good and you?"

"Good. I didn't think you were going to call; I was just about to leave."

"Oh, you weren't even going to call, huh?"

"Well, you told me you were going to call me when you got finished. Besides, you didn't give me your number."

"I like you and everything, but I'm not going to be sweating you to go out with me. If I tell you that I'm going to call you then I will."

"Yeah, well, you know how you girls do sometime."

"I don't know what kind of girls you've been used to, but I ain't her."

"I hope not."

"So what's up, we still going out?"

"Yeah, I'll be over to get you in a few."

"You don't even know where I live."

"You're going to tell me, aren't you?"

"Yeah, I guess."

"You don't have to if you don't want to."

"Ease up; I'm just playing with you."

George arrived and came to the door. Her dad answered the door.

"Hi, is Sheila here, my name is George."

"Hi, I am Mr. Jones. Sheila, your date is here."

Sheila's mom comes in and says, "Hi, I'm Mrs. Jones."

"Hi, I'm George, nice to meet you. I see where Sheila gets her looks from."

Her dad called for her again. "Sheila, your date is here."

"Here I come, Dad."

Sheila and George leave. They get to the car and he opens the door for her.

"You really smell nice, Sheila."

"Thank you, George. Where are we going?"

"Do you like Pappadeaux?"

"Sure I do."

"I thought we would go there and then maybe to the club or a movie, whichever you want."

That sounds good.

They get to the restaurant and go in and get seated.

The waitress comes and says, "My name is Joyce, may I get you all started with some drinks?"

Sheila said, "Yes, I will have a Grey Goose and cranberry."

George said, "I will have the same. So I see we have something in common—we both like the same drink."

"Yeah, ain't that something."

"Why are you so cold?"

"I'm not cold, you are just too sensitive."

"Sensitive, huh? I guess I am because I feel attitude all over you."

"No, I'm just cautious of slick-ass niggas like you."

"What makes you think I'm slick?"

"I've seen my share and you look like the type."

"What type is that?"

"The type that is always looking to get something out of a woman."

"Please don't judge me by your past relationships. I'm not them."

The waitress comes with their drinks and asks, "Are you ready to order yet?"

George says, "Give us a minute." George was about ready to take her ass back where he found her. Back to what we were talking about before. "I don't have to use a woman for anything, I have my own."

"Well, the other guys did too. One was a lawyer with a nice practice, he had property, and he had his hands in a lot of stuff, legal and illegal. That didn't stop him from trying to pimp my roommates and I."

"Well, some people are just greedy. They want it all and don't care who they hurt to get it. I don't have to have it like that."

By that time Sheila had finished her drink.

The waitress came to take their order. They ordered their food and a couple more drinks. George was still on his first one.

Sheila said, "What are you going to do, babysit your drink all evening?"

"No, I just don't drink a lot."

"Oh, a choir boy, huh?"

"Not quite, I do have some things that I do on occasion."

"And what might that be?"

"In due time, if you stick around long enough maybe you'll find out."

"I figured as much. Everyone has something they like to do."

By this time their food and drinks came.

"Tell me a little more about yourself."

"Like what?"

"Whatever you want to tell me."

"Well, I'm from Cincinnati. I graduated from Hughes High. Then I went to Spelman and graduated from there. Then I came back home and went to work for P&G."

"That sounds pretty good. I want to know more about you, like what made you so cold at such a young age."

"Just life's experiences."

"You haven't lived long enough to have too many experiences."

"You would be surprised."

"Try me."

"Maybe one day if you stay around long enough."

"Okay."

They finished their food and drinks and left.

"What do you want to do now? Do you feel like dancing?"

"Sure. Where are we going?"

"There is a club not far from here called Rhino's."

"What kind of club is it?"

"It's pretty nice. It's not a teenybopper club. You got to be twenty-five and up to get in."

"Cool."

They get to the club and once inside, Sheila said, "This is nice."

George said, "It's still a little early yet."

"That's good—we can get a good seat."

They sit down near the dance floor.

"How is this?"

"This is fine, where is the waitress? Here she comes."

"What can I get you all?"

"Can I have a double Grey Goose and cranberry?" as she looks at George.

He nods and says, "I'll have the same."

"I thought you didn't drink that much."

"I don't. I order like this because it gets harder and harder to get a waitress as the night goes on. It's still early yet. I'll have this for a while. You can have what you want. I got you."

"You're just trying to get me drunk."

"No, you're going to get yourself drunk."

"I don't think so. I have to watch you."

"You're safe with me."

"Yeah, that's what your mouth says."

"I would never do anything you don't want me to."

"See, that's that bullshit. I have heard that too many times before."

"Ease up, Sheila. I keep telling you I'm not that guy."

"Tell me about you, George."

"Let's see, where do I start? I'm an only child."

"Me too."

"I thought this was about me? You had your chance. It's my turn," as he laughs.

"I'm sorry," Sheila said. "Go ahead."

"I grew up in Walnut Hills. My dad is a Pastor and my mother is an RN. I graduated from Walnut Hills. Then I got a full ride to Ohio State on a football and academic scholarship. I hurt my knee in my junior year and that was the end of football. So I finished my Psychology Degree and got a job back here."

"How do you like it?"

"It's a job, it pays the bills."

"What part of town do you live in?"

"Price Hill."

"Price Hill?"

"Yeah, Price Hill, what's wrong with that?"

"Price Hill has some nice parts."

"Enough about me. Tell me about you."

"I did."

"I want to know everything."

"That could take a while."

"I've got plenty of time. I know you told me the basics. I want to know why you think everyone is out to hurt you."

"I didn't say everyone was out to hurt me. I am just real skeptical of you men and your intentions."

"I assure you my only intention is to get to know you and see what happens."

"Okay. When I was in high school, my first boyfriend and I had sex and I didn't like it. We went to the drive-in one night and he wanted me to do it again and I wouldn't. He got an attitude. When he dropped me off at home, he didn't even kiss me goodbye, let alone walk me to the door. He knew I was leaving to go to school the next day. It made me feel that all he wanted was sex.

"My freshman year in college, one of my girlfriends went to a party with one of her male friends. He and his boys raped her and killed her. It was Christmas Eve. They did her so bad. They even threw her body in the river.

"Then I met this guy named Ralph. He was a lawyer. He had property, cars, clothes, money. He had everything going for him. Me and my girls were looking for an apartment. He let us rent one of his town houses dirt cheap. He even furnished it for us. Turns out he did all that because he wanted us to entertain his clients. I mean do whatever it took to please them. He even wanted us to fuck them. Excuse me but I still get pissed when I think about it. And after that it seems like it's been one thing or another."

"Damn. I'm sorry you've had it so rough with men."

"It's okay, I really learned a lot real fast."

"I guess you did, but you can't give up on love. All men aren't the same. I would like to think I'm nothing like that."

"Really?"

"Yeah, really. Seems like all the girls that I've met in Cincinnati are gold diggers. They see you driving a nice car, dressing nice, and have a nice house. Right away they think you're supposed to take care of them. It's refreshing to meet someone that's got her own and not looking to take yours. They think just because you sleep with them you owe them something. I tell them quick, I gave you some too.

"It's still kind of early, do you shoot pool?"

"A little."

"Do you want to shoot a couple games?"

"I'm not very good."

"That's okay, I'll help you."

"Okay."

"Come on, the tables are back here."

"They have everything here, huh."

"Not everything. They do have some pretty good food, though, if you get hungry."

"I don't think so, I'm still stuffed from dinner."

"Are you having a good time?"

"So far so good, I'll let you know when you're out of bounds."

"Fair enough."

"Okay, come over here and pick out your stick. All of their sticks are pretty straight. You just have to find the right weight for you. I just grab a stick. If you shoot for a while you'll get used to it. Grab the waitress and order us some more drinks while I put some money in the table.

"Do you want to break?"

"No, you go ahead."

"Okay, here it goes. Alright, nothing fell so it's an open table. Normally we call pockets, but I'll go easy on you."

"No, go ahead and play your game."

"Alright."

"I don't know what I should shoot at."

"Here, I will show you. First of all, I need to show you how to hold the stick." George got behind her. "You take it in your hand and lean over the table."

"George, I thought your stick was over there. You can get off my ass any time now."

"Oh, I'm sorry."

"Yeah, right. I know how to hold it. You think you got a free ride; I'm going to have to charge you for that one."

Sheila starts shooting; she's calling her pockets and everything.

"I thought you couldn't shoot."

"I didn't say I couldn't shoot. I said that I wasn't very good."

"Either way you lied to me, you cleared the table on me."

"I figured I would get my lie in before you. I'm sure you will catch up."

"Awe, that's cold. That's my song, let's go dance."

They get to the dance floor. Sheila says, "I love this song."

"What do you know about old-school music?"

"That's when music was music. Do you like hip-hop and rap?"

"Some of it, but this is what's happening. There is nothing like a little Zapp to get a party started."

"I like Cameo myself. It was a lot of good groups back then. Earth Wind and Fire, the Ohio Players, Lakeside. I could go on and on. How old are you?"

"Twenty-four, I grew up on this stuff, that's all my dad and mom listened to."

They danced and danced until it started getting late.

George said, "Let me know when you get ready to go."

"Okay. George, do you get high?"

"What do you mean?"

"You know, smoke weed, cocaine."

"Sheila, do you get high?"

"I haven't in a while but I'm feeling kind of rowdy tonight."

"I smoke weed but that's about it."

"Cool, you got some?"

"Yeah, but we have to stop and get some papers."

"You don't smoke blunts?"

"I think that's the biggest waste when you got some good bud."

"Okay, stop at the store and I will buy some papers."

"Okay. Are you hungry? We can hit the Waffle House."

"No, I'm good."

"Cool."

"Where is the bud?"

"Here you go."

"You could have at least been breaking it up for me."

"I didn't know you were going to roll it. You are just full of surprises tonight, aren't you?"

"Don't let the smooth shit fool you."

"I knew there was more to you than meets the eye. I like you, Sheila, and I want to get to know you better."

"We'll see, where is your lighter?"

"Here, be careful, that's not your average bud."

"Yeah, I could tell when I was rolling it."

"You think you know something, don't you?"

"I know about this here."

They got on 75 and Sheila lit the joint. She coughed so hard she told George to pull over so she can throw up. She wipes her mouth and says, "Damn, what was that?"

"I told you to be careful, but you know," as he laughs.

"Now I do, that's some good shit."

"I've noticed you use a lot of profanity."

"That's something I'm working on. I just got like that in Atlanta. If it bothers you we don't have to go out anymore."

"Why are you so hard? You need to chill out."

"I'm sorry, I'll work on that as well."

"I really like you, Sheila, and I'm not going to do anything to hurt you. You seem like the woman I've been waiting on. I like your style and class. You are intelligent, independent, and that little touch of gangsta in you just sets me on fire."

"Don't get too close, you might get burned."

"Just set me on fire, baby," as he laughs.

They get to Sheila's parents' house.

"Well, this is my stop. I really enjoyed myself tonight. It's been a long time since I've been out on a date."

"I can't believe you don't have someone to take you out."

"If I did I wouldn't be with you. I am a one-man woman."

"That's a good thing to know. Come on and I will walk you to the door."

They get to the door and George gives her a hug and a peck on the cheek.

"Have a good night, Sheila."

Sheila got in the house and her mind was racing. She had a nice little buzz going on. She thought to herself it would be nice to have a hit of rock. It had been a while since she had done it. Getting high that night brought it all back. She didn't know where to get it or have anywhere to do it so she put it out of her mind. She thought about George. She said to herself he was pretty nice. He didn't try to get her to go home with him or anything. He didn't even try to kiss her at the door. Then she thought it was because she had just thrown up. Then she went upstairs and went to bed.

Chapter Nine

The Good Times

It's Monday and it's back to work. This was not an ordinary Monday. Sheila was pretty happy today. She had a nice weekend. Her date with George went well, and she had some pretty good prospects for an apartment, and she liked her job. This was a good day.

About eleven o'clock George called.

"Hello, Sheila speaking."

"Hi, Sheila."

"Hi, George, how are you?"

"I'm good and you?"

"I am great. I really enjoyed myself Friday night."

"Good, I'm glad you did."

"Did you? I haven't heard from you all weekend."

"Yes, I did. I didn't call because I've been real busy, and besides I don't want to be a pest."

"You wouldn't be a pest; I was looking forward to talking to you. Why didn't you call me?"

"I didn't want to appear too anxious."

"Oh, okay. Well, I'm glad you had a good time, maybe we can do it again sometime."

"That sounds good."

"Do you go to church?"

"I haven't in a while."

"Maybe we can do that sometime."

"That sounds good."

"Okay, I have another call so I'll talk to you later."

As the day went on, Sheila is conducting business as usual. Taking care of clients, giving directives to her employees, all of a sudden she caught herself daydreaming. It was like she just went off into La La Land. She was thinking about the weekend and how nice George was. She thought she had never had a man like him. The next thought was she wondered if he was a good lover. It had been a while since she had been touched in that way. She started getting a little horny. She said, "I hope no one's at home when I get off."

Sheila gets off work and heads home. The hornies were all over her like white on rice. She could hardly wait to get home. She is listening to her music, something nice, sexy and slow. She was so hot that she was almost ready to play with herself in the car. She could feel herself getting all juicy.

Sheila gets home and almost sprints to the door. She was praying that no one was home. They had a garage so she never knew until she got in the house if her parents were there. She opens the door and runs through the house, "Mom, Dad, are you home?" She got no answer. "Yes," she said with a sigh of relief.

Sheila went to her room and closed the door. She was so anxious, she could hardly wait. It was like she was about to make love to a lover she hadn't seen in years. She through her clothes everywhere, turned on the stereo, and jumped on the bed and got busy.

She touched herself in that sweet spot and had an explosion instantly. She said, "Oh, shit." Then she started talking to herself like she was talking to her lover. "Oh, no, you're not getting away that easy." She started playing with her breasts. She said, "Damn, my nipples feel like bullets." While playing with her breast with one hand, she slid the other hand down to her vagina and started playing with her clit. Stroking it gently up and down side to side. As she applied a little more pressure her hips started gyrating more and more.

As the excitement was building, she took one hand and opened her clit to expose it more. Then she placed her palm on it and slid her two middle fingers inside her vagina. Her body tensed and she said, "Yeah, baby, that's it." With her rubbing her palm on her clit, her fingers were working in and out at the same time. "Oh, shit," she sighed and all at once her body started to shutter as she reached the climax she was looking for. Her vagina started gripping her fingers, she let out a moan and it was over.

She laid there for a minute, weak from the excitement. She said, "Damn, that was good." Thoughts went through her head how Ralph used to get her off while she was taking a hit. She missed that and wanted that feeling again. She thought about George and wondered if he would do that. She knew he smoked weed but wondered if he would be game for that.

As she laid there she heard, "Sheila, we're home."

"Okay, Mom, I will be down in a minute."

"What are you doing?"

"Nothing. Just relaxing, getting ready to change clothes." She jumped in the shower, put on some clothes and went downstairs.

"Hi, Mom and Dad. What you all been up to today?"

"Not a whole lot, baby, just been out doing some shopping."

"What did you all buy?"

"Nothing yet, we were doing a lot of looking."

"Oh, okay. What were you looking at?"

"Now you're being nosey."

"Oh, excuse me."

"You're excused. How is your apartment hunting going?"

"It's going good. Do you all want to go with me?"

"Where are you looking?"

"One is in Price Hill, one is in Western Hills, and the other one is in Rose Lawn."

"Those don't sound like very good areas."

"You would be surprised, Dad."

"I guess, I haven't been in those areas in a while let alone looking for apartments."

"Yeah, they've got some really nice areas."

"How much is the rent?" her dad asked.

"It ranges anywhere from six hundred and fifty dollars to eight hundred dollars per month. Of course the nicer one is the most expensive, and that's the one I like the most."

"That figures, you're just like your mother."

"What about you, Dad?"

"We're not talking about me; we're talking about you and your mother."

"Whatever, Dad, let's go."

Off they went to look at the apartments.

"Let's start at the least expensive one and work our way up."

"That makes sense," said Sheila's mom.

Her dad said, "Yes, that makes sense. Looking at the nicer one first will only make the other ones less attractive."

They went to Price Hill first.

"Okay, what is it that you like about these apartments?"

"Well, they have an exercise room, a pool, and a great view of the city. It is also close to my job, you know how this Cincinnati traffic can be. There are a couple ways to get off the hill so that will make it easier to get to work."

"Okay, let's go to Western Hills."

They get to Western Hills and her dad says, "Now tell me what it is you like about these."

"They have the same amenities as the last ones without the view. They have a little better floorplan."

"Okay, these don't look bad, but one thing I do know, you're farther away from work and coming out from over here in the mornings is going to be rough."

"This is true. Let's go look at the other one."

They get to Rose Lawn. As they are coming up the driveway her mom says, "These are nice. Now how much are these?"

"Eight hundred a month for a one-bedroom."

"Wow, that's expensive for a one-bedroom anywhere. What makes these so special?"

"Dad, they have everything. Two pools, tennis court, clubhouse, fireplace, and Dad, they are huge inside. They are bigger than most of the two-bedroom apartments I've seen."

"You know, with bigger apartments bigger utility bills come with it."

"Yeah, I know."

"Well, I'll tell you this. If you can afford it get it. It's better to spend a little more and be happy than to settle."

"I knew you would say that, Dad. What do you think, Mom?"

"I agree with your dad and you know we got your back."

"Yeah, I know, I'm gonna come and sign the lease tomorrow."

They get home and Sheila calls her girlfriend Stephanie.

"What's up, girl?"

"Nothing, what's up with you?"

"Just got back from looking at apartments with my mom and dad. That's what's up."

"What did you decide on?"

"These apartments over in Roselawn, do you want to go see them?"

"Sure. You got some trees?"

"You know I do."

"Do you want to come and get me?"

"Hell no. I've got the weed, I'm not driving too."

"Alright, here I come."

"Okay, pick up some beer or a bottle or something."

"Damn, girl, alright."

Sheila pulls up at Stephanie's and blew the horn. Stephanie came out and said, "Ain't no car hops in here, bitch."

"Come on, hoe, let's go."

Now Sheila is an educated young lady but when these two get together, Stephanie really brings the hood out of Sheila. These two were as thick as thieves. They could talk to each other like that, but if anyone else would try this it would be a fight.

Stephanie gets in the car and off they go.

"What's up, girl?"

"Not a whole lot, just trying to pick out an apartment. I wanted to take you and show it to you. Let's go."

"You got a blunt?"

"No, but we can stop and get one. I have to get something to drink anyway."

"Cool."

They pull up to the store and get out. They go into the store and guess who she runs into? Troy and some of his friends.

"Hi, Sheila, how are you?"

"I'm good, and you?"

"I'm good. I heard you were back in town."

"Yeah, I've been back for a few months now."

"Is that right? What are you doing these days?"

"Not a whole lot, just working at P&G."

"That's great."

"It was good seeing you, Troy, take care of yourself."

"You too, Sheila."

They get their bottle and a couple blunts and leave.

Once in the car, Sheila tells Stephanie to roll the blunt while she pours the drinks.

"So Sheila, what's up with you and Troy?"

"Nothing, why do you ask?"

"It seems like he still has a thing for you."

"Girl, that was a lifetime ago."

"What happened?"

"He came down to Atlanta while I was in school and I was seeing someone else."

"Oh, okay. Here is your drink. So what has been going on with you? I don't get to see you much anymore."

"I have been working, looking for apartments, and just hanging around the house."

"Why have you been hanging around the house?"

"There hasn't been anything else to do."

"You're not seeing anyone?"

"I hadn't been, but I went out on a date with this guy from work."

"What's up with him?"

"He seems pretty nice, but you know how these niggas are. They're cool for a while then the real person shows up."

"You can't just give up, though."

"I'm not. I kind of like him so far. We'll just see what happens."

Sheila's phone rings and she says, "Speak of the devil. Hi, George, how are you?"

"I'm good, what you up to?"

"Hanging out with my friend, going to show her my apartment."

"Oh, yeah, you got an apartment?"

"I have to go sign my lease tomorrow. If you can take a long lunch tomorrow you can take me."

"I'll see what I can do."

"Alright, I'll talk to you later."

"Okay, you girls have fun."

"Here it is, Stephanie."

"Yeah, these are nice. I looked at these one time but they were too much for me. They wanted sixteen hundred dollars to move in and I didn't have it."

"I wouldn't have it either, that's a lot. They are having a move-in special for people that have a good rental history."

"They had that when I was looking but it was going to be my first apartment."

"Maybe you can move over here now and we can be neighbors."

"Why don't we just get a two-bedroom?"

"I don't think so. That may ruin our friendship."

"You're right, I like having my own. I will check into it, though."

"That's some good weed, girl. Where did you get that from?"

"My dude in Bond Hill."

"Can you get me some?"

"Come on and I'll introduce you to him."

"You sure that's going to be okay?"

"I'll call him and make sure."

"Yeah, I think that would be best. Those boys get kind of funny when they see new faces."

Stephanie calls her guy.

"Boo, what you doing?"

"Who is this?"

"You know who this is, stop playing."

"Oh, what's up, girl, what's good?"

"I need to come and see you."

"Damn, girl, you better slow down."

"No, I don't want that. I got my girlfriend that wants to meet you to see if you can cut some trees for her."

"How tall are they?"

"About twenty feet."

"Okay, bring her by."

"Where are you?"

"At the crib."

"Okay, here we come."

"Okay, he said it's cool."

"What did you mean you didn't want that? What are you talking about? You know, you told him you didn't want that I wanted to get some trees."

"You don't know anything about that. You don't know what I know. Okay, every now and then I get some rock to sprinkle in my weed."

"You think he has some?"

"Sheila, are you sure you want to get some of that?"

"Yeah, I haven't done it in a while."

"You've done that before?"

"Yeah. My boyfriend in Atlanta used to cook it for us."

"Damn, girl, I would've never known."

"I would've never known you did it either. That shows that you have control."

They get to the house. Stephanie says, "Come on, Sheila, this is it."

"Damn, this is it?"

"Yep."

"You never would've known."

"He keeps a pretty low profile. He doesn't like a lot of in and out. Only a select few people can come by, and when they do, he likes them to stay for a little bit."

Stephanie knocks on the door. A voice from inside says, "Who is it?"

"It's Stephanie."

"Okay, here I come. Come on in, Stephanie. Who is this you got with you?"

"This is Sheila, my home girl. Sheila, this is Boo. Boo, this is Sheila."

"Damn, Stephanie, where you been keep'n her?"

"We graduated from high school together, then she went off to college in Atlanta."

"Is that right?"

"I stayed in Atlanta for a bit."

"Where did you go to school?"

"I went to Spelman."

"Yeah, you look like one of those Spelman girls."

"What does that mean?"

"Nothing, just that y'all were some of the classiest women I've seen. So what do you do here?"

"I work for P&G."

"Good, that's a good company to work for. What can I do for you ladies?"

"She wants to get a twenty of both."

"Both; you don't mess with that stuff, do you?"

"Every now and then."

"That's how it always starts out, every now and then."

"I did it when I was in college and haven't done it in a while. I heard Stephanie talking to you on the phone and put two and two together."

"And what did you come up with?"

"Four."

"I like her, Stephanie. She seems like good people. You know Boo loves the ladies. I treat them right."

"I bet you do," Sheila said.

"Okay, ladies, here you go. Y'all can use the room back there if you want."

"Do you have some papers?"

"Everything's back there that you need. You girls can stay as long as you want. I'm not going anywhere until about ten-thirty."

"We're gonna do this and go."

"Yeah, okay."

"Stephanie, he seems pretty nice."

"He is, just don't mess with his money."

"Damn, he wasn't lying; he does have everything back here. He's got papers, pipes lighters, and everything."

"Here you go."

"Damn, he gave us all that for forty dollars."

"He treats me real good. Here, roll some up, make a nice one."

"Okay. Let me see that pipe."

"Sheila, are you serious?"

"Yes, I have been wanting a hit for a long time. Do you think he will let us have some ice and a glass for our liquor?"

"I'm sure he will. I'll be right back."

"Here you go. Pour us a drink while I take a hit." Stephanie watched her as she put a piece on the stem. "Sheila, you don't need that much."

"I want to get a good one and then I will pass it to you." Sheila lights it and takes her hit and passes it to Stephanie.

Stephanie said, "Okay, you do know what you're doing."

Sheila laid back in the chair and her legs started shaking.

Stephanie said, "What's wrong?"

Sheila said, "That hit made me cumm."

Stephanie said, "Hell no. I've heard of that but it never happened to me. Okay, come on, girl, let's finish this shit and drink this liquor so we can go."

"Okay."

It is now 11 o'clock by the time Sheila got home. She was still high from the liquor and crack. She was praying that her mom and dad weren't up. She made it in the house and went to her room. As she was getting ready for bed, all she could think about was how good that dope was. She laid there and tried to go to sleep but she couldn't. her mind was just racing. She said, "Shit, it's 12:30, I have to go to work in the morning. Maybe if I take a shower I'll be able to go to sleep." Sheila got up and took a shower and got back in bed and went to sleep.

Sheila had no idea what she had just done. She thought she was just having fun. She hadn't smoked any cocaine in a while. Before she had some control over it. She had no idea about the disease of addiction, how progressive it is. See she had stopped using cocaine but kept drinking and smoking weed. That rarely ever works for long. It leaves the gate open. Sooner or later she will be saying, "Who let the dogs out?"

Six o'clock came early. When her alarm went off she didn't hear it. Her mom came in and said, "Sheila, get up, your alarm is going off. Man, what did you drink last night? This room smells like alcohol."

"Okay, Mom, I'm getting up."

"If you're going to drink you should wait until the weekend."

Her mom had no idea what was about to happen to her baby girl. The advice she should have given her should have been totally different.

Sheila got up to go to work but she could barely make it. She had to stop and get a big cup of coffee. As she was driving to work she noticed how run down she was feeling. She blamed it on how late she stayed up not the drugs. She said to herself, "I'm not staying up that late during the week anymore. I am going to wait until the weekend the next time." Damn, that shit was good, though.

Sheila got to work and was feeling a little better right now. She walks into her office and says good morning everyone. Her coworkers said, "Good morning, Sheila. You all ready for the day, so let's satisfy some customers." They noticed something was different about her but didn't know what it was. They thought she was just in an exceptionally good mood. What they didn't know was she was trying to overcompensate for how she really felt.

About 11:00, George called.

"Good morning, George, how are you? I'm fine, just a little tired."

"You and your girl must have had a late night."

"Yeah, you could say that. I've had a couple of those before. Listen, I took off for the rest of the day. I can go with you to sign your lease if you like."

"Okay, cool, I'll take off too and we can hang out. Do you mind driving?"

"No, I don't."

"Okay, I'll take my car home. Just follow me to my house."

They get to her house, Sheila says, "Come in for a minute, I want to change."

"Okay."

"You can sit and talk to my mom and dad while I change."

"I don't know if I'm ready for that yet."

"Come on, they don't bite."

"They got teeth, don't they?"

"What are you trying to say, George?"

"Just playing. Come on, silly."

"Hi, Mom and Dad."

"What are you doing home?"

"George is taking me to sign my lease."

"Hi, Mr. and Mrs. Jones."

"Hi, George, good to see you again."

"Likewise. I certainly see where Sheila gets her looks from."

Her dad said, "Well, thank you."

They all laughed and her mom said, "Well, she must have got her brains from me."

They were sitting talking while Sheila changed clothes. "What's your last name, George?"

"Daniels," he said. "George Daniels Jr."

"Who are your parents?"

"Bishop George Daniels Sr. and Marlene Daniels."

"Oh, okay, I've heard of your dad before. He is the Pastor of Tabernacle Christian Center in Walnut Hills."

"Yes, sir, that's him."

"He is a powerful man. He has a lot of clout downtown."

"Yeah, he's pretty strong."

"What about you, are you going into the ministry?"

"That's what they say. Right now I work at P&G with Sheila."

"Where did you go to school?"

"I graduated from Ohio State University."

"Oh, okay, good school."

About that time, Sheila came down. "Okay, I'm ready."

"Goodbye, Mr. and Mrs. Jones, it was nice to see you again."

"You too, son, come back and see us sometime."

"Will do."

"Where are we going, Sheila?"

"Lake View Estates, do you know where it is?"

"Yeah, in Rose Lawn. I have a partner that lives over there."

"A life partner?"

"Oh, you got jokes."

"A girl has to be sure these days. There is so many of you guys on the DL it's not funny."

"No, he's a guy I went to high school with. Are you hungry? Do we have time to get something to eat?"

"Sure, we probably should but I don't know how long this is going to take. We can just grab something from Wendy's if you want."

"Sounds good to me."

Sheila lets out this big yawn and says, "Damn, where did that come from? You must really be tired."

"Yeah, I guess I am."

They get to the apartment complex. George says, "My friend lives right around the corner."

"Does he? Do you come over here a lot?"

"Every now and then. I haven't seen him in a while now. He works some crazy hours. Do you want me to go in with you?"

"You can if you want to."

After Sheila signs her lease she says, "Come on, George, let's go look at the apartment."

"Okay, let's go."

They get to the apartment and George says, "My dude lives right over there."

"What's his name?"

"John, John Smith."

"Okay, maybe I will get to meet him one day."

"Maybe."

"Come on in and let me show you around."

Once inside the apartment, as she is showing him around, he grabs her and kisses her.

"Wow, what was that for?"

"I've wanted to do that for a while."

"Is that right? You better watch yourself, young man."

"You didn't resist."

"You caught me by surprise."

"Yeah, okay, let that be the reason."

They get in the car and Sheila's phone rang. It was her dad.

"Sheila, are you finished signing your lease?"

"Yes."

"Good, can you meet your mom and I at Furniture Fair?"

"Hold on. Let me see if George minds bringing me out there. Do you mind taking me out to Furniture Fair?"

"Sure, which one?"

"Which one, Dad?"

"The one on Rte. Four."

"The one on Rte. Four."

"Okay."

"Okay, Dad, George is going to bring me out there."

After they pick out furniture for her apartment, George asked if she wanted to get something to eat.

"Sure, where?"

"We are right here at your favorite spot, Pappadeaux."

"Okay, let's go. You know I can eat there anytime."

They get to the restaurant, get seated, and the waitress comes.

"Can I start you all off with some drinks?"

Sheila said, "Sure, I'll have a double Grey Goose and cranberry and water."

George said, "I'll have the same." As they were sitting there talking, George asked, "Do you drink every day?"

Sheila said, "Not every day and if I did, what's it to you?"

"Slow down, baby, it's just that you and your girl were out late last night and I can see that you are a little tired. Sheila, I like you a lot and I just want you to take care of yourself."

"Well, thanks for your concern but I'm fine."

"Yes, you are."

They laughed and by that time the drinks came and they ordered their food.

On the way home, Sheila was so excited. She said, "You know I like you, George. Once I get my furniture in my apartment we're going to have to celebrate."

George said, "Bet, what do you want for a housewarming gift?"

"I don't know, let me think about it."

As they were riding home she was having all kinds of thoughts. She was thinking about her and George having their own private party. She was wondering if she could get him to smoke some rock with her. She wanted him to do that one thing while she took a hit. Sheila was remembering how that felt when her and Ralph got down like that.

That's the way addiction will do you. It will let you remember the good times. The thing is she hadn't suffered any real consequences from her using yet. Just hold on, we'll get to that. She had no idea where she was headed. It always seems fun at first, but it always ends in disaster.

Friday came and it was Sheila's first weekend in her new apartment. She had some big plans. She went and bought a new teddy to wear for George. She had plans of getting him to do that thing for her. She called Stephanie and told her she needed a hook up. She told her to get her fifty and fifty and bring it to the apartment. Sheila stopped at the liquor store and bought a half-gallon of Grey Goose.

She got to the apartment and it wasn't long before Stephanie pulled up. She knocked on the door.

Sheila said, "Come on in, girl, it's open."

"How did you know it was me?"

"I saw you pull up and I unlocked the door."

"Oh, okay."

"You got my stuff?"

"Yeah, I got it. Boo must really like you. He hooked you up."

"Cool. I hope you brought some tools. I want to get a hit before George gets here."

"I got you."

"Can you leave it here with me? I'll give you some money to get you another one." "Okay, let me get a hit and I'll leave."

"Okay, here you go."

Sheila called George to find out where he was. When he answered she asked him to stop and pick up some chicken.

He said, "Don't you want to go out?"

"Not tonight," she said, "I have something else planned."

He said, "Is that right?"

"Yeah, that's right."

By that time, Stephanie was finished with her hit. Sheila did hers and let Stephanie out.

Sheila's mom called.

"Hi, Mom."

"Hey, Sheila, what you doing?"

"Getting ready to get in the shower."

"Are you okay? You sound a little funny."

"Just trying to get this place straightened up a little before George gets here."

"Oh, George is coming over, huh?"

"Yes, ma'am."

"Well, you kids have fun but not too much," as she laughed.

Sheila got out of the shower and put on a top and some jeans with no panties. She was pulling out all the stops. She knew George wanted her and she wanted him too. Not to mention she had already had a drink and a hit. By now she was on fire.

Sheila rolled a blunt and just as she lit it, there was a knock at the door.

"Who is it?" she said.

"It's George."

"Okay, here I come." Sheila opens the door and says, "Come on in."

George's eyes focused right in on her erect nipples. He noticed right away that she wasn't wearing a bra.

"Okay, stay with me, George."

"I'm sorry, you are just so sexy."

"You were looking at my titties, stop lying."

"What do you expect walking around like that?"

"I'm at home; I can walk around however I want. Come on in and have a seat."

"It smells good in here, what you smoking?"

"It's in there in the ashtray. Go ahead and fire it up and I'll get you a drink."

Sheila got his drink and comes and sits beside him. "Did you get some plates with the chicken?"

"No, I didn't."

"Then I guess you're going to be washing dishes."

"That's cool. I don't mind…I'll do anything for you."

"Is that right? I'm going to hold you to that. Are you ready to eat?"

"Sure."

"Okay, let's eat and I'll show you around."

They finished eating and put the plates in the sink.

Sheila said, "Come on and let me show you around."

"Okay."

"This is my kitchen. This is my washroom. This is the patio, I'm going to like sitting out here. It already has a privacy fence. This is the downstairs bathroom. Come on upstairs, let me show you the rest of it."

"Okay."

As they got to the steps, Sheila got on the first step and George grabs her and kisses her.

Sheila said, "Okay, that's going to cost you."

"I'll pay it."

"I bet you will."

They head up the stairs; Sheila was a few steps ahead of him. Her ass was right at eye level.

George said, "This is really nice."

"What, my ass or the apartment?"

"Both."

"Come on, boy; get your mind out of the gutter."

"You put it there."

"Not yet. This is the extra room, this is going to be my computer room. This is the master bath; it connects to my bedroom. This is my bedroom."

"Wow, this is so sexy."

"If you're a good boy you might get to experience it."

They get back downstairs; Sheila asks, "Are you ready for another drink?"

"I don't know, I'm driving; I might need to take it easy."

"It's early yet, what are you afraid of?"

"I'm not afraid of anything."

"Yeah, we'll see, that's what you're mouth says. Here, smoke some more of this. I'm going to go and get comfortable. I'll bring back some more treats when I come back."

She left and went upstairs. While she was gone, George was sitting there boiling with anticipation. Sheila had him right in the palm of her hands and she knew it. She had big plans for George and he was falling right into her trap. He had no idea what was about to happen to him. He had no idea that the most pleasure he had ever experienced in life was going to be the beginning of the most painful part of his life.

Sheila comes back downstairs in her robe. She said, "This feels a lot better. Relax, George," Sheila said. "You can get comfortable if you want. Do you need to take a shower or anything?"

"No, I just took one before I came over."

"Okay. Are you ready to party with me?"

"Yeah, let's get it on."

"Are you sure?"

"I guess, you aren't going to go crazy on me, are you?"

"No, silly. It's a special night and I wanted to do something special. Have you ever smoked primos before?"

"Yeah, a time or two."

"That's what I want to do."

"Okay, have at it."

Sheila rolls a primo and pours herself another drink. She fires up the joint.

George said, "Damn, you laced that heavy."

"That's the way I like it. Here, get this shotgun."

She blows the smoke into George's mouth and sticks her tongue in at same time. This really turned him on. She gave him the joint and slid over next to him and started rubbing on his leg as he hit the primo. She noticed his penis was hard and rubbed it.

George looked at her and smiled and said, "You like that?"

She said, "Yeah, that's kind of nice. It's been awhile since I've felt one of those."

"Is that right?"

"Yep."

They get finished smoking the primo and Sheila stands up and takes her robe off. George was stunned as he sat there looking at her toned body. She walked over to him and straddled him. She sat on his lap and started grinding on him. She started kissing on his neck and his ear saying, "Damn, George, I am so hot." She slid backwards off his lap as she was kissing on his chest. She made it to his penis and put it in her mouth. At the same time, she started fingering herself.

He said, "Damn, Sheila, what are you doing?"

Her body started shaking. She got she and George off at the same time. She didn't expect him to cumm in her mouth. It made her gag. She got up and ran to the bathroom and spit it out. She came back in the living room and went at it again.

She said, "I want you to do something special for me."

"Anything, baby, anything."

"Come on upstairs."

They get upstairs and get in the bed. Sheila jumped right on him. George rolled her over and started kissing on her neck. He worked his way down to her breast. As he started sucking on her breast. She started panting like she had been running a race. He was working his way down her stomach. Her body started flexing. She said wait George, I have to get something before you do that. She reached over in her nightstand and got out her pipe and some rock.

George said, "Sheila, what are you doing?"

"You said you would do anything for me. Well, I want you to eat my pussy while I take this hit."

"What??"

"Yeah, that's what I want you to do."

"Well, okay."

Sheila sat on the edge of the bed. She said, "Come over here and rub my pussy while I put this on here."

George said to himself, *Hell no, this bitch is crazy. What the hell, let's see what happens.*

"Okay, when I take this hit I'm going to lay back on the bed and I want you to start sucking it. It intensifies it though if you have some smoke in your mouth."

As George was rubbing on her clit, Sheila took a big hit. She gave him the pipe as she lay back on the bed. He said, "What the hell." He took a hit and gave it back to her and started sucking her pussy. Instantly, her body started shaking. As he was sucking on her pussy she came so hard she squirted on his face. She screamed so loud it startled George. He had never experienced anything like that before. This turned him on even more. This was his first time ever hitting the pipe.

Sheila said, "Damn, that was good. Now it's your turn. Sit on the bed."

"Now what do I do?" George said.

"Here, hold this and I am going to put you a piece on the pipe. Now take a hit and give it to me and lay back."

George took a hit and gave Sheila the pipe. As he lay back on the bed Sheila took a hit and went down on him. This was feeling so good to George he could hardly contain himself. Sheila was working him so good he tried to jump up and get away. She pushed him back down and jumped on top of him and started riding him like there was no tomorrow. George couldn't believe it. This was the wildest sex he had ever had.

About that time Sheila's body started shaking again. She said, "Shit, George, I'm cumming again. Cum with me, George. Cum with me."

"Okay, Sheila, here it comes. Damn it, here it comes. Damn it, this is the best pussy. There it is, Sheila, there it is."

They came together and collapsed in each other's arms.

"Damn, Sheila, that was wild. That is the first time I have ever done anything like this. That was also my first time ever hitting the pipe. Do you do this often?"

"I haven't done this since college," said Sheila.

"Well, how did you know where to get dope?"

"I am from Cincinnati, you know."

"I never would have thought you knew anything about that."

"Why, because I'm a career girl with a corporate job? Don't let the smooth shit fool you."

"I guess not."

"Do you want to finish this with me?"

"I don't know, Sheila."

"You did that with me and it didn't kill you. Come on, let's finish it and we can throw the pipe away."

"Okay, Sheila, I guess it won't hurt this time."

Neither one of them had any idea of what they had just done. It all seemed like fun, but that's the trap. The adversary comes at you with his pleasures to set you up to kill you. With George being a preacher's son, that makes the adversary even happier. Sheila is caught up in a vicious cycle and doesn't even know it. Just because she hadn't done it since college and haven't had any problems behind it, she thought she was okay. She didn't know that this was the beginning of the end.

Chapter Ten

The Message

Sheila had no idea that the seed of addiction had been planted in her years ago in college. When Ralph topped it off with the best sex she had ever had, it made it that much worse. She had such a great orgasm when they mixed the two together, in her mind she couldn't reach those heights without it. She had dated other guys since Ralph; she just didn't have the nerve to ask them to do what she had asked George to do. This set them both up for a slow death.

George really liked Sheila; there was nothing he wouldn't do for her. Sheila was a little more advanced than George was. Sheila had a power over him that he didn't understand. She was all he could think about. Sheila liked him a lot also, but she had such a mistrust of men so it was hard for her to let go.

Monday came and it was back to work as usual. Sheila walked in and said, "Good morning, everyone."

"Good morning, Sheila," they replied.

Natalie, one of her employees, asked, "How was your weekend?"

She paused for a second and with a big smile she said, "It was great."

Natalie said, "That good, huh?"

Sheila said, "Yes, it was."

"Wow, what did you do?"

"Girl, my man and I had a private party in my new place."

"Oh, you moved in?"

"Yes, I did."

"So what did you all do?"

"I told you it was a private party. It's a secret, if I tell you I would have to kill you."

"Never mind then."

Sheila went to her office and closed the door. She sat in her chair and leaned back with a big grin thinking about Friday night. It crossed her mind how George made her feel. Then she thought how she talked him into it. She realized what kind of power she had over him. This made her smile even harder. She hadn't got to the part where the same thing that makes you laugh can make you cry.

About that time George called.

"Sheila speaking, may I help you?"

"Hi, Sheila, how are you?"

"Hey, George, what's up?"

"Not a whole lot. I was just sitting here thinking about you."

"Is that right? What you thinking about?"

"I was thinking about how much I like you."

"George, you don't even know me."

"I know it hasn't been that long, but I can't stop thinking about you. I don't know what you've done to me."

"I haven't done anything."

"Yes, you did. I don't normally act like this, but you are something special."

"Well, thank you, George, I've been thinking about you too."

"What have you been thinking?"

"Now you're being nosey."

"Alright. What are you doing for lunch?"

"I don't have any plans. Do you want to take me to lunch?"

"Yes, I do."

"Okay, let me get some work done and I will see you at noon."

"Okay, I will see you then."

George had been thinking about Sheila all weekend. That episode they had Friday really excited him, but something in him told him that they couldn't continue like that. He really liked Sheila, but this part of her that she showed him concerned him. He had made up in his mind that he wanted something more permanent with her. He thought he could change her. He didn't know this was going to be something that she had to do.

It was now noon and Sheila was kind of excited about her lunch date with George. As Sheila was headed out the door Natalie asked, "What are you doing for lunch? The other girls and I are going to Chipotle, would you like to go with us?"

"Not today," she replied, "George is taking me to lunch." She had such a big smile when she said that.

Natalie said, "Okay, girl. George must be something special, I see that big Kool-Aid grin."

Sheila said, "He is kind of nice," as she left the room.

When she got downstairs, George was there waiting on her. As he opened the door for her he said, "Hello, beautiful," and gave her a peck on the lips.

She said, "You can't do that out here."

He said, "You kissed me back," as he laughed.

"No, I didn't."

"Okay, whatever."

George came around and got in the car. He said, "So where do you want to go?"

"I don't know, you pick. You asked me out for lunch."

"You want to go to Bootsy's?"

"That's fine with me, I'm with you."

"Okay, that's where we'll go. Sheila, I really like you a lot."

"Is that right? Well, I can't stand your ass."

"You are just so damn sweet," as she laughed.

"Oh, you got jokes?"

They get inside and get seated. The waitress comes over and asked, "What can I get you all to drink?"

Sheila said, "I'll have water."

George said, "The same for me." The waitress left and he said, "What, no Grey Goose?"

Sheila said, "No, it's too early and besides, I have to go back to work. If I was going home, it might be a little different."

The waitress brought their water and took their order. As they were sitting talking, George said, "Sheila, I want you to be my girl."

"Why is that, George?"

"I've never known anyone like you. You are beautiful, smart, independent, and have just that right amount of hood in you. You didn't get an education and forget who you are. Instead, you let it enhance who you are."

"George, there is a lot you don't know about me."

"I know and there is a lot you don't know about me. I think as we spend more time together we will learn and grow together."

"That sounds good, but I have been through so much it's hard for me to trust anyone."

"Sheila, it has been the same for me. So many girls have just wanted me for what I had and what I could do for them it's not funny."

"Well, I have and can get my own. That was one of the things that I learned early. When I start allowing men to take care of me they think they own me."

The waitress came with their food and they continued the conversation.

"When I was in college, I met this lawyer and he tried to turn my girlfriends and I out. He put us up in this nice town house and furnished it. With the amount of rent he was charging, it sounded like a good deal. He would take us out, supply us with drugs and alcohol and everything. Then one day he wanted us to go out with some of his clients. He got upset when we wouldn't screw them. I've had a lot of guys that seemed real nice at first then turned out to be crap."

"Well, Sheila, I have to tell you I'm not them. I have had some of the same experiences in reverse. Women would look at me and see dollar signs. I had a girlfriend that I let move in with me. I did everything for her. I even bought her a car. She had a job of her own but she didn't make enough to live like she was living. I had suspected that she was messing around on me. One day I found out. I got off work early came home and she was in our bed screwing some other guy. After that, it's been hard for me to trust also. When you wouldn't let me rent you one of my places, something told me you were the one. So many women would have jumped at that chance. I learned my lesson with that one; I will never do that again. Sheila, I want you to go to church with me Wednesday night."

"Wednesday night?"

"Yeah, we have a Wednesday night service."

"I don't know, George; I have never been to church on Wednesday."

"Maybe it's time you tried something new."

"I don't know, I'll let you know."

They finished eating and it was back to work.

George gets Sheila back to work and says, "I want you to think about what I asked you."

"What, being your woman or going to church?"

"Well, both actually. I really like you, Sheila, and I want to be with you."

"I like you too, George. We'll just have to take it one day at a time and see what happens."

"What are you doing after work?"

"I don't know, why?"

"I want to cook dinner for you."

"I don't know, call me later. I have to see how my day goes; I might not feel like being bothered."

"Oh, it's like that."

"Just call me."

About four o'clock George called. "Hey, Sheila."

"Hi, George."

"How was the rest of your day?"

"It wasn't bad, what about yours?"

"Mine was great after seeing you."

"You need to stop. You know it's not that serious."

"You just don't know how I feel about you."

"I believe it's more like how you feel about my coochie."

"Well, that's good too."

They both broke out laughing.

"No, seriously, what are you doing after work; I want to cook for you."

"Oh, you can cook?"

"Baby, I got skills."

"Okay, but I have to go by my parents' first."

"That's fine. What do you want?"

"Use your imagination; I want to see what kind of skills you have."

"Okay. Dinner should be ready about seven."

"Alright, I'll see you then."

Sheila gets over her mom and dad's house she goes in the house and says, "Hi, Mom and Dad. Something smells good, what's cooking?"

"Hi, babe," her dad said.

"Hi," Sheila said to her mom.

"It seems like forever since we've seen you."

"I know, I really miss you two."

"We miss you too. How have you been?"

"I've been good, just a little busy."

"Busy doing what? You too busy to come and see your mom and dad?"

"I've been getting my place together and tryin' to enjoy it. I call you all every day."

"That's well and good, but we need to lay eyes on you every now and then."

Sheila sat down at the kitchen table while her mom was cooking. Her dad came in and joined them shortly afterward.

He said, "So what's been going on, baby girl?"

"Not a whole lot, Dad. I've been working pretty hard."

"How is work going for you?"

"Work is good. I am managing the call center."

"Oh, really? What do you all do there?"

"We handle customer orders and complaints."

"That's great, baby girl. Have you thought about going back to school?"

"I have but not right now. I want to enjoy life right now."

"Well, don't get to enjoying it too much. You will look up and time has just passed you by."

As they were sitting there talking her dad got up and fixed himself a drink and came and sat back down.

Sheila said, "Where is mine?"

He looked at her and said, "I guess you are old enough to have a drink with your dad. You are going to have to fix it yourself, though."

"Not a problem, I know how to do that. Mom, do you want one?"

"No, hun, not right now."

Sheila came back to the table and sat down.

Her dad said, "So how is Stephanie?"

"Fine," Sheila said.

"You and her have been hanging out a lot lately, huh?"

"Not a lot, why do you ask?"

"I've just heard a few things."

"Like what?"

"Just that you all were hanging out late pretty often."

"We've hung out a couple times."

"You just be careful. You know that girl gets into all kinds of stuff."

"Okay, Dad, I'll be careful."

"Sheila, are you hungry?" asked her mom.

"I already have dinner plans with George."

Her dad said, "He seems like a nice young man."

"He's alright."

"Where does he live?"

"Price Hill."

"Why don't you bring him by sometime?"

"I'll see what I can do."

"Where are you all going for dinner?"

"He is cooking dinner at his house."

Her mom said, "Oh, he cooks, huh?"

"That's what he said, but we'll see."

"So what's for dessert?"

"Mom, what do you mean?"

"You know exactly what I mean; I'm not ready to be a grandmother."

"Don't worry, Mom, that's not going to happen."

"Just be careful."

"Okay, I will talk to you all later, I got to go."

"Okay, babe, have a good time."

"Not too good a time," her dad said.

Sheila chuckled as she left.

Sheila makes it to George's house. She walks up and rings the doorbell. George comes to the door in an apron covered with flower.

"Wow, what are we having, fried George?"

"Ha-ha, very funny, come on in."

"Something smells good, what you cooking?"

"Fried chicken, greens, and cornbread."

"You had time to make greens?"

"I put them on last night."

"Oh, okay. You think you're smart, huh? You were planning on getting me over here all the time, huh. I love it when a plan comes together."

"You didn't bring anything to drink."

"No, I thought you might already have some."

"I have some beer."

"I don't drink beer, where is a liquor store?"

"Right around the corner if you want to go around there."

"Okay, I will be right back."

Sheila gets to the liquor store and goes inside. As she is standing there she notices this guy checking her out pretty hard. She tells the clerk to give her a fifth of Grey Goose.

The guy steps up and says, "Hey, pretty lady, you gonna drink all that by yourself?"

"No, I'm not."

"My name is Flip, what's yours?"

"Sheila."

"Good to meet you, Sheila," as he reached out his hand.

She knew he was a thug but he had a little class about him.

"I haven't seen you around here before."

"I am over a friend's house."

"Looks like you all are having a little party."

"Not really, just dinner."

"You aren't the police, are you?"

"No, why do you ask?"

"I was going to give you my number just in case you want to turn your dinner into a party."

"Okay, thanks.

Sheila got back to George's house. When she walked in the door he grabbed her and kissed her.

She said, "Wow, what was that for?"

He said, "Just because."

"Because what?" Sheila said.

"Because, that's how I feel about you. You just don't know how you make me feel."

"I guess I don't."

"Are you ready to eat?"

"Yes, I am hungry."

"Okay, just have a seat and I will bring the food out."

"Okay. It smells good."

"I hope you like it."

"I need to wash my hands."

"The bathroom is right through there."

Sheila came back and sat down at the table. George brought the food out.

Sheila said, "That really looks good. I hope it tastes as good as it looks."

"I'm sure it will. I told you that I have skills."

"Everyone says that about themselves."

"Yeah, but when I say it it's true."

Sheila fixed her plate, then George fixed his.

"Be careful, Sheila, it's real hot."

"Kind of like me, huh?"

"Oh, yeah, it's spicy too."

They laughed.

George said, "Let me say grace. Lord, thank you for the food we are about to receive and bless the company I am receiving it with. Amen."

Sheila said, "That was nice, thank you."

"I told you that I want you to be my woman. I want you to be blessed as well as myself."

As they start to eat, Sheila coughed.

George said, "Slow down."

"My food went down the wrong way. It is good, though."

"Thanks. I told you I had skills."

"Yes, you did. How did you learn how to cook so good?"

"My mother taught me how to cook at an early age. She also taught me how to clean, wash clothes, and iron. She said she was teaching me these things so I could take care of myself and not rely on someone else to do it for me. I think that intimidates some women when they see I am self-efficient."

Sheila said, "They are probably a little insecure. I like that myself."

"Good, because I think I want to keep you around."

They get finished eating and start clearing the table. George is following her into the kitchen.

He says, "Umm umm."

Sheila said, "What's wrong?"

"Nothing," George said, "nothing at all."

"Well, what was that for?"

"I was just admiring the view. You have the nicest ass."

"Is that all you see when you see me?"

"No, but that is definitely one of your good qualities," then he chuckled. "This ass is going to get you in trouble one day."

"I welcome that kind of trouble," and then they both laughed.

Sheila asked, "Do you want me to help you clean the kitchen?"

"You can if you want to."

"Okay, I'll help you."

George said, "I'll wash and you can dry."

"That's fine."

George started the water. He turned to Sheila and pulled her to him. He said, "Sheila, I'm starting to like you a lot."

Sheila said, "Me too."

Sheila put her arms around George's neck and starting kissing him. When they were finished kissing, she pressed her body tightly against his and said, "What's wrong with your pants? They seem to be a little stiff."

George said, "That's not my pants." He backed away and said, "We better get this kitchen cleaned up before something happens."

They get finished with the kitchen and go into the living room.

"Are you ready for a drink?" George asked.

"Sure, you know how I like it."

George fixed the drinks and came in and sat down.

Sheila said, "I really like your place."

"Thank you."

"How long have you been living here?"

"I have been here for about three years now."

"This is a weird area," Sheila said. "You have these nice houses here and you get up the street and it's like another world."

George said, "I know. They are working on it slowly but surely. Would you like to walk up to the park?"

"Sure, let's go. Let's finish these drinks and we can go."

"I'm not going to get jumped by any of your women, am I?"

"Not today," as he laughed.

"Oh, you got jokes."

"A few."

They start walking to the park. George reaches over and grabs her hand. The thought went through Sheila's mind that this is different. This is the first time that she had held hands with someone and walked to the park. She was feeling this. This was turning into a nice evening. She was starting to feel that George really liked her. George asked her why she was so quiet.

"Oh, I'm just thinking."

"About what?" he asked.

"Now you're being nosey," as she laughed.

They get to the park and George says, "Let's walk more towards the back so we can blaze this blunt."

"That sounds good to me."

They find a bench in the back and sit down.

"Here, fire this up."

"I didn't know you had some weed."

"That just goes to show that you don't know everything."

"Oh, you got a smart mouth today."

"I am smart every day."

"I met a guy at the store. He gave me his number and told me to call him if we wanted to turn this dinner into a party."

"What was his name?"

"Flip."

"Oh, okay, I know him. That's where this came from."

"Is that all he sells?"

"No, but that's all I get from him."

"Oh."

"Are you enjoying yourself, Sheila?"

"Yes, I am. I love the way you say my name."

"How is that?"

"It's like how you say it with so much feeling."

"That's because I like saying your name. You have no idea how I feel about you."

"No, why don't you tell me?"

"We don't have enough time, but if you give me the rest of your life I will show you."

"Oh, that's some smooth shit there."

"No, that's some real shit."

"George, you don't even know me. You don't know where I've been."

"I don't care where you've been. What's important is where you're going. I like you a lot, Sheila."

Then they held each other and had a deep passionate kiss. Sheila had her hand on his thigh. She said, "See, there goes your pants again."

"Do something about it."

"Here?"

"Let's go back to the house."

"Okay, can we finish this first?"

"Okay."

As they walked back to the house holding hands,

Sheila said, "You know, George, I like you too. It's just so hard for me to trust."

"I'm not asking for all your trust at one time. All I'm asking for is a chance to show you."

"I think I can do that."

"It would make me so happy if you could. I like you so much. It has been a long time since I've felt like this about anyone. Most of the girls I've dated only wanted me for what I could do for them. I'm tired of helping women that don't want to help themselves."

"George, trust and believe, I won't ask you to do anything for me. In fact, it's hard for me to accept gifts from anyone. I've had very well-to-do men in my life. When I let someone call themselves taking care of me, it came with stipulations. I told you about my lawyer friend. Every boyfriend I had after that was pretty much the same. I got to the point that I didn't want to be bothered. There is a lot you don't know about me."

George said, "I don't care about your past, all I care about is our future."

"Oh, that was some real slick shit there."

"You liked that, huh?"

"Yeah, I did."

"You need to know that I mean every word. I can show you better than I can tell you."

"That's what I'm talking about."

When they walk in the house, George closes the door with one hand, grabs Sheila with the other, and pulls her to him and kisses her.

Sheila says, "Wow, that was nice."

"Did you like that?"

"You are a great kisser, George."

"Want me to kiss something else for you?"

"Don't start none and it won't be none."

They both laughed.

"Have a seat. Would you like a drink?"

"Sure."

"I'll be right back. Let me get some glasses and ice."

"Okay, I'll be right here."

"Turn the stereo on."

"What do you want to listen to?"

"It doesn't matter, just pick something."

Sheila said, "You have so much music it's hard to decide. Ahh, here we go, Luther, that's one of my favorites."

"Yeah, it's a shame that he died. He really made some good music. Here you go, my dear. Do you want to smoke a blunt?"

"Sure, do you have something else to go with it?"

"You see it, vodka."

"No, I mean some rock."

"No, I don't have any of that. I told you I don't do that much. The other night when we did it, it was the first time in a long time. It was the first time I ever smoked it out of a pipe."

"You're lying. I know that wasn't your first time."

"Yes, it was."

"Man, you mean I showed you something? Did you like it?"

"I did. It was kind of different, especially doing it while we were having sex."

"I know, it intensified it, didn't it?"

"Yes, it did."

"You want to do it again?"

"Not tonight. I have to go to work in the morning."

"I do too."

"Maybe you can handle it but I can't."

"Okay."

They sat there listening to music having their drinks and smoking their blunt. George slid over close to Sheila and kissed her. She wasn't very responsive.

George said, "What's wrong, Sheila?"

"Nothing," she said. "I guess I'm just a little tired." Really she had smoking crack on her mind.

George said, "I want you to go to church with me."

"When?"

"I generally go on Wednesday and Sunday. I'm going Wednesday night if you want to go with me."

"I don't know, George, I haven't really been much of a church person."

"It's never too late to start. I would really like for you to go with me."

"I'll think about it. Well, I'm getting ready to go. Thanks for dinner and everything. I really enjoyed myself."

"Not a problem. I enjoyed having you here. I'll walk you to your car."

"Okay."

They got to the car, she kissed him goodbye and he went back to the house.

Sheila got in her car and reached for Flip's number. She found it and pulled off so George wouldn't see her sitting dialing the phone.

She started dialing as she pulled off.

"Hello, who is this?"

"It's Sheila from the liquor store earlier."

"Oh, what's up, pretty lady?"

"I need to see you. Where are you?"

"I'm at the apartments on Price Street down from the liquor store."

"Okay, I'll be there in a second."

She pulls up in front of the apartments and he gets in the car.

"What can I do for you, pretty lady?"

"It's Sheila."

"Okay, I'm sorry."

"No, I said that just in case you forgot my name."

"I'm not a dummy, I can remember from a second ago. In fact I have been thinking about you since I met you. I'm not a fool, though. I know you wouldn't want to be bothered with someone like me."

"I don't judge people. Just because you sell drugs doesn't mean you're a bad person."

"I'm not. This isn't the only thing I do. I'm just trying to make ends meet while I'm in school."

"Really, what are you studying?"

"Architecture."

"Wow, that's great. Listen, I want to get some crack but you can't tell George. I told him I met you at the store."

"Yeah, that's my dude. What can I get for you?"

"Give me a twenty."

"Are you sure? They say this is some good shit. You're gonna be calling back for more. I will make you a nice deal on a fifty."

"Okay, let me have it."

"Okay, I'll be right back."

Flip came back and gave her the dope and she pulled off.

George called and asked, "Have you made it home yet?"

"Not yet, I stopped at the store. I'm almost there, though."

"I really enjoyed having you over for dinner."

"I enjoyed myself also."

"Sheila, I really would like for you to go to church with me Wednesday night. I think you'll really enjoy it."

"I'll think about it, George, but don't try to push me."

"Okay, Sheila. I'll talk to you tomorrow."

"Goodnight, George."

"Goodnight, Sheila."

Stephanie called when she was pulling up at home. "What you doing, girl?" she said.

"Just getting home from over George's having dinner."

"Did you have a good time?"

"It was okay. We ate, walked to the park, had some drinks, and smoked a blunt."

"Is that all you smoked?"

"Yeah, that's it."

"Boo has been asking about you."

"Oh, yeah?"

"He asked where you've been."

"I met someone else today. I just picked some up."

"You weren't even going to call me?"

"I really didn't think about it, but since you called, come on over."

"I'll be there in a bit."

Sheila pulled up to her apartment and bounced out of the car. The anticipation was so strong; it made her stomach start bubbling. She ran inside and went straight to the bathroom. After she used the bathroom she couldn't wait to get that first hit. She got her pipe out and put a big piece on it. She hit it and as soon as she blew it out her knees buckled. She started shaking and said, "Oh, shit." She instantly grabbed her vagina and started playing with it. When she got finished her hand was wet as hell and cum was running down her leg. She said, "I'd better take a shower before Stephanie gets here." She took another hit and took her clothes off and got in the shower.

She got out of the shower and put on some shorts and a t-shirt. About that time the doorbell rang. She opened the door and let Stephanie in. She told her to go ahead and get some glasses and ice and fix some drinks while she goes and gets the stuff.

Stephanie asked, "Is it good?"

"Girl, it's some panty dropper."

"That good, huh?"

"You'll see."

Sheila comes back downstairs and gives Stephanie the pipe and says, "It's still some in there."

"Get that out of there." Stephanie said, "Shit, girl, I want a fresh one."

Sheila said, "Okay."

When she pulled the rock out, Stephanie asked, "How much was that?"

"This a fifty," Sheila said.

Stephanie said, "Damn, you got hooked."

Sheila broke Stephanie off a piece and gave it to her.

"You might not want to put all that on there at one time."

"I'm a big girl. I can handle it."

"You're going to make my pipe harsh."

"I brought my own."

"Good," Sheila said.

Sheila was pouring herself a drink. Stephanie took her piece and put it on and took a hit. When she blew it out she laid back on the couch and said, "Damn, girl. This shit is good."

"I told you."

They sat there drinking and getting high. They were almost half-way through. Stephanie asked Sheila if she wanted a shotgun.

Sheila said, "Sure. It really gives you a rush."

Stephanie took a hit and blew it into Sheila's mouth. She sat back and blew it out and said, "Damn." She started playing with herself.

Sheila said, "Either this shit is making me extra horny or your lips are soft as hell. I wish George was here to lick this for me."

"I'll do it for you," Stephanie said.

"Stop playing, girl."

"No, seriously we can have some fun and no one will ever know. Shit, I'm horny as hell too." Stephanie stood up and took off her pants.

Sheila said, "You're serious, aren't you?"

"Yeah, let's do this."

Stephanie sat down close to Sheila and said, "Put a hit on your stem and lay back."

Sheila put a nice piece on and laid back. When she lit it Stephanie started playing with her clit. Sheila blew it out and said, "Oh, shit, that feels so good."

Stephanie said, "Take another hit," as she got down on her knees.

Stephanie started licking and sucking on Sheila's vagina while she took her hit. Sheila started shaking and screaming. Cum went all over Stephanie's face.

She said, "Damn, girl, you trying to drown me."

"Sorry, but that shit was good. Let's go upstairs and get in the bed."

"Okay, let's go."

They got upstairs and got completely naked.

Stephanie said, "Damn, I'm so horny."

They grabbed each other and started kissing. They fell on the bed. Sheila started sucking on Stephanie's nipples. Stephanie started moaning. Sheila worked her way down her stomach. She said, "Okay, now you get a hit."

Stephanie took a hit as Sheila licked on her clit and stuck her finger in her vagina. Stephanie's body tensed and she started cumming instantly. They licked and sucked on each other and got high until about two in the morning.

When they got finished, they laid there in the bed talking. Stephanie said, "This wasn't your first time doing this with a woman."

"No, it's not my first time being with a woman. It is my first time doing it while getting high. That was wild. I know it wasn't your first time either."

"No. I'll be honest. I like women and men. I have always wanted to do you." Sheila said, "I knew you were looking at me awfully strange sometime but I blew it off. Well, this was cool, but I like a stiff dick."

"Girl, they've got toys for that."

"You're crazy."

"When was your first time being with a woman?"

"My first college roommate and I got it on."

"How did that happen?"

"I heard her masturbating one night after we got back from a party. The sound of her doing it turned me on so I started masturbating too. Our eyes met while we were masturbating. She asked if she could help me with it and I said yes and we did each other."

"You mean to tell me you haven't done it since then?"

"No, and I probably wouldn't have tonight if it wasn't for the drugs."

"Yeah, right, you know you wanted me."

"No, really, I like men and it's time for you to go."

"Just put me out then."

"No, I have to get some sleep so I can go to work."

"Can I stay until you go to work?"

"Who has your kids?"

"My mom. They're asleep now anyway."

"Okay, I'm going to sleep. I'm tired, goodnight."

Sheila was supposed to be at work Tuesday morning but she didn't make it because she overslept. When she woke up, she called in sick. This was something different for her. Sheila had always had a strong work ethic. The events from the night before had taken a toll on her. She had never partied like this on a weeknight before. The progression was starting to set in.

Sheila woke Stephanie up.

"What time is it?"

"It's nine o'clock."

"Oh, shit, I've got to get home. My mom is going to raise hell. Why didn't you wake me up earlier?"

"I just woke up myself."

"Aren't you supposed to be at work?"

"Yeah, I called in. I haven't taken a day off since I've been there. Besides, I still get paid anyway."

"What are you going to do today?"

"I have no idea, probably sleep. I am so tired."

"Well, I'm out. I'll talk to you later."

Stephanie left and Sheila got back in the bed. It was hard for her to go back to sleep at first. She was lying there thinking about the events of the night before. She didn't understand how it happened. All that was on her mind is how good it felt. She told herself that she wasn't going to let it happen again. She said to herself, "I'm not gay. I have to have more control over myself than that while I'm getting high." Soon she drifted off to sleep.

Chapter Eleven

The First Warning

Sheila got to work Wednesday morning and everyone gave her a warm greeting.

"Are you feeling okay? What's wrong?"

Sheila replied, "It must have been something I ate."

Natalie said, "Yeah, with this heat you really have to be careful, you can't just eat anything. You still look kind of tired."

"I know, I didn't sleep very well last night either."

"What? George keep you up," as she laughed.

"No, girl."

Sheila got to her office and started working. Shortly after she started working her phone rang.

When she answered, "Sheila, where have you been?"

"Hello to you too, George."

"I tried to call you all day yesterday."

"I had my phone off because I wasn't feeling well."

"Why didn't you call me and let me know?"

"I didn't want to burden you with my stuff."

"Sheila, I care about you."

"Thanks, George, but it's really not that serious."

"I just didn't know what happened to you."

"I'm okay but I have to get to work now."

"Okay, I'll talk to you later."

"Okay, bye."

A little while later, her cell phone rang and it was her mother.

"Hello, Mom," she said.

"Well, hello, Sheila, how are you?"

"I'm good."

"I can't tell. I tried to call you all day yesterday."

"I was asleep and I had my phone off."

"What was wrong with you?"

"I wasn't feeling very well and I wanted to get some rest. I am feeling better today."

"That's good. I just wanted to call and check on you. There is a lot going on out there today and your father and I just wanted to make sure you were okay."

"I'm good, Mom. You all don't have to worry about me. I am going to have to call you back later, though. I have some work I have to catch up on."

"Okay, babe. I will talk to you later."

Sheila hung up the phone and sat back in her chair. As she stared off into the ceiling, a million thoughts were running through her head. She began to feel ashamed of her and Stephanie's encounter. She thought about what led up to it. She couldn't believe that she had stayed up until two o'clock in the morning on a work night getting high not to mention freaking with her best friend. She shook her head and said, "I'm never doing that again."

Sheila went on through her day making good progress on her work. It was now getting close to time to go to lunch. Natalie came in and asked Sheila if she had plans for lunch.

"No," she replied.

"You want to hang out?"

"Sure, we can do that. Where do you want to go?"

"Do you feel like doing Bootsy's?"

"That's fine. Let me get finished with this and I'll be right out."

Sheila came out and they started to the elevator. Her boss came around the corner and asked how she was feeling.

She said, "I am better today. Thank you."

Her boss said, "Good…just try to give us a little earlier warning the next time."

"Okay," Sheila said, "I apologize, I won't let it happen again."

Sheila and Natalie get on the elevator and start talking junk.

"I can't believe it, you take one day off in seven months and it's like I committed murder."

"It's not that serious," Natalie said.

They get outside and are walking down Walnut St.

Sheila said to herself, "Shit, it's Flip."

"Hey, girl," he said, "how are you?"

"Hey, Flip, how are you?"

"I'm good."

"Oh, Flip, this is Natalie. Natalie, this Flip."

"Hi, Natalie, nice to meet you."

"You too."

"What are you two ladies up to?"

"Just on our way to lunch."

"Oh, okay, me too. I'm in between classes. I came out to get something to eat. Can I hang out with you two?"

"Sure," Natalie said.

"Where are you all going?"

"Bootsy's."

"Cool, I like Bootsy's."

Sheila said, "Oh, shit," to herself.

They get to Bootsy's and Flip rushed ahead and opened the door for them. Sheila thought to herself, *At least he has manners.* The hostess comes and seats them.

As they are sitting there Natalie asks, "So did your momma name you Flip?"

"Oh, you got a fly mouth, huh? No, she didn't."

"So what is your name?"

He said, "Why you want to know my government?"

"You know mine."

"Okay, Natalie, it's Marcus."

"Now was that so hard? Where did you get that name anyway?"

"I've had that name since high school. I used to be real good in gymnastics."

"Where did you go to school?"

"Elder. What about you?"

"I went to Princeton."

"I know a few people that went there."

About that time the waitress came. "What can I get for you folks to drink today?"

Sheila said, "I'll have water."

Natalie said, "I'll have the same."

Flip said, "Give me a Grey Goose on the rocks with a cranberry back."

Sheila said to herself, *Hmm, that sounds good,* but she was going back to work.

"What are you going to school for?" Natalie asked.

"Architecture. What do you do?"

"I'm an accounts rep at P&G."

"Oh, okay. Is that where you work too, Sheila?"

"Yep."

Natalie said, "That's my boss."

Sheila said, "Natalie, he didn't ask you all of that."

"Well, excuse me, grumpy."

"No, I'm just saying I don't want everyone knowing all my business."

"I'm sorry. I thought you two knew each other."

"We do but not like that. We met through George."

"Oh. Speaking of George, did you all have a good time the other night?"

"Yes, we did."

"Good."

The waitress brought their drinks and took their order. They were sitting there talking and everything was going well. When Sheila and Natalie ran into Flip, the first thing that ran through Sheila's mind was that he was going to say something wrong. As they sat there talking and eating, she saw a side of Flip that she didn't expect. It was quite pleasant, in fact. She said to herself, *He's not half bad. A bad-boy gentleman,* then she snickered.

"What are you laughing about, Sheila?"

"Nothing, I just thought about something." Then she made eye contact with Flip.

"Okay, it's time to go back to work. It was nice having lunch with you, ladies"

Natalie said, "It was nice meeting you, Marcus."

"Don't say that too loud," and he laughed as he walked them to the door. "You ladies have a good rest of the day."

"You too, Flip," said Sheila.

As they walked back to work, Natalie said, "I saw the way you looked at him. What's up with that?"

"He was nothing like I thought he would be. He is one of George's thug friends but he doesn't act anything like that. He's actually kind of nice."

"Yes, he is," said Natalie. "I never would have known. I like me a bad boy so why don't you hook a sista up?"

"We'll see."

They get back to work and all her coworkers are looking at her. Sheila thought to herself, *What's up with this?* She goes to her office and she notices a kind of fresh smell as she got to her door. When she opened her door, her office had about four dozen roses in it.

Natalie walked up and said, "Damn, you got somebody sprung."

All Sheila could say was, "Wow." She pulled the card off of the flowers, it said, "Thinking of you, George." She picked up the phone and called him.

"Hey, Sheila. I guess you found your surprise."

"Yes, I did, and they are beautiful. Thank you so much."

"Sheila, I want you to go to church with me tonight."

"Okay, what time?"

"I'll pick you up around seven."

"Okay, I'll be ready."

Now that was a first for her. No one had ever sent her roses like that. She said to herself, *Damn, he really likes me.* She sat down in her chair and thought about it. *George is a nice guy, but I don't know if I'm ready for that. He's got a good job, he's good looking, the sex is okay, but I think he's just a little too good. He doesn't like to party like I do so this may cause problems. He's really into church and I'm not, but maybe that's what I need.* Then she thought about running into Flip at lunch. He wasn't anything like she imagined. She was kind of turned on by him. She liked his swagger. She thought man, he had some good dope. Soon, that took over her thoughts. She thought it would be nice to get some when she got off. *Damn, I told George I was going to church with him, oh well.*

Sheila got off work and was on her way home and her phone rang, it was Flip.

"What's up, girl?"

"Who is this?"

"It's Flip. I saved your number from the other night."

"Oh, okay, what's up?"

"Nothing, I just wanted to tell you that I enjoyed having lunch with you today. How did you like that thing the other night?"

"It was great. Did you need something else?"

"Not right now. I will call you when I'm ready."

She hung up the phone and she said, "That was nice of him." Then her stomach started flipping. She said, "Man, I've got to use the bathroom all of a sudden."

Sheila got home and ran into her apartment. She threw her stuff down and ran straight to the bathroom. While she was in there her phone started ringing. *Who the hell is that?* It was her mom.

"Hey, Mom, what's up? I was going to call you but I had to run to the bathroom."

"Your dad and I wanted to know what you were doing for dinner. We don't get to see you much anymore."

"I can't tonight. I'm getting ready to go to church with George."

"Church?"

"Yes, ma'am. He's coming to pick me up at seven."

"Okay, call me and let me know how it is."

"Okay, Mom, love you, bye."

Sheila was getting in the shower and thought she didn't know what to wear. She wasn't one to go to church so her subconscious was looking for a way out. Really she was thinking about Flip and would rather be getting high. She got on in the shower and got cleaned up. When she got out, she called George to ask him what she should wear. She wanted to cancel but something wouldn't let her. He told her some women wear dresses, some wear jeans. "It really doesn't matter, as long as you get there."

Sheila got dressed and made a sandwich while she was waiting on George. Her mind was still in a quandary. Sheila was changing and she didn't even know it. Others would notice the change in her before she did. George taking her to church was an intervention and she had no idea. God was trying to spare her from what she was about to go through, but she was being defiant.

The doorbell rang, it was George. Sheila went to the door and opened it.

"Hmm, seven o'clock. You're right on time."

"I don't like to be late for anything, especially church."

"You are so good. Maybe too good for me."

"Baby, I'm just what you need. You just don't know it yet."

"Is that right?"

They got to church at about twenty after.

He said, "Come on in; I want to introduce you to my mom and dad."

"Why didn't you tell me? I would have worn something else."

"They don't care about what you have on, besides they are expecting you. All they care about is that you are here."

"This is my first time meeting your parents."

"Trust me, they will see past your clothes. Mom, Dad, this is Sheila. Sheila, this is my mom and dad, Bishop and Pastor Daniels."

"How are you, baby? It's nice to finally meet you. We've heard so much about you."

"I am fine, and you all?"

"We're great, God is so good. You two go ahead and get your seats, service is about to start."

The praise team came out and started the service. "Okay, everybody, on your feet and let's give God some praise."

Everybody started standing up. Sheila was looking around; she didn't know what was happening.

George grabbed her hand and said, "Stand up, baby."

She whispered in his ear, "What's going on?"

"This is called praise and worship. They do this at the beginning of every service."

"Oh, okay."

The praise team started an up-tempo song. People in the church were clapping, jumping up and down, and praising God. Sheila was looking like this was so strange. She hadn't been in church for so long and when she did, it wasn't like this. She was trying to get into it, but her mind was elsewhere. She had a lot of confusion going on even though she was clapping like everyone else.

The praise team sat down and George's father Bishop Daniels got up. He welcomed the visitors and got into his sermon. His topic was on the wages of sin. He said the wages of sin is death but the gift of God is eternal life. He talked about how the things we do seem fun at first and then it turns bad. He used drug and alcohol addiction as an example. He explained how it starts out as fun, innocent partying, and then it turns into something you can't do without. He talked about how the devil sets the trap and makes it look good and inviting.

"One day you look around and you are in so much mess that you just want to die. You don't have to go down that path. You can surrender your life to Christ right now. There is someone in here right now that is in a struggle and doesn't even know it. God is telling me to tell you to come out now before you sink too deep."

Sheila started getting nervous because it seemed like he was looking right at her. She thought about how she was getting high. She couldn't put the progression together. She didn't remember the first time. She couldn't see how she was thinking about it more and more. She didn't think about what she had just allowed to go on while getting high. The message was for her but she couldn't see it, but she would.

The whole time Sheila was sitting there with getting high on her mind. She couldn't hear the message that was meant for her. She may have heard it, but she wasn't listening. She didn't think any of it pertained to her. She had a great job, nice apartment, and a nice car. She was just partying a little. She couldn't see how the amounts and frequencies were increasing. So she just blew it off.

Service ended and they were about to leave.

"Let's go say goodbye to my mom and dad."

"Okay."

They make their way up to the front.

George's dad asked, "How did you enjoy the service, Sheila?"

"I really enjoyed it, Bishop Daniels."

"That's good and I'm glad you came. I hope you come back and visit with us again."

"I will, if George brings me back."

"I will," said George. "Alright, Mom and Dad. I will talk to you later."

"It was nice meeting you all, Bishop and Pastor Daniels."

They get to the car and George asks her if she wanted to get something to eat.

"No," she replied. "It's after nine o'clock; I need to get my things ready for work tomorrow."

"Okay, it is kind of late; I'll just take you home."

About that time Sheila's phone rang. "Hello?"

"Hey, Sheila."

"What's up, Stephanie?"

"Not a lot. What are you doing?"

"I went to church with George and we are on the way home."

"Is he staying with you tonight?"

"I don't think so."

"Okay, call me when you get home."

"Alright."

They pull up at Sheila's apartment.

"Are you coming in for a minute?"

"No, I'm going to let you get your stuff together for tomorrow. I need to get my stuff ready also. I enjoyed you going to church with me; we have to do it again sometime."

"I look forward to it."

"Okay, I'll talk to you tomorrow."

"Okay, goodnight, George."

"Goodnight, Sheila," as he kissed her. "Man, that was so sweet."

Sheila giggled as she opened the door. "Bye, boy."

Sheila got in the house and called Stephanie back.

"Hey, girl, what's up?"

"Girl, Boo has been asking about you."

"Oh, really. What does he want?"

"Girl, you know what he wants. What do all men want?"

"Girl, you know he's not my type."

"Girl, Boo is the biggest trick in Cincinnati. You can get anything you want from him."

"Stephanie, you know what happens when you let men start giving you stuff."

"Do you want to get high? I've got some money so let's go over there."

"It's ten o'clock."

"Come and get me, we don't have to stay long. He'll hook us up. Come on and let's go."

"Okay, I'll be there in a minute."

They get over Boo's house and go to the door. Stephanie knocks on the door. His doorman opens the door. He says, "Boo, it's Stephanie and some other fine-ass babe."

"Let them in."

Stephanie said, "What up, man? I brought somebody to see you. I told her you've been asking about her."

"Hey, Sheila, how have you been?"

"I've been good."

"To who?" he said.

Sheila laughed and said, "That was cute."

"Come on over here and sit down beside me and tell Daddy what you need."

Stephanie nudged her as if to say, "Go on, girl."

Sheila sat on one side and Stephanie on the other.

He said, "See, dog, this is what I'm talk'n 'bout. I'm sitting between two of the finest women in Cincinnati. What can I do for you ladies?"

"You know what we want."

"How much?"

Stephanie said, "I have twenty," and

Sheila said, "Me too."

"Here you go, girls. Here is a gram on me, keep your money. You gonna do it here or take it with you?"

"Can we use your room?"

"Sure, go ahead. It's some tools back there in the drawer."

"Cool."

The girls got up to go to the room.

Boo said, "Damn, you fine, girl, let me know if you need something else."

They get to the room.

Stephanie said, "See, girl, I told you."

"I'm not going to make this a habit, Stephanie. I know what he wants and I ain't feeling him like that."

"Girl, all you have to do is rub his leg every now and then."

"Girl, that shit will get you fucked up. That's not some old man that you can play with like that. Sooner or later he's going to expect you to pay up."

"Girl, he ain't gonna take it. He's a dope dealer, not a rapist."

"Girl, he's a criminal. You don't know what he might do if he feels someone is trying to play him."

Stephanie said, "Well, I would just enjoy the ride."

Sheila said, "Yeah, that's what he wants us to do," as she laughed.

Sheila took a piece and put it on the stem. When she hit it, she laid back and said, "I have been waiting on that all day."

Stephanie took the stem and asked, ":How is it?"

Sheila said, "It's pretty good."

Stephanie put a piece on there and hit it. She laid back and said, "Yeah, it is." She handed it back to Sheila.

Sheila said, "I want a nice one." She put a bigger piece on the stem. She took a big hit and instantly her leg started shaking. She laid back on the couch and started playing with herself.

Stephanie said, "There you go with that shit again."

At that time Boo walked in and said, "Damn, what the hell is going on back here?"

Stephanie said, "That's what happens when she gets a good one."

"She needs to get high over here all the time. She won't have to rub it herself. You girls want something to drink?"

"What you got?"

"Beer or Grey Goose."

Sheila said, "Grey Goose."

Stephanie said, "Me too."

Boo brought the drinks in and sat down between them. He picked up the stem and put a piece on it. He hit it and sat back and passed it to Sheila. She hit it and gave it to Stephanie. Sheila was getting uncomfortable. She knew what smoking did to her. With Boo walking in catching her in action, she could only imagine what was on his mind. They sat there talking and drinking for a minute.

Boo said, "Here, Sheila, put you a good one on there."

She did and when she hit it he touched her leg. Sheila jumped up and said, "Don't do that. If I don't offer for you to touch me, please don't. I get high but I'm not the one."

"I'm sorry. It won't happen again. Come on, Stephanie. Let's go. It's still some more dope left here."

"It's after eleven and I have to go to work in a few hours."

"Okay." Boo said, "Here, you girls can take this with you, and again, I'm sorry, Sheila. Can I call you sometime? I'd like to take you out to dinner sometime and make it up to you."

"I'm good. We'll get at you later."

The girls left. On the way taking Stephanie home, Sheila was kind of pissed. She said, "See, that's what I was telling your ass. When you start taking stuff from men they have expectations."

"Don't get mad at me, I didn't touch you."

"I'm just saying. I'm not mad at you. I knew he was up to something when he came and sat down between us. I didn't know he smoked."

"That was news to me too. I don't think he does it a lot but I don't know."

They pull up to Stephanie's house. When Stephanie goes to get out she said, "Oh, here is your half of what was left."

Sheila said, "It's twenty minutes till twelve. I have to be at work in the morning. We'll save it until tomorrow."

"Alright, give it here."

"Alright, I'll holler at you tomorrow."

"Cool."

Sheila gets home and she is still a little hyped. She goes in the kitchen to fix a drink. She always keeps some Grey Goose around. She turns off all the lights and makes her way upstairs. She goes in the bathroom to start her shower water. She comes back into the bedroom and starts to undress. She takes another sip of her drink and says to herself, "I could use a good orgasm." She tells herself, "No, it's too late; I have to be at work at nine." She looked at the clock and said, "I still got time to get some sleep so what the hell. Let me go ahead and get rid of this stuff so I won't have to worry about it tomorrow."

Sheila turned on some music and took the rest of her clothes off. She grabbed a towel and put it on the chair. She went to her closet and got her stem out and sat it on the nightstand beside the chair. She got the piece out that Stephanie gave her. She sat in the chair and took a drink and then laid back and started rubbing on her clit until her hips started gyrating. She reached over and grabbed her stem and put half of what she had on it. She lit it and laid back in the chair. She took her fingers and went to work. She had her stem in one hand and pussy in the other. She stroked her clit and then ran her fingers inside her vagina and it started gripping. She was moaning and sighing like someone was really putting it to her. She was almost to the point of exploding. She put the rest on and lit it and laid back. She took a big hit and started rubbing her clit. She squirted halfway across the room and then sat there trembling. She got up and her legs were weak from the excitement. She took a shower set her clock and went to bed.

She couldn't go right to sleep because her mind was still running a million miles a minute. She was telling herself, "Man, I've got to get some sleep." She tossed and turned for the longest. Everything was running through her mind from the sermon to what happened over Boo's, she just couldn't quiet her thoughts. Then she had the thought it would be nice to have another piece. She said to herself, "Hell no, it is too late." She finally dozed off around one-thirty.

Seven o'clock rolled around real fast. Her alarm went off and she hit the snooze. It was seven-thirty before she finally rolled out of bed. She jumped up and ran downstairs to fix some coffee. Then she ran back upstairs to take a shower. By the time she got upstairs she was pouring sweat. She said, "Damn. I'm sweating like crazy. I need to take a cold shower so I can cool down." She realized the drugs in her system had her body hot. She jumped in the shower; she couldn't take the coldness so she warmed it up a little. "Ahh, that's better." She got finished and got out and got dressed. She got her coffee and out the door she went.

Sheila got to work and hurried from the parking garage to the office. Once again, she started sweating. It's a good thing she didn't wear a lot of makeup because it would have been running everywhere. She hurried through to her office.

Natalie came in and asked, "Sheila, are you okay?"

"Sure, why do you ask?"

"Well, you're always early and you never just rush in. You came through and barely spoke. And you're sweaty."

"I was out a little late last night and had a little too much to drink."

About that time her office phone rang. "Sales and marketing department, Sheila speaking."

"Sheila, can you come to my office, please?"

"Yes, Mr. Franklin. I will be there in a minute."

Sheila got herself together as best as she could. She got a bottle of water and drank it down trying to cool her pipes. She headed up to Mr. Franklin's office. Mr. Franklin was the Sr. V.P. On her way up to his office, she was wondering what he wanted. She was nervous as hell.

Sheila gets to his office and knock on his door.

"Come in," he says.

Sheila goes in and he reaches out his hand to shake hers.

"Have a seat, Sheila. You don't have to be nervous. I called you up here to give you some good news. You are doing a great job in your department. Profits are up. You have one of the lowest absentee rates in the company. I am very pleased with your performance. I have decided to give you a two-percent raise. You can stop sweating now." He thought he had made her nervous when it actuality it was the drugs from the night before.

She said, "Thank you, Mr. Franklin," and got up and left.

"No problem, Sheila, keep up the good work."

She got back to her office and sat down to catch her breath.

Natalie came in and said, "Well, what did he want?"

"Girl, he gave me a raise."

"You go girl, so where we going for lunch?"

"You pick."

"You know where I like to go."

"Yeah, Bootsy's."

"That's my favorite spot."

"I know. I like it too. It's so classy and has a good food too."

"I agree, it's probably the nicest place downtown to have lunch. They are pretty live on Friday nights also. Tell Barbara and Terry I'm taking everyone out for lunch. Let me make these calls and I'll be ready to go."

Sheila started making her calls and sleep started coming down on her. It was almost ten o'clock. She had another two hours before lunch. After all of the excitement died down, she started feeling the night before. She was talking to a client on the phone and started dozing. She caught herself and shook it off. She got up and got some coffee.

When she was on her way back through, Natalie said, "You must have really had a rough night. I have never seen you drink this much coffee before."

"Yeah, it was a long night."

Sheila got back to her office and called George. "Hey, honey, how are you."

"Who is this?"

"Oh, you got jokes. Who else calls you honey?"

"I was just playing. Hi, Sheila, how are you?"

"I'm good and you?"

"I'm great."

"That's good."

"What's up, why are you in such a good mood?"

"My boss called me in his office and gave me a raise."

"How long did you have to sit on his lap?"

"Oooh. You know what, you almost made me tell you something."

"I was just playing, baby. I'm sorry. Will you accept my apology?"

"Okay, but don't let me have to bust you up. I want to celebrate tonight. I think I'm going to take a long weekend. Can you take off tomorrow?"

"Why? What do you have planned?"

"A weekend that you'll never forget."

"I'll see what I can do."

"Okay. Meet me at my apartment when you get off, I want to take you to dinner."

"Okay, bet."

It is now twelve o'clock. Sheila goes out into the main office and asks if they are ready to go to lunch. They said sure. They are headed out and they get to the elevator.

Barbara says, "Thanks for taking us to lunch."

"Not a problem. They gave me a raise today and you all are responsible for it. That's why I am rewarding you all."

"Are we going every week?"

"Don't push it."

They all laughed.

They get to the restaurant and go in. When they get upstairs, the hostess greeted them and asked if they wanted a table or a booth. Sheila asked if it was crowded in the back. The hostess said not yet. They started toward the back. The hostess said, "How is this?"

"This is fine,"

Sheila said.

The hostess said, "Taylor will be your waitress," and left.

Taylor came and asked, "May I start you all off with some drinks?"

Sheila said, "Yes. I'll have a Grey Goose and cranberry. Go ahead, girls, get what you want."

They all ordered cocktails.

Sheila said, "Don't make this a habit when you go to lunch, ladies. They gave me this bonus for productivity and I would hate to disappoint them."

"We won't. We're only drinking because you're buying. We can't afford to drink like this."

Natalie said, "I'm surprised to see you drinking at lunch."

"I normally don't, but I'm celebrating. I think I'm going to take a long weekend."

"Must be nice."

"Work hard and you can get there too."

Taylor brought the drinks over and asked, "Are you all ready to order?"

The girls all ordered their food and sat and talked while they were waiting.

"So what do you have planned for the weekend?" Terry asked.

"First I'm going to take George out to dinner. Then we may go to a movie. Then I'm going to take him home and rock his world."

"Aww, you are bad."

"Don't let the business suit fool you. I get down to business with it off also."

"That is TMI." They started laughing. The food came and they ate and went back to work.

Sheila got back to her office and was hanging on the best she could.

She caught herself nodding a couple times. That drink she had at lunch set off some feelings inside of her. She had forgotten all that she had said that she wasn't going to mess with drugs today. As the day progressed, the urge was getting stronger. Then she thought about being with George and how she wanted him to do that one thing. Sheila looked at her watch; "Damn, it's only two-thirty. Let me call Mom and see what she's doing."

"Hey, Mom, what's going on?"

"Oh, hey, baby, how are you?"

"I'm good."

"What have you been doing?"

"Not a lot, just working. George and I went to church last night."

"You told me you were going; how was it?"

"It was good. The choir was awesome. I didn't know that many people went to church on Wednesday night. I also met his mom and dad. His dad is the Bishop, you know."

"Oh, girl, you have to watch those preachers' kids. They are usually the worst ones."

"I got a raise today at work."

"Really, how much?"

"Two percent."

"Well, some is better than none."

"That's what I said."

"Are you coming by tonight?"

No. George and I are going out to dinner after work."

"You have to bring him by this weekend."

"Okay, Mom, I'll see what I can do."

When she got off the phone, she called her boss and told him that she was going to take Friday off.

He said, "Okay, Sheila. You got some big plans for this weekend?"

"No, not really. Just going to spend some time relaxing with my man."

"I didn't know you were involved with someone."

"Yeah, it just kind of happened."

"Well, you have a great weekend, you deserve it. See you Monday."

Sheila got off the phone and her stomach started flipping. It was going on four o'clock. About that time George called.

"Hey, Sheila."

"What's up, George?"

"I was calling to see what the plans were."

"Well, I've never been to Jeff Ruby's. I heard that it was really nice."

"Yes, it is."

"Have you been there?"

"Yeah, I've been there a time or two."

"What is their specialty?"

"Their steaks are off the chain and their service is excellent."

"Do they have a bar?"

"Yes, they do and the drink prices aren't too bad either."

"I didn't ask you that. I got something for you; I'm going to rock your world. Do you have some weed?"

"I can get some."

"Okay. Try to have it already set up so you can meet me at my house by six."

"Okay."

When Sheila got off the phone she looked up Flip's number. She wanted to get some crack from him because of what Boo tried last night. She found the number and called him. She knew she had to move quickly because she didn't want to run into George. She knew that's who George got his weed from. She knew he would be meeting him when he got off work.

Sheila dialed his number.

"Hello."

"Flip, what's up, man?"

"Who is this?"

"It's Sheila."

"Oh, what up, pretty lady."

"I need to get with you."

"What do you need?"

"An eight ball, how much?"

"A hundred and fifty."

"Okay, where you at?"

"At the spot."

"On Price?"

"What other spot do you know?"

"Alright, smart ass, I'm on my way. Can you have it ready?"

"Yeah, where you at?"

"At work."

"Okay, see you in a few."

"Okay."

It was now four o'clock. Sheila got up from her desk and put all of her papers away. She went out on the floor and told the girls to have a good weekend.

Barbara said, "Give a sista a raise and she's slacking already."

"Whatever, don't hate. See you all Monday."

"Bye, Sheila," they all said.

Sheila got to Flip's at about four-thirty.

"Hi, Sheila. Damn, you got here quick, and you look real nice too. Do you always look this good? I'm gonna steal you from old boy."

Sheila just smiled.

"What you gonna do with all this?"

"I'm getting enough to last a couple days."

"You must plan on having a party."

"Yeah, a private party."

"I would love to have a private party with you."

"Be careful what you wish for."

"No, you be careful. I put you a little extra in there."

"Cool, I appreciate it. Here is your money. I'm out."

"Alright, holla if you need me."

"Alright."

Sheila headed home. She wanted to stop by the liquor store but she didn't want to go to the one down the street. She didn't want to risk running into George. She was trying to hide the fact that she had got some crack from Flip. In the back of her mind she kind of liked him but didn't want George to know.

It was now about five-fifteen when Sheila got home. She hurried in the house and put her bags down. Sheila ran upstairs to the bathroom. The urge to smoke some crack was on her so hard that it made her have to use the toilet. She got finished and grabbed her pipe out of the drawer. She had to hurry because she knew George would be there soon. She put a piece on the pipe and lit it. When she blew the smoke out, she said, "Damn, that was good." She started getting that same horny feeling. She glanced at the clock, it was now about 5:35. That's enough time. She kicked off her shoes, pulled up her skirt and slipped her panties off. She rubbed her clit and her knees almost buckled. She sat down and played with herself. She lit the pipe one more time as she played with herself. She started to reach her climax. She put the pipe down and finished what she was doing.

Sheila had to rush around spraying air freshener. She had to fight herself to keep from picking up the pipe again. She knew George would be there soon and she had to get ready. She didn't want him to know that she was getting high. She was so hyped, she felt jittery. She remembered that she had a piece of a blunt left. She grabbed it and lit it and took a couple pulls. When she blew the smoke out she calmed down almost instantly.

Sheila got finished getting dressed. Then, there was a knock at the door. She opened it.

"Hi, George," she said, "come on in and have a seat while I put on my makeup."

"Nice scent, Sheila."

She got nervous for a second. She thought that he smelled the crack. Then he said, "What's that scent, Herbal Essences?"

"Oh, you got jokes? Here, finish this blunt while I get ready. Fix us a couple drinks." Sheila got finished getting ready and they left.

Once in the car, George said, "You look real nice, Sheila."

"Thanks, George, so do you."

"It seems like it's been forever since I've seen you."

"Stop, George, it's only been since yesterday."

"I know but it seems like forever."

"Awe, poor baby." She reached over the console and slid her hand up his leg to his crotch. She rubbed on his penis and it got hard as a rock. She said, "I see someone else missed me."

George said, "What's going on with you? This is different."

"I just want you to think about what you're going to get when I get you back to my place."

"Oooh, wee."

They get to the restaurant and park. George gets out of the car and comes around and opens Sheila's door for her. When she got out, he pulled her close and kissed her.

"What was that for?"

"That was for being you. I like you a lot, Sheila."

"I like you too, George. Now let's go get something to eat."

They get to the door and he opens it for her. As she went in, she gave him a kiss and said, "I'm going to tear you up when I get you home."

George just laughed and asked, "What are you going through?"

They went in and the hostess said, "Hi, my name is Tammy, welcome to Jeff Ruby's. Will there be just two for dinner?"

"Yes," Sheila said.

"Would you please follow me?"

Sheila said, "Wow, this is nice. Thank you."

"Is this your first time dining with us?"

"Yes," Sheila said.

George said, "I've been here before."

"Well, I hope you two enjoy your dinner. How is this?"

"This will be fine."

"Sherry will be your waitress and she will be with you shortly."

Sherry came over and said, "Hi, I'm Sherry, welcome to Jeff Ruby's. I understand that this is your first time dining with us. Let me tell you a little about our menu. We have an extensive wine list if you like that is second to none. We were rated best all-around restaurant in Cincinnati. We are one of three five-star restaurants in Cincinnati."

"Wow, that's nice," said Sheila.

"May I start you all off with something to drink?"

"Yes, I'll have a double Grey Goose and cranberry."

"And you, sir?"

"I'll have the same."

"Okay, I'll be back in a second."

"George, I really like this place. I have heard so much about it."

"Yeah, this is the nicest five-star restaurant in the Cincinnati area."

Sherry came back with the drinks. "Do you all need more time?"

"No, I think I'll have the 16-ounce T-bone medium with a baked potato and asparagus."

"And what for you, sir?"

"I think I'll have the same thing. I'll have my steak medium also."

"Okay, coming right up."

Their food came and they ordered a couple more drinks and left.

They got to the car and George opened the door for Sheila. She put her arms around his neck and kissed him.

"Thanks for having dinner with me."

"Thanks for asking me out."

"I am not a selfish woman, George. I just wanted to share my good fortune with you."

"Thank you, Sheila."

"That was nothing, wait until I get you home."

They were driving out of the parking lot. George thought that there was something different about Sheila this evening. She seemed kind of anxious when he picked her up. The way she rubbed on his penis, she had never done that before. She seemed kind of rushed at dinner, she didn't even eat all of her food and she was ready to go. He had no idea that she had smoked some crack before he picked her up. Her behavior was changing and neither one of them could see it. George just thought that she was being extra frisky. The change was so gradual Sheila wasn't paying attention.

They were getting close to the bridge to go back across to Ohio. George said, "The lights in Cincinnati are beautiful."

Sheila said, "You focus on the lights and I will focus on this," as she grabbed his zipper.

George looked at her in disbelief. *Who is this woman?* he thought to himself as she pulled his penis out and put it in her mouth. He didn't try to stop her, though.

As they headed up I-75, Sheila was doing her thing. Up and down and round and round. It was getting good to George about this time. He reclined the seat a little more. He thought to himself, *What the hell is going on with her?* She was working him like a pro.

Just as they were coming up to the Norwood exit, George said, "Sheila, you better stop, you're gonna make me cum."

Then she started working him harder. Then his toes curled in his shoes.

He said, "Sheila, Sheila," and then he grabbed her hair and let it go.

She took it all.

He said, "Okay, stop, I can't take it anymore."

She rose up and just smiled at him and said, "Round one goes to Sheila." He just looked at her and laughed.

They get to the house and George gets out and goes around and opens her door. She walks around him and towards the door and he grabs her ass and says, "I'm ready for some of that now."

She looked at him and smiled and said, “Oh, you’re gonna get all you can stand. Did you bring the weed?”

“Yeah, I brought it in when I picked you up.”

“Cool.”

Once in the house Sheila said, “Turn on some music and fix us a drink while I go get comfortable.”

“Okay.”

George was pouring the drinks and thinking to himself, *What the hell has gotten into her?* He said to himself, *Whatever it is I like it. I’m going to tear that ass up tonight.* Little did he know what she had planned for him.

Sheila came down the stairs. She had on a red teddy and a red silk robe. George was mesmerized. He said, “Damn, Sheila, you look good.”

“Thank you.” She put the bag down that she had in her hand and started kissing him. He pulled her over on top of him. She was kissing and grinding on him. She leaned back and unzipped his pants. She pulled his penis out and slid her panties to the side and put it inside of her. He said, “Damn, Sheila, you are so hot and wet.”

She said, “I guess I missed you too.” She made a few gyrations and up and down motions then her body tensed. All at once it seemed as though she was going a thousand miles an hour. Then she said, “Here it comes, George, cum with me.”

“Okay.”

“Now, George, now.”

“Okay, Sheila, here it is.”

They exploded and she collapsed in is arms.

Sheila sat on the couch beside him and said, “You made a mess on your pants.”

He laughed and said, “No, I believe we made a mess.”

Then they both laughed.

She said, “You may want to take them off. I’ll get a blunt ready while you do that.”

She got the blunt ready and George sat back down on the couch. Sheila sprinkled the weed in it and then she pulled her rock out of her bag. George said, "Damn, where did you get all that?"

"I've got my connections."

He said, "I see what kind of night this is going to be."

"Yep, do you have a problem with it?"

His mouth said no but everything inside him was saying don't do it. He remembered the last experience and said what the hell.

She got the blunt rolled and said, "Here, fire that up."

They sat there, smoking the laced blunt and drinking. George said, "How often do you do this?"

"Not very often. I'm celebrating tonight and this is what I wanted to do and I wanted to do it with you."

"Why did you get so much?"

"I wanted to get enough to last."

"That looks like it will last for a while."

"I hope it lasts at least a couple of days."

"A couple days?"

"Yeah, you're going to stay off with me tomorrow, aren't you?"

"I don't know, Sheila. You know I'm not into this like that."

"If you're scared say you're scared."

"Okay, let's do it."

"That's what I'm talking about."

Sheila stood up and got naked. She grabbed George's hand and put it on her vagina. She said, "Ooh, you see how wet I am. I want you to do that thing for me."

"What thing?"

"You know what thing." Then she reached in her bag and grabbed her pipe. He said, "Oh, that thing."

"She said, "Yeah, that thing."

"Okay, let me take my clothes off."

"Yeah, you do that."

Sheila laid back on the couch with her back half on the armrest and half on the back of the couch. She put one foot on the couch and one on the floor. Her vagina was so wet, he could almost see himself. As she was getting her hit ready, George went down on her. She said, "That's it, baby. Now suck on my clit real slow and steady. Yeah, that's it." She took a big hit and started trembling.

"Wait, baby, I don't want to cum yet."

"Here, put you a piece on there and suck it with the smoke in your mouth." She put a big piece on the pipe and lit it for him. He got a big hit and then she took the pipe and laid back again. She lit it and he went down on her. This time she couldn't hold it. Her back arched and she started trembling. She screamed and said, "Shit, I'm cumming and I can't stop." She squirted on George's face. She flexed one more time and balled up, trembling.

She got herself together and said, "Okay, big boy, it's your turn. Lay back on the couch. Do you know how to do this?"

He said, "Yeah, I think so."

"Here, take the pipe and grab you a piece."

He got a small piece and she said, "No, take this one." He laid back and she put his penis in her mouth and started working him. He lit the pipe and got a big hit. She said, "Now hold it and give me the pipe." She lit it and gave it back to him. He laid back and she started sucking on his penis again. He said, "Oh, shit, Sheila, here it comes." She started going crazy on him. They went on like this all night. Drinking, getting high, and having sex. She was really working him over.

Somehow George woke up in the morning so he could call in. He sat up for a while looking at her sleep. He thought to himself she is so beautiful but he wasn't on all this getting high, it was a little too much for him. He didn't know what he was going to do. He really liked her but he didn't know if she could stop getting high. He had never seen her like that before and it kind of scared him. Part of him liked it, but the other part knew it couldn't go on like this.

Sheila woke up finally and said, "Hey, you, are you okay?"

He said, "Yeah, I'm okay."

She got out of bed and came and sat on his lap and put her arms around him and kissed him. She said, "You were really amazing last night."

George asked, "Was it me or the dope?"

She said, "It was a combination of the two."

"Do you think we can be just as good without the dope?"

She got agitated with him and said, "Didn't we do it before we got high?"

"Well, yeah, we did." He didn't know she had got high before dinner. "Do you want some breakfast?"

"Yeah, that will be nice. Yeah, I need you to get some strength. Oh, no. Oh, yeah, I'm not finished with you yet."

Sheila got up and took a shower. When she got out, she gave George a towel and washcloth. She said, "You can take a shower while I cook breakfast."

George got out of the shower and went downstairs and ate. Then they went and got back in the bed and started all over again.

Although this was kind of exciting to George, he knew in the back of his mind that this wasn't what he wanted. He was thinking this was the only way she could get off. He was wondering how much of a hold the drugs had on Sheila. He really liked her, but he didn't want her like this. It was now about one o'clock in the afternoon. They had just got finished having sex again. They had smoked their last piece of dope. George said, "Man, Sheila, I am so tired."

"Lay down and get some rest, George."

"This was crazy. We got high and had sex all night and half of today."

"I know. That was wild, wasn't it?"

"Yeah, it sure was. Did you enjoy it?"

"Yeah, Sheila, but we can't keep going like this."

"I know, I just wanted to celebrate with you this weekend. Maybe we can get some more later."

"I don't want any more and you shouldn't either. I'm going to sleep. We can go out to eat later."

"Okay, George, I'll be good. Let me clean up this mess and I will lay down with you."

Chapter Twelve

Caught Up

Things were going pretty good for Sheila. She was doing well on her job. She and George were getting along pretty good. She was spending time with her parents. She was really holding things together it seemed. It seemed as though she was controlling her drug usage.

Sheila went over her mom and dad's house one day after work. She was sitting there talking to them and her mom asked, how is George? We haven't seen him in a while. George is fine. We went out a couple of weeks ago. He seems like a nice young man. He is. He is probably the nicest guy I've ever met. Her mom said hmm, that sounds pretty serious. I do like him but we have our difficulties. Like what? Nothing really, he just keeps trying to push this church thing on me. Well that's not a bad thing. Your dad and I have started going. Really? Yes. We are just visiting different churches until we find one to join.

About that time her phone rang. Hello. Hi Sheila. Speak of the devil; we were just talking about you? Who was just talking about me? I'm at mom and dads. Oh ok, tell them I said hello. Mom and dad, George said hello. Oh ok, tell him we said hello. What is he doing? Tell him to come over and eat with us. Mom and dad said why don't you come over for dinner? Okay. I was working on one of my houses. Let me get cleaned up and I'll be there shortly. Okay see you then.

Sheila and her mom and dad sat talking for a bit and a knock came at the door. Sheila got up and went to the door. It was George at the door. Hi honey. Honey? Okay what's going on Sheila? Nothing, I'm just happy to see you. Come on in. Hi Mr. and Mrs. Jones. Hi George, it's good to see you. It's been a while. Yes it has, it's good to see you-all also. What smells so good? That would be dinner. Josephine cooked some chicken, greens, macaroni and cheese, and cornbread. On Tuesday? Yes sir. No wonder you all have been married so long. Yeah my baby knows how to treat her man. Let's go into the dining room.

Man, this looks even better than it smells. Yeah my Josephine can really burn. I haven't tasted Sheila's cooking yet. If she learned anything from her momma she'll be fine. I don't mine cooking myself. George you cook? Yes mam. My mother made sure I knew how to do everything I need to do in the house. Cooking, cleaning, doing my own laundry. She said she didn't want me to have to depend on a woman to do those things for me. That's a good thing. Ronald can cook. Every now and then I'll let him in my kitchen. I like to take care of my man. And I like her taking care of me too.

Okay let's say grace so we can dig in. Let me go wash my hands first. The bathroom is right back there. Sheila I like him. You better try and hold on to him. He's ok. Alright girl, I don't see how you could do much better than that. Okay mom stop, I'm not trying to get married yet. I'm just saying that seems like a pretty good candidate. He's ok.

George would you like to say grace? Sure I would be honored. Father, thank you for this food that we are about to receive. May it nourish our bodies for Christ sake and bless the hands that prepared it Amen. Sheila's mom gave her a big smile and a nod. Sheila gave her mom a look like stop it mom.

Wow this really looks good Mrs. Jones. Thank you George. There is plenty so don't be shy. Oh I love to eat so you don't have to worry about that. This is probably my favorite meal. This is like a Sunday dinner. I don't necessarily wait until Sunday to cook like this. The mood can hit me any time. Well I'm glad it hit you today. You saved me some money. I was calling Sheila to see if she wanted to go out to eat. Sheila's mom gave her a smile and a nod again. Sheila just shook her head.

George didn't you have to work today? Yeah I took off early. One of my tenants had a problem with their plumbing and I had to go fix it. How can you just take off like that? Well I've been with P&G for about six years now. I don't miss a lot of work so I have some time saved up. That's pretty smart; I used to do the same thing. How long did you work at Ford Mr. Jones? 35 long years. I figured I'd better come on out while I was still young enough to enjoy myself. That's what I plan to do.

Sheila tells us that you two went to church the other week. Yessir, we went to a Wednesday service. Do they have service every Wednesday? Yes sir. Maybe we can go sometime. I would love to take you all with me. I try to get Sheila to go more often. Okay you all can get off me now. I was just saying. Well stop saying and eat. Okay, ok. Dang what's wrong with you? I told you don't be trying to force church on me. I'm not trying to force anything on you. Good. Sheila it's not a bad idea. Okay mom stop.

Wow the food was great. I really enjoyed it. Thanks for having me over. Not a problem George. We enjoyed having you. Hey let us know when you're going to church again. We would like to go. I'm going tomorrow night if you all would like to come. What time? Service starts at seven thirty. That sounds good. How do you know I wanted to go to church tomorrow night? Nobody asked you to go. You don't have to be there for your parents to go. Oh you're gonna eat my parents' food and now you're gonna get smart with me huh? You can leave. I am. Mr. and Mrs. Jones do you know where the church is? Yes we know where it is. Okay. I look forward to seeing you tomorrow night. See you there. Bye Sheila. Later.

Sheila why are you acting like that? I told him about trying to force me into going to church. Sheila, he isn't trying to force you into anything. We asked him if we could go. I know you did. It felt like a set up. Sheila why are you so dead set against church? Because there is so much hypocrisy in church. People going up in there, acting like they're all perfect and stuff. Like they have never done anything wrong. Sheila no one is perfect. Yeah well they don't act like it. Sheila you don't go for the other people you go for you. It's about your own personal relationship with God. The way times are now, it couldn't hurt. See that's what I'm saying. If there is a God why does he allow all of this stuff to happen? Okay we're going to stop right there. One day you're gonna wish you knew God. Okay mom and dad… I will talk to you all later. Bye honey, have a good night.

Ronald what's gotten into that girl? I don't know Josephine. It seems like ever since she came home from school she's been different. I wonder what happened to her. She's just growing up Ronald and finding her own way. Do you think if we had taken her to church more when she was younger it would be different? I don't know Ronald. Look at some of the children that grew up in church and turned out bad. I believe everyone just has their own path they have to take. All we can do is pray for her. I guess you're right.

On the way home Sheila's phone rang. Hello. Hey Sheila. What's up George? I was wondering what was up with you. Nothing George. Oh it's something. You got so agitated with me for no reason. You know how I feel about being pressured to go to church. Sheila, I am not trying to pressure you. Your parents asked if they could go to church with me, what was I supposed to say? In fact, they brought it up not me. I know George, I'm sorry. Okay I accept your apology. Are you gonna go with us tomorrow? How can I not? How would that look? My parents going and I don't come. Sheila, you don't have to go if you don't want to. I'll go George. Good I'm glad. Talk to you tomorrow. Good night.

Just as Sheila was pulling into her apartment complex her phone rang again. She looked at her phone and said whose number is this? Hello. Hey Sheila. Oh hi Tonya, I didn't know whose number this was. Yeah it's me girl. I had to change my number to stop this nigga from calling me. I guess you got to do what you got to do.

What's been going on with you Tonya? Not a lot, working and going to school. You still going to school? Yeah, my dad wanted me to go to law school. He has his own firm now and he wants me to come and work with him. Daddy's little girl huh. Don't hate the playa hate the game. As long as daddy is going to pay the bills I can handle the rest. You are so spoiled. And you're not? We aren't talking about me though we're talking about you. As they laughed. Tonya let me call you back when I get in the house. Okay.

As she got in the house her phone rang again. Damn who is this? She looked at the phone, it was Stephanie. Shit- what does she want? Hello Stephanie. What's up Sheila? Nothing, I'm just getting home from over my mom and dad's. You mean you were in the neighborhood and didn't even say hi. Girl I was so pissed when I left there, all I wanted to do is get home. What happened? George came over and ate dinner with us and the whole church thing started. He knows I don't like him pushing church on me. Well, you know, he could be trying to push much worse on you. There you go. No really I've been thinking about it myself lately; I'm just not ready yet.

What's going on? I called to let you know that Boo has been asking about you. What does his fat ass want? He wants to see you. You know I ain't trying to mess with him after that last time. I don't like people touching all on me like that unless I want them to. He told me he was sorry about that and wants to make it up to you. Let me get my clothes changed and I'll call you back.

Damn I wasn't even thinking about getting high and then Stephanie called. What time is it? Okay it's nine o'clock. I can get changed and be over Stephanie's by nine thirty and be at Boo's by ten and home by twelve thirty. Okay that sounds like a plan, let's do it. Damn I was supposed to call Tonya back. I'll call her tomorrow.

Sheila and Stephanie got over Boo's house at about nine fifty. Sheila tells Stephanie ok we aren't going to be in here all night. By twelve o'clock we're out of here. I have to go to work tomorrow. Okay Sheila I know. Whenever you get ready, I'm with you. I hope he don't try to put his hands on me again. If he does I swear to God we're gonna be fighting up in here. Stephanie just looked at her and said come on girl it ain't going down like that. I'm just saying Stephanie.

They get to the door and Boo opens the door and says come on in ladies. He starts right out apologizing to Sheila. Sheila I'm sorry about the other night. When I walked in and saw you playing with yourself, I thought it was on. Let me tell you something right now. I like to get high and sometimes it makes me kind of horny, but I'm not that kind of girl. I don't like people touching me unless I want them to. Understood. Good. I accept your apology.

What can I get for you ladies? We've got fifty dollars. Okay, I told Stephanie I would take care of you to make up for the other night. Here is a sixteenth. Wow thanks. Do you girls want something to drink? Sure. What do you want, beer or liquor? What kind of Liquor do you have? I bought some Cîroc. I wanted to try it out. It tastes pretty good. Let me try some of that. I've wanted to try some of that. That's Puffy's company isn't it? Yep. I like to support my brothers.

The girls fixed their drinks and proceeded to the backroom. They were back there doing their thing. Boo knocks on the door and said is it cool? Yeah come on in it's your house. I know it's my house but I don't want to make anyone uncomfortable. You're ok with me Boo. You really showed me a lot tonight. I'm not a bad guy. You just see so much in this business that it makes you kind of jaded. I understand, believe me I know. What do you know? I tell people all the time, don't let this nice girl image fool you. You know you can come by here anytime Sheila. I'll remember that. There was a knock at the door. Boo's partner said there is someone here to see you. Okay, here I come. You ladies enjoy yourself and I'll check on you in a minute.

Sheila looked at her watch and said, "damn time flies when you're having fun." This is some good stuff. He always has some good stuff. I have been trying to control myself but you know what this stuff does to me. Stephanie looked at her and laughed and said yeah I saw your leg wiggling. Let's get some more and go over your house. Girl, you are crazy. Besides, when we do that I still want some dick. Oh I got just what you need. Oh you've grown one since the last time I saw you? You can call it that if you like as she laughed. What are you talking about? You'll see. It's getting late and I have to go to work in the morning. Drop me off on your way to work. Do you have any more money on you? We only have a couple hits left. I got about ten dollars. I got twenty. See what he will give us for thirty. Okay.

Sheila went to the door and called for Boo. He came to the door and said what's up.

Sheila said, " we've got thirty dollars. What can we do with that? I got you, hold on a minute. The girls grabbed their coats and were headed out of the room when Boo came to the door. Here is a gram. Where are you girls going? It's late we got to go home. I have to go to work in the morning. I know with this you ain't getting ready to go to bed right now, or are you?" as he laughed. Can I go with you all? Not tonight. I can't leave anyway. I got to get this money. On the way out there was another guy sitting in the front room. He said damn Boo who is that? Don't worry about it. I think I know that one girl. She used to be with my boy Troy when they were in high school. Man she's come a long way from there. She is fine as hell. I hope she stays that way.

On the way home Sheila told Stephanie that she recognized that guy in the front room. Oh yeah, where from? I think he used to be with Troy. You know I thought he looked familiar. Isn't that Robert or something? Yeah that's him. He looks kind of bad. Yeah he did didn't he?

They get to Sheila's apartment and go inside.

Sheila said, " Stephanie you go fix us a drink while I go get the pipe. Okay Sheila. Stephanie pours the drinks and comes and sits down. About that time, Sheila comes downstairs with her bag. So what were you talking about at Boo's? Stephanie reached down and grabbed her purse. She stuck her hand inside and pulled out a bag. What's that Sheila asked? Stephanie reached in the bag and pulled out a two headed dildo.

Sheila said, " what the hell. I told you I had something for you. Oh my God it is so big. Why does it have two heads? Stephanie said shit I be wanting some dick too. This way we can both get some at the same time. Girl you are a real freak. And you like it so what does that make you as they both laughed? Well let's do this.

Sheila hit the stereo remote and turned on some music. Stephanie said we might as well come out of these clothes. Sheila took a drink and said might as well. By the time she put her drink down Stephanie was already naked.

Sheila said, " damn girl. Stephanie said I've been waiting to get a hold of you since the last time. You're a trip said Sheila. More like a journey Stephanie said.

They started getting high and slid close to each other. They started playing with each other's clits. They both were starting to moan and groan. They both were getting wet as hell. Stephanie got up and got on her knees in front of Sheila. She said ok Sheila lay back and scoot your ass out. Put you a nice hit on the pipe. Sheila grabbed the pipe and put a hit on it and gave it to Stephanie and said you start it. She did and handed it to Sheila as she laid back. Stephanie started licking and sucking on her clit and flicking her tongue in and out of her vagina. Stephanie said light it and get you a good hit. As she did Stephanie sucked on her clit and slid the dildo inside her.

Sheila said, " oh shit and started shaking uncontrollably as Stephanie worked it in and out. I'm cumming she screamed oh shit my pussy is so hot. Sheila went limp and was panting she said damn that was good. Stephanie said ok my turn.

Stephanie sat up on the couch and Sheila said, " ok wait a minute let me catch my breath. She was still shaking. She said damn you fucked me up with that one. I told you I had something for you. You weren't lying. Okay I'm ready, lay back. Stephanie did and Sheila did her. When she got finished Stephanie said ok let's go get in the bed. Okay help grab this stuff.

They got upstairs and put the stuff down. They started kissing and caressing each other's breasts and nipples. Stephanie said ok let me show you how this two head thing works. They got in the bed and put their asses toward each other while lying on their backs. Stephanie grabbed the dildo and slid it in Sheila and said scoot this way as she slid it in herself. Stephanie grabbed her pipe and Sheila grabbed hers. They each took a hit as they were gyrating their hips and working back and forth. Soon they were both screaming and cumming. When they were finished, there was a big puddle in the bed.

Sheila said, " I have never felt anything like that before. Stephanie said I'm glad I could share it with you. I'm glad you did. I still like men better though.

Sheila looked at the clock and said damn its two o'clock. I'm gonna be tired as hell tomorrow. I have to get some sleep. I got to have you home before I go to work. What is your mom gonna say? I asked her to watch the kids for me. I told her it would probably be late before I came in or maybe in the morning. Alright I'm going to sleep.

Sheila couldn't see how things were starting to unfold. She was only concentrating on what she thought was fun. She couldn't see that she was addicted to the drugs. She didn't see how her lust kept pouring gas on the fire. When she got high, it made her sex drive even greater. Stephanie saw this and was starting to exploit it. Sheila thought Stephanie was a friend, but she really had it in for Sheila. She really couldn't stand the fact that Sheila was so successful and she wasn't. Sheila was caught in a vicious cycle and couldn't see it.

Sheila woke up the next morning around six. She sat on the edge of the bed and thought to herself- damn I'm tired. She went and got in the shower and started washing herself. When she washed her vagina she realized she was sore. She immediately remembered what had taken place and said what the hell am I doing. I have to stop this shit. I'm not gay, am I?

Sheila got out of the shower and woke Stephanie up and said it's time to get ready to go. The dildo was still lying in the bed. She looked at it and just shook her head. Stephanie asked what time is it. "Six forty five," Sheila said. "Get up and get ready to go."

"Okay, did you enjoy yourself last night Sheila?"

"That was wild," said Sheila.

"Yeah we have to do that again sometime."

"I don't think so Stephanie. I like men too much."

"You didn't act like it last night."

"Whatever, just get your ass up and get ready to go."

Sheila went downstairs to make some coffee. She hollered up the stairs and asked Stephanie if she wanted some. She said hurry up Stephanie we got to go. She said ok I'm just trying to straighten up a little for you. I'll get it when I get home. Okay here I come.

They get in the car and her neighbor came out and gave them a funny look and a smile.

Sheila said, "did you see that? Stephanie said what. The look that he gave us. I wonder if he heard us last night. I don't know but we were sure loud enough. Man I have to cut this shit out. Don't worry about what your neighbors say. Shit I have to live here Stephanie. Did you get all of your stuff? Yeah, but I left a little something for you. What? I left you a little something to play with. What that dildo? I don't need that. You might. Whatever.

Sheila got to work and walked into the office. Hey girls as she passed through. Barbara and Terry said good morning Sheila. After Sheila went to her office, they went to Natalie and said Sheila isn't looking good. Natalie said I know. I'll go see what's up with her.

Natalie gets into Sheila's office. What's up Sheila? Are you okay? Yeah girl I'm just a little tired. What did you do last night? Girl I was at the hospital with my dad last night. My mom called me about eleven o'clock and said she was taking him to the hospital because he was having chest pains. I sat out there until three o'clock this morning. Is he okay? Yeah, they kept him for observation. I guess he'll be home today. I was just wondering because you didn't look very well. I'm good girl. I'll just have to drink a bunch of coffee.

Sheila was now starting to lie to cover her tracks. This should have given her a sign as to where she was headed. She couldn't see the trouble that laid ahead for her. She didn't see the progression yet. All she could see was the pleasure. She hadn't come face to face with the destruction that she was about to cause, but she would.

Sheila got her day started. First she was sitting there and sat in a certain position and she noticed her vagina was still a little sore. She thought about last night and how her and Stephanie had used the dildo. She thought that wasn't bad. In fact, it was pretty good. She said I can't start liking that stuff. Am I gay? Sheila was starting to get confused about her sexuality. She knew she liked George but he didn't really like everything that she liked. She enjoyed getting high with Stephanie because she could get as freaky as she wanted. So she justified it and said she would keep George for appearances and get high with Stephanie.

She was sitting there trying to do her work and started crashing. She was sitting there and noticed herself nodding. She said to herself damn I'm tired. It was early in the day and she had a long way to go. She had a call come in. When the girls had situations that they couldn't handle, they sent it to Sheila. The customer was explaining the problem and Sheila went straight to sleep on them. She woke up to hello, hello are you still there? She dozed off on the customer while they were on the phone. She got through that situation just barely.

Sheila got up and got some coffee. She looked at her watch and said; damn it's only ten thirty I have a long way to go. She got the coffee and went back to her desk. The girls were watching her. Natalie came into her office and said why don't you just go home and get some rest Sheila? She said you know I think I will. She called her boss and told him the lie that she had told Natalie. She explained to him that she was too tired to stay at work. Okay Sheila we'll see you tomorrow.

On her way home her phone rang. Hello. Hey Sheila what's up? Hey George, how are you? I'm good, how are you. I tried to call you at work and they said you had left for the day. Yeah I got sick at work so I came home for the rest of the day. Do you need me to bring you something? No I'm good. I'm going to stop at the store and pick up something for my stomach. Are you still going to church later? I don't know. I'll have to see how I feel.

Sheila was driving home and a craving came over her. She thought I can get some crack and go home and enjoy myself. She pulled out her phone and called Flip. Hello. Hey Flip what's up. Sheila? What are you up to? Hey do you have a ride? Yeah I just bought a car yesterday. What's up? I need to see you and I was wondering if you could bring it to me. It's kind of early for you ain't it? Can you bring me something or not? What do you need? How much is a sixteenth. Eighty bucks. Okay bring it to me. Where at? Twenty two thirty Lake Shore Apartments. Okay I'm near there now. Okay, I have to stop by the ATM and I'll be there in about ten minutes. I should be there about the same time. Cool, see you then.

Sheila pulled up into her apartments. By the time she got to her parking spot a car pulled up beside her. She looked over and it was Flip. She got out and so did he. He approached her and gave her a hug and said how are you? She said I'm good come on in. Nice car. Yeah I just picked it up yesterday. I had to go back by the lot and sign another paper and drop off some money.

They get inside the house. Have a seat Flip. What you got for me? Here you go. That looks nice. You know I look out for you. Yeah I know, that's why I called you. Oh I thought you called me because you liked me. You're alright. Alright, I see the way you look at me. How is that? Like you want my body. They both laughed. You're kind of cute. Besides you know I'm seeing George. I won't tell if you don't. She just looked at him like maybe. Do you have something to drink? What do you want? Water, soda, Juice or a real drink. I've got some Grey Goose. Let me have some of that. Okay I'll have one with you. Cool.

Sheila poured the drinks and sat down. Flip took a sip and said that's some good stuff there.

Sheila said, "yeah, it is kind of smooth. Sheila what are you doing calling me so early? I thought you were at work. Last I checked, I was a grown woman. My bad, I was just saying. I got off early and thought I would get me a little something. Okay, I was just asking. It's just a little out of character for you that's all. I'm good, just enjoying myself today that's all. Okay thanks for the drink; I'm out so you can enjoy yourself. Holler at me if you need me. I will. Just for the record I do like you but I'm involved right now. Like I said if you need me holler at me, I mean for anything as he laughed.

Flip left and Sheila couldn't wait to get upstairs. She grabbed her pipe and put her a piece on there and took a hit. She sat down in her chair and said yeah that's it. She instantly got horny and started playing with herself. She thought damn I should call Flip back. Then she remembered that Stephanie had left that dildo. She immediately took her clothes off and got busy.

All of a sudden after a couple hours she realized that she wasn't feeling it anymore, Sheila got scared. She thought what the hell is going on? She heard noises in the house. She put the pipe down and ran downstairs. There was no one in the house. She looked out the window and no one was outside. She went back upstairs. Her heart was racing and she was nervous as hell. She grabbed everything and put it up and laid down. She thought, am I going crazy? I have been getting high too much. I have to stop this. I am masturbating like crazy. I'm having a lesbian relation, that's not me. I even left work to do this. I have to quit. Soon she dropped off to sleep. She just ran out of gas.

At about six George called. Hello. Sheila are you still sleep? Yeah I was. Are you still going to church? Yes I'm going. How are you feeling? I'm a little tired but I'll be ok. Okay I'll be there to get you around seven. Okay George I'll be ready. See you then. Okay.

Sheila got up and took a shower. She was still kind of disturbed by what was going on. She started thinking maybe God is what she needed, he just wasn't sure. At this point she was so scared she was about ready to try anything. She said she can't let anyone know what was going on with her, that would just be too embarrassing. She had no idea how sick she really was.

Sheila was getting dressed and her mom called. Hey babe what are you doing? I just got out of the shower and getting dressed. I was wondering if you were going. Yes mam I'm going. Are you ok Sheila? Yes mam I'm fine. Why do you ask? You just sound different that's all. I just woke up. Just woke up? Didn't you have to work today? I wasn't feeling well so I came home and laid down. Oh ok. We will see you later. Okay.

George got to Sheila's and she came out and got in the car. Hi baby how do you feel? I'm ok, just a little tired. You look like it. What did you do last night? Stephanie and I hung out for a little bit. On Tuesday night? Yeah we went out and had a couple of drinks. Where did you all go? We went to Vito's for a little bit. What time did you get in? Why all the questions George? Damn baby I was just making conversation, I didn't mean to offend you. What's wrong with you? I just don't like getting the third degree. Okay I'm sorry.

The rest of the way to church was pretty quiet. George had a million thoughts going through his mind. He noticed that Sheila had been tired a lot lately and he didn't know what was going on. He noticed she was starting to look tired also. Something was changing but he couldn't quite put his finger on it. Was it another man? He didn't think that was it, they talked too much. He just let it go and didn't question her anymore. He realized that God would reveal it to him sooner or later.

Sheila's mind was racing. She was wondering what George was thinking. She was really troubled in her spirit. She was ashamed of the fact that she was having sexual encounters with a woman. What was worse is that she liked it. She knew that she liked men and didn't understand why this was happening. She had no idea that it was the drugs. Her life was changing right before her eyes and she couldn't see it.

They got to church and parked. Her mom and dad were just getting there also. They waved as they drove by. Her mom and dad waited while they parked. George parked and he and Sheila got out and started toward the church.

Hi Mr. and Mrs. Jones -glad you could make it. Good to see you George. Hi mom and dad. Hey baby girl as they hugged. Her mom felt Sheila trembling as they embraced. Baby are you ok? Yes mam, I'm just a little tired. You look a little tired. You need to get more rest.

They get in church George says let me introduce you to my mom and dad. Okay. Mom and dad these are Sheila's parents, Mr. and Mrs. Jones. How are you? Glad you could join us this evening. I am Bishop Charles Daniels and this is my first lady Celia Daniels. It's good to meet you all. Then they took their seats.

Service started and everyone got up out of their seats as the praise team came out. It was really upbeat. Everyone was clapping and enjoying themselves. Sheila's mom and dad were really getting into it. Sheila's mom looked at her and she had a blank expression on her face. Everyone could sense that something was wrong with Sheila but didn't know what it was.

Bishop Daniels came out to speak. His topic was; Time for change. He talked about his life and how he used to be in the streets. He said he hasn't always been Bishop Daniels. He said that people used to call him all kinds of names but Bishop wasn't one of them. He said that God gave him all kinds of warning signs that it was time to change but he didn't listen. He talked about how it wasn't until he hit rock bottom that he decided that he was going the wrong way. God sent me here to tell someone it's time for change. You don't have to suffer anymore.

Sheila felt as if he were talking directly to her. She was sitting there squirming in her seat. She thought did he know something about her? Had he seen her coming out of somewhere she shouldn't have been? No he couldn't have. I make sure I'm real careful. He can't know about me and Stephanie. In her mind, that was the worst thing she was doing. As a tear started coming from her eyes, her mom reached over and hugged her. Are you ok babe? I'm ok mom, just tired that's all. You know you can talk to your dad and I about anything. She thought to herself- not this.

Service ended and they went up to talk to George's parents. How did you enjoy the service Mr. and Mrs. Jones? It was fine, I think we'll be back to visit again. What church do you all belong to? We don't. We are visiting different churches to see where we want to join. Well we would love to have you here. We will consider it. Sheila it was good seeing you again. It was good seeing you again also. George you are going to have to bring them by the house sometime. Yes sir I will. Okay talk to you all later. Goodbye.

They get outside and Sheila's dad ask, what are you all going to do?

Sheila said, " I'm going home and going to bed. George said I'm doing the same. I have a busy day tomorrow. I was just wondering if you two wanted to go get something to eat. Not tonight, maybe some other time. What about this weekend? That sounds good. Okay we'll talk to you later. Yes sir. Sheila's mom said Sheila call me with concern in her voice. Yes mam I will. I mean tonight. Okay.

They get to Sheila's and she asked George if he would stay with her tonight. He told her no he didn't have any clothes with him to wear to work. I'll call you when I get home. Okay George goodnight. Good night Sheila. Are you ok? Yes I'm fine. I'll talk to you later. They kissed good night and Sheila got out. George left after she got in the apartment.

Once inside she called her mom. Hey mom you wanted me to call you. Sheila your dad and I are concerned about you. Are you ok? We know you've been hanging out with Stephanie a lot lately. I know that girl gets into all kinds of stuff. Mrs. Martin told me that she saw you dropping her off a couple mornings. I know you should have been on your way to work. Mom, Mrs. Martin, should mind her business. We hung out a couple of nights and she stayed over here. On a work night Sheila? That girl doesn't have a job and if you keep that up you won't either. I'm fine mom. You didn't feel like it at church when I hugged you. I could feel you trembling and you don't look good either. I'm just tired mom. I'm going to bed now. Okay good night babe.

Sheila went to bed. She was thinking about what her mom said. She asked herself was she starting to look like a lesbian? All that was on her mind is what had been going on between her and Stephanie. She started to feel ashamed and then she thought about getting high but she was just too tired to get up. She started crying. She cried so hard that she cried herself to sleep.

Chapter Thirteen

The Cover-up

It is Thursday morning; Sheila wakes up to get ready for work. She goes to the bathroom. As she is brushing her teeth, she looks in the mirror. She noticed that her eyes were starting to get dark rings around. She was starting to notice herself that she was looking a little tired. She said to herself that she needs to get more rest.

Sheila jumped in the shower. As the water was running over her body, she started reflecting on the sermon of the night before. She felt like he was talking directly to her. It had convicted her in her spirit about the way her and Stephanie were carrying on. I'm not doing that anymore she said. I'm not gay. I have a boyfriend and that's what I'm going to stick with.

Sheila couldn't see how the drugs were starting to affect her. She was so ashamed of her behavior that she couldn't see what was causing it. She couldn't see that these things only happened when she got high and George wasn't around. She blew right past how she felt the day after getting high for hours. She didn't associate getting high with the way she was starting to look. She couldn't see that she was addicted. She had a good job, making good money. As far as she was concerned, she was just partying a little. That little was starting to become more and more frequent.

She gets out of the shower and gets dried off. She looks in the mirror again and says a little make up will fix that. She fixes her hair and then puts her makeup on. She goes out and puts her clothes on. She puts a pant suit on that used to fit very well and she noticed the waist was getting a little loose. She thought to herself, I'm trimming down.

It must be all that walking I'm doing at work. She looks in the mirror and says looking good girl and out the door she went.

Sheila got to work and passed through the office. Good morning ladies she said. Good morning Sheila, are you feeling better today? Yes much better. How is your dad? My dad, oh he's fine. He came home yesterday. She had almost forgotten that she had lied about her dad going to the hospital.

She got into her office and sat down behind her desk and said to herself-life is good. She dove into her work as usual. Getting through her paper work like it was nothing. She was very smart and talented. She had a way with their customers like no other. Everyone loved her. She made this job seem so easy. Today would prove to be kind of different.

Sheila was sitting there doing her work and the phone rang. Sales and marketing Sheila speaking. Hi Sheila. Oh hello Mr. Franklin. I was just calling to see if you were feeling better today and how your dad was doing. We are both doing better today, thanks for asking. Good deal, I just wanted to make sure everything was okay with my star employee. Thanks Mr. Franklin, everything's fine.

Sheila was sitting there working when Natalie came in. Sheila, you need to take this call. We have a customer that claims his order was messed up and I can't get it resolved. Thanks for the warning, send it through.

Sheila speaking may I help you? I hope you can. This is Mr. Johnson from Kroger. How are you Mr. Johnson? I'm not too good right now. What can I do for you? We were supposed to have a delivery of Tide two days ago and no one seems to know where my shipment is. Well let me see if I can find out what's going on. Mr. Johnson I don't have an order for you. Well that's some bullshit; I know we placed an order. Please don't use that type of language with me. This is the third time that I've called and I keep hearing the same shit. Mr. Johnson I asked you not to use that type of language with me. I will talk to you how I damn well please. I don't think so, click. Sheila slammed the phone down.

Natalie came back into the office and asked if she had got him taken care of. He started cursing at me. I don't have to take that from anyone. Yeah he was a little rude with me also. We don't have to take abuse from anyone. Thanks for the warning.

A few minutes later her phone rang again. Sales and marketing Sheila speaking. Did you just hang up on me? Yes I did, and if you continue to use that type of language towards me I am going to hang up again. Who do you think you are? The question is who do you think you are that you can talk to people like that. Lady do you know that we are one of your biggest customers? I don't care who you are. You can't call here and talk to me or my staff anyway you want. Who do you think you are talking to? I don't have to listen to this shit. I want my order and I want it now. Click. Sheila hung up on him again.

Sheila knew this wasn't going to turn out good. She couldn't think of any other way to handle it because her head was still cloudy. Her judgment was starting to get impaired. She had always been able to keep her composure when it came to dealing with customers. This time the situation was getting a little out of hand.

Her cell phone rang and she looked at it, it was George. Hey George, what's happening? Hi Sheila, I was just thinking about you. What about? Well last night you seemed kind of different. You were nodding in church. Why are you so tired? I told you that Stephanie and I hung out the other night. Yeah I know you told me that, but you were so tired it seemed like you had been out all night. Is there another guy? Look George I'm a grown ass woman. I'm not about to start explaining myself to you. If you don't like it you can step. Then she hung up on him. He tried to call her back but she wouldn't answer the phone.

Sheila was changing. Her thoughts and her actions were starting to be affected by the drugs; everyone except her was starting to see it. Her patience was getting short and her attitude was getting kind of nasty. If she kept going down this path, soon her physical appearance is going to change.

Sheila took a little time to get her composure together. She thought to herself that she had better call Mr. Franklin before Mr. Johnson did. She was trying to do damage control. She knew in her heart that she didn't handle that well.

Sheila picks up the phone to call her boss. The phone was feeling like it weighed two hundred pounds. Hello, Mr. Franklin speaking. Hi Mr. Franklin. Hello Sheila, I was just about to call you. Yes I knew you would be getting a call. Yes I did. I need you to come to my office. Okay Mr. Franklin I'm on my way.

Sheila hung up the phone, she was nervous as hell. She sat there for a minute and her stomach started turning. She had never been in trouble before, this was a new experience for her. She sat there and was trying to think of what to say. She said hell I'll just have to tell him the truth and let the chips fall where they may.

Sheila gets up to Mr. Franklin's office and knocked on the door. Come in she heard through the door. She opened it slowly and walked in. Come on in Sheila and have a seat. She walks over toward the desk. She was very nervous. How are you today Mr. Franklin? I am well Sheila. The question is how are you? I'm good. Are you sure? I received a very serious complaint this morning from a very important customer. That is the second complaint that I have had about you this week. The second? Yes the second. Okay, I know about this one but what's the other one? A customer said they thought that you were falling asleep on the phone. Oh ok that must have been from the other day when I was at the hospital all night. Yes that's why I didn't say anything because you told me what was going on. So what happened this time?

Well Mr. Franklin. I received a call this morning from Mr. Johnson. He asked about an order. I checked the system and didn't see an order for him. I came back to the line and told him that and he started cursing at me. I asked him not to use that type of language and he did it again so I hung up on him. Then he called back and I informed him again that he couldn't talk to me or my staff in that manner and I hung up on him again. You see Sheila that's where you went wrong. I was with you up until that point. The proper thing would've been to say, "let me see if I can get someone else to help you. "

Sheila is there something else going on with you? How are things with you and George? Sheila looked at him with a puzzled look. Yes that's right I know your boyfriend's name. I have been with this company a long time and know a lot of different people. I just sense that there may be something else. I can sense something changing in you. I need you to know that there is a lot you don't know about me. I also need you to know that you can come and talk to me about anything. I like you Sheila. I think you are a great employee, you can go far with P&G, I don't want to see you mess it up. Now I have to give you a verbal warning but understand I have to cover my butt as well. The next time I am going to have to write you up. Thank you Mr. Franklin, it won't happen again. See to it, have a great rest of the day.

Sheila got up and left Mr. Franklin's office. Her knees were shaking like drug store dice. She thought it was like he could see right through her. The fact that he knew about George tripped her out. The thing that she didn't know was that Mr. Franklin was a recovering addict. He had almost lost his job and they gave him another chance. He could see something in Sheila but didn't want to make accusations. He knew whatever it was would expose itself sooner or later.

Sheila was starting on a downhill slide and couldn't see it. She thought she was just having fun. She was starting to lose control. She was getting high more often. Her sexual activity was becoming more and more perverse. She was becoming more unmanageable with her job. Soon everyone was going to see it.

Sheila got back to her office and sat down. Her palms were still a little sweaty. Natalie came in and asked; Sheila are you ok? Yes Natalie I'm fine. What did Mr. Franklin say? He gave me a verbal warning. Wow, it could've been a lot worse. Yeah tell me about it. It's almost lunchtime. Do you want to go somewhere? I don't care like where? I don't know, let's do Chipotle or something like that. That sounds good. Let me tie up a few loose ends and we can go.

Sheila and Natalie get up to Chipotle and order their food. They get their food and go out on the square. They get a table and sit down. Natalie said, so what all did Mr. Franklin say to you? Girl it was a trip, it seemed like he could see right through me. Girl you'd better be glad that he likes you. He can be a real piece of work. I heard. What tripped me out is that he knew about George, he even called him by name. Girl, Mr. Franklin knows everything that goes on around here. I see. Sheila thought; I hope he doesn't know everything.

The girls were sitting there eating. Natalie said, "hey isn't that your boy Skip?" You mean Flip as Sheila started laughing. Flip walks up and says what's so funny? Natalie said isn't that your boy Skip. Oh that's real funny. Do I look like a Skip? I don't know, what does a skip look like. Whatever. Can I sit here with you ladies? Yeah sure pull up a chair.

How have you ladies been? I haven't seen you two in a while. Sheila thought that was cool how he said that. We've been good. What's up with you? Just staying in my lane, doing what I gotta do. How is school going? School is going good. I will be finished in a year and a half. I am trying to find an internship now. You'll get one. You picked a good field. Yeah I think so. It's good to get paid to do something that you like to do. I agree. Well it's been fun but I gotta run. You girls have a nice day. You too Marcus. He laughed and said bye Natalie.

What's up with you two Sheila? What are you talking about Natalie? You know exactly what I'm talking about. I see the way he looks at you. He looks at you like he wants to eat you alive. Girl that's George's friend. That doesn't mean anything. Well it does to me. Eat and let's go. Whatever, and they both laughed.

Once back to the office Sheila's phone rang. She looked at it and noticed that it was Flip. She thought what could he want.? She had just left him. He knew she was at work. Why would he be calling me?

Hello. Hey Sheila, what are you doing? Working what do you think? What's up? I was just thinking about you. Oh really. Yeah really. I really enjoyed having lunch with you all. I would like to take you out sometime. Flip what would George think about that? I wouldn't tell him as he laughed. I thought you and George were boys. Nah it's not like that, he just cops from me. You know he's my man. I know but I can do things for you that he can't. Like what? I can give you excitement. I don't know Flip, that may be a little too exciting. Well at least think about it before you say no. I'll holler at you later. Okay bye Flip.

Sheila got off the phone and sat back in her chair. She was thinking about what he said. Sheila was kind of attracted to him. She said to herself that she kind of liked his bad boy appeal. She said to herself he is kind of cute. It might be kind of fun. It may be a way to get high for free. She said to herself, I can't do George like that. She said oh shit I'd better call him. I was kind of mean to him earlier.

Sheila finished some of her work and picked up her phone and called George. Hello. Hey George what you doing? I'm working what's up with you? I was just thinking about you and wanted to call and apologize. Oh really? Sheila you were really mean earlier. I don't deserve to be treated like that. I have only tried to be nice to you and you treat me like a sucker. I don't have to put up with that shit from anyone. I know George and I'm sorry. Do you want to have dinner later? No I don't think so Sheila. I'll talk to you later. George do you accept my apology? Yeah Sheila, I accept your apology. I got work to do; I'll talk to you later.

Sheila hung up the phone and said damn he's pissed. Oh well I said what I had to say if he can't accept it ,the hell with him. She said I don't know who he thinks he is. I don't need him, he needs me. I got plenty of niggas that want me. I can have anybody that I want.

She was thinking all this stuff. But she really felt rejected. Sheila was starting to lose touch with reality. She was becoming emotionally unmanageable and couldn't see it. As far as she could see, she was normal. The change happens so gradually that it's normally too late when you figure it out.

It was now about four thirty she was starting feel a little antsy. It would be nice to go have a drink. She said I wonder what Stephanie is doing. Nah I need to give her a rest. We are getting too close; I need to give that a rest. I think she is gay for real and I'm not trying to go that way. I'm gonna call Flip and see what's up with him. She picked up her phone and called him.

Hello Sheila. Hey Flip. How did you know it was me? I got your number and name programmed in my phone. Oh really? Yeah really, what's up? I wanted to go and get a drink after work. Is that right? Yeah what are you doing? I wasn't doing anything. I got somebody coming by in a few and then I'll be free. Do you want me to meet you somewhere? We can go to Applebee's if you want. We can have a drink and get something to eat also. That sounds good. Do you want me to bring something with me? Do you have some bud? Yeah. Cool bring me some of that and the other. How much? I don't know, fifty of each I guess. Okay. Which Applebee's do you want to meet at? Western Hills I guess. Cool I'll see you there.

Sheila got to Applebee's and went in. The hostess asked how many? I'm going to be meeting someone. Would you like a table or a booth? A booth will be fine. She took Sheila to her booth and sat her down and said your waitress will be with you in a minute. Okay thank you.

While she was sitting there she started feeling antsy again. She was feeling a little nervous and excited at the same time. She knew in her mind that this was probably something that she shouldn't be doing but she couldn't stop it. She kind of liked Flip but she liked what he had even more. All kinds of stuff was running through her mind. Her mind went from thinking about getting high to getting caught. Soon Flip walked in and she waived him over.

Hey Sheila as he kissed her on the cheek. Thanks for asking me out. I was about to get off work and wanted to have a drink and get something to eat. I didn't want to call my girlfriend so I called you. What's up with George? Why didn't you call him? I did, but he's a little pissed at me right now. Just my lucky day huh? I guess so. What happened? I didn't ask you here to talk about me and George so just let it go. Okay, ok I'm sorry. Damn girl you're kinda mean aren't you? No, I'm just direct and don't put up with any bull shit. Well I don't either so we have something in common. At that point the waitress came over.

Can I start you two off with something to drink? Yes. Do you have Cîroc? Yes we do. Okay I'll have that and cranberry. And what about you? I'll have the same but on the rock no chaser. Okay I'll be right back with your drinks. Okay thanks.

How was the rest of your day Sheila? It was good, today wasn't too bad. I had a little problem with a client but I got through it. That's good. How was your day? Long as usual. I have so much to do in a day it seems that there is never enough time. A lot of times I'm up late at night taking care of my business, and then I have to study and go to school. It makes for a really long day. That's one of the things I like about you Flip. What's that? You're not trying to make the streets you're life. Oh no, I'm not the one. I'm not trying to sling it toe to toe. Ain't no future in that.

The waitress brought the drinks and took their food order. Flip said go ahead and get whatever you want. Really? Yeah I got you. I asked you out. I have wanted to go out with you for the longest. Is that right? Yeah, ever since I saw you at the store. I noticed you checking me out. I was hoping you did. You are so fine. I want to do all kinds of things with you. Like what? Anything you want me to. Is that right? Be careful what you ask for. I can handle anything I ask for. Yeah that's what your mouth says. I like you Sheila. You're not too bad yourself Marcus I mean Flip and they both laughed.

As they were sitting there her phone rang, it was Stephanie. Hey girl what's up? Hey Sheila what are you doing? I'm out having dinner with a friend of mine. You out with George? Now you're being nosey. I was just seeing if you want to get into something. I think I'm already into what I'm going to be into for the evening. Flip looked at her and gave her the biggest grin. Boo has been asking about you. I'm cool on that for a minute. I'll holler at you later.

They sat there and ate and talked for a while. They seemed to be enjoying each other's company. At least Flip was enjoying her company. Sheila had other things on her mind. She was sitting there thinking about getting high and wondering if she could get him to do that thing for her. All of a sudden they were looking at each other and he licked his lips.

Sheila said, " is that for me? If you want it. Oooh wee. I take it that means yes. Come on let's go to my place.

On the way to her house her phone rang. Hello. Hey Sheila how are you. Hi George, I'm good. Sheila I really need to talk to you. About what? About us and what went on earlier today. Okay but not today. Why not? We need to talk about this. There you go again George. I said not today. Don't be questioning me about everything. I don't understand, you seem so different. I love you Sheila. Okay George we will talk about it tomorrow. Alright Sheila. Bye George.

They pull up to her apartment and go inside.

Sheila said, " go in the kitchen and get a couple of glasses and pour us a drink. I'll be right back; I'm going to get comfortable. Where are the glasses and the liquor? The glasses are in the cabinet over the microwave and the liquor is in the cabinet beside the refrigerator. Okay I got it.

Flip poured the drinks and came into the living room to sit down. At that time, Sheila came down the stairs. She had on some loose fitting sweat pants and a tube top. Flip looked at her and was like a deer in headlights. To him it was like she just floated over to the couch. What's wrong Flip she said? Absolutely nothing Sheila. Are you ok? Yeah Sheila

I'm fine. You are just so beautiful to me. In this old stuff? Thank you Flip. Not a problem. You bring my stuff? Yeah I got you.

Sheila sat down and grabbed her drink. She took a sip and sat the glass down. She picked up the sack and said this is a fifty. This is big for a fifty. For you it's free and so is this, he put about a sixteenth on the table. Wow, don't start anything that you aren't willing to keep up. I got you babe. All you have to do is be my girl and I will give you the world. That sounds good Flip but I've been there before. I know nothing comes for free. I got you Sheila. You know I'm involved with George. Well what am I doing here? We are going to have some fun. Okay I'm with it. Do you get high? I drink and smoke weed that's it. You don't mind if I do do you? Do you babe.

Sheila rolled a blunt and laced it with some of the crack that he had given her. Flip said that's how you do it huh? Sometimes, sometimes I hit the pipe. I just wanted to get some weed in me. I do too. Let me see that sack so I can roll me a blunt. How long have you been smoking Sheila? Not too long. I just started back. I had tried it once in college and didn't do it anymore until this year. What made you start again? I like the way it makes me feel. How does it make you feel? You'll find out. You're not going to get all crazy on me are you? Well that all depends on what you call crazy. He said oh shit and they both started laughing.

Sheila had lit the blunt and had smoked it down about halfway. They were sitting there talking and smoking weed for about an hour or so. It was getting to be about eight thirty.

Sheila said, " I'll be right back. She went upstairs and got her pipe and brought it back downstairs. She said you're going to be ok with this aren't you? As long as you don't go crazy on me I'll be cool. She just laughed.

Sheila pulled her pipe out of the bag and grabbed a piece of crack and put it on there. Flip was sitting there watching her to see how she reacted. She lit it and instantly she grabbed her vagina and started rubbing herself. She said your shit is always good. Flip said oh shit. She said yeah this is how it makes me feel. Flip sat there watching her and he was getting turned on himself.

Come here Flip. What, I told you all I do is smoke weed. I don't want you to hit this, I want you to lick this, as she stuck her hand in her pants and rubbed her clit. Oh that's what you want. I got you. That's one of my favorite things to do. I bet you've never done it like this. There is a first time for everything.

So he went over and kneeled down in front of her and slid her pants down. He noticed that trimmed muffin was wet as hell. He said damn girl did you already cum? Yeah and now it's your turn to bring it out. Okay here I come.

They got busy. This went on for hours. Getting high and having sex. Having sex and getting high. She did him and he did her. He said damn Sheila you just don't stop. She said this crack just sets my pussy on fire. I see, you're not normal. Are you complaining? No I'm just saying.

About twelve o'clock Sheila ran out of crack. She asked Flip if he had some more. He said he didn't have any more on him. She told him to go and get some more and come and spend the night with her. He said I don't have it like that to give away. She said I'll pay you for it. Don't you have to go to work in the morning? Yeah, but its Friday. It's going to be a light day I may not even go. I don't think I need to do that. I thought you said you would do anything I wanted. Okay Sheila how much do you want? Bring me a gram. Okay I'll be right back. Okay hurry up.

Flip was gone about thirty minutes and started getting real tired. He thought about that he had to go to school tomorrow. He knew that he had told Sheila he was going to bring her something back. He said to himself, shit I ain't going back over there. I have to get some sleep so I can go to school. He picked up his Phone and called Sheila and told her that he was going home and going to bed. She went off on him. She started cursing him out and told him that's why I don't like fucking with you motherfuckers. All you motherfuckers do is lie. She was going off on him then he just hung up on her.

She sat there for a minute steaming. She was caught up in the grip. Her mind was just racing. It was getting close to one o'clock. She said fuck him. I am going to call Boo and see what's up with him. I don't have to take this shit from anyone. This motherfucker is never going to get any more of this pussy. Sheila picked up her phone and called Boo.

Hello, who is this? It's Sheila. What's up girl? Where you been? I've been around. You ain't been around here. I miss you. What's up with you man? Just chill'n, what's good? I wanted to come and see you. Okay come on, I'm at the spot. Okay I'll be there in a few. She put on her clothes, grabbed her shoes, a jacket and her keys and she was out the door.

She got to Boo's place and knocked on the door. He came to the door and let her in. What's up girl? What you doing out so late. I could n't sleep and I decided to get me one. What do you need? Give me a gram. Okay. Can I use your room? Sure anything you want.

He gave her the dope and said you know where everything is. Do you want a drink? Sure. He had never seen her like this before. He knew that she was different. He had been in the game for a while. He could tell when someone was tweaking. He knew how crack made her act and was hoping this would be his lucky night.

Sheila went to the back room. This was different. She had the room to herself. She had never been over there before without Stephanie. She got the pipe out of the drawer and sat down. She put a piece on the pipe and lit it. She sat back in the chair and stuck her hand in her pants and started playing with herself. About that time Boo walked in with her drink. He said oh shit you don't have to do that baby, Let me suck it for you. She looked at him and threw the fact that he wasn't her type right out the window. Okay motherfucker, come on. She was so hot she didn't care.

He took the pipe from her and she laid back in the chair and slid her pants down. He took a big piece out of his pocket and put it on the pipe. He got on his knees in front of her and lit it. He passed it to her and she lit it while he sucked on her pussy. When she hit it her body instantly got as stiff as a board. She was lying there trembling and he kept on. She said damn Boo you make that shit feel so good. While he was sucking on her, he slid his pants down and pulled out his dick. All at once he rose up and stuck it in her. She said shit Boo, it's so big. Oh shit I'm cumming again. She didn't even pay attention to the fact that he wasn't wearing a condom. She was so high that she didn't care.

After they were finished, he brought her a towel to clean herself up. She just sat there and finished the dope and drinking liquor. Boo sat beside her and was getting high with her. He asked, Sheila what's going on with you? This isn't like you. I got me, besides you got what you wanted. Yeah but it doesn't feel good. You are a good girl and I would hate to see you throw your life away like this. I've seen it time and time again. A girl with everything going for her just throw her life away for this shit. You need to check yourself. I got me. Alright I'm out of here.

It was now five o'clock in the morning and she had to be at work at eight. She was on her way home and started thinking about the night. It was after five and she hadn't had any sleep. How was she going to go to work like this? She thought to herself, was she going crazy? All she could hear ringing in her head was what Boo had just told her. She also heard the voice of George's father's sermon. She thought, what am I going to do? I can't take off work. I need a doctor's excuse. I'm going to go to urgent care. She knew that she would be there for a while and this would give her an excuse.

She got home and sat around thinking about everything. She was trying to calm herself down and come up with an excuse to go to urgent care and get a doctors excuse. She knew that she had taken too many days off in the last few weeks. The paranoia was starting to set in. What can I tell them? I twisted my ankle, yeah that'll work.

Sheila was starting to show the signs of addiction but she couldn't see it. The disease was progressing faster and faster. Soon she would be gone beyond recall if she didn't get it in check. The lying, manipulation, changes in behavior were all telltale signs. Other people were starting see it but she couldn't.

Chapter Fourteen

Exposed

This behavior of Sheila's had been going on for a while now. She would straighten up for a week sometimes two, but now everything was coming to a head. Her runs were starting to get longer. Before she would use and go to work. Now she is missing days at a time. Everyone was starting to have questions about her. From her boss Mr. Franklin to her mom and dad.

It was Monday morning. Sheila had taken off work Friday. When she got to work Natalie and the other girls had a strange look on their faces. As she passed through the office they all spoke, but it was kind of dry. Not the warm welcome that she was used to.

Sheila got to her office and she had an uneasy feeling in her stomach. Her phone rang, it was Mr. Franklin. Sheila speaking. Good morning Sheila. Good morning Mr. Franklin. Sheila I need to see you in my office please. Yes sir I'll be right there. She hung up the phone and that feeling got worse.

Sheila got to Mr. Franklin's office and knocked on the door. Come in. How are you Mr. Franklin? The question is how are you Sheila? Have a seat. She came around and sat down. Mr. Franklin had a serious look on his face, not warm and friendly like before.

Sheila I'm going to get right to the point. Do you know why you're here? In her heart she did, but the words would not come out of her mouth. Well I'll tell you. Your work has been suffering and you have been taking too many days off work. I told you before that there was a lot you didn't know about me. I think it's time you know.

I am a recovering addict. Sheila I haven't always been in this position. There was a time when I was strung out on drugs and I was the last one to know it. I thought I was just having fun until one day my boss called me in his office just like I'm doing you. I had someone give me a break so I am extending the same courtesy to you. I am going to give you a chance to come clean with me. If you lie to me and I send you to take a drug test and it comes back dirty I'm going to have to let you go. If you tell me the truth and agree to go to treatment I'll work with you. You are a good employee and I would hate to lose you. I believe if you can get clean you'll be back to the same Sheila we all know and love.

Sheila broke down crying. Mr. Franklin I am so sorry. I have been using drugs. She told him her whole story. She told him how it started in college with her boyfriend. She told him that she hadn't done it in a while after that. When she got her apartment she wanted to celebrate her success and that's where it started again. She told him that she thought she could handle it but it just took over. She didn't get completely honest with him. She felt he didn't need to know about the sex, but that was as much a part of her problem as the drugs.

Mr. Franklin came around the desk and hugged her. He gave her a tissue and told her to dry her eyes. He told her that everything was going to be alright. He explained to her that at one time he was in the same situation and everything worked out for him. This is what we're going to do. I need you to go take a drug test and I will handle the rest. I thought I wouldn't have to take a test. Yes that's how we document it and get the company to pay for your rehab. Now Sheila you're going to have to complete this and stay clean to keep your job. Yes Sir Mr. Franklin I will and thank you. You're welcome Sheila. I'm glad you came clean with me. Take the rest of the day off and go take the test and we'll get the process started.

Sheila left Mr. Franklin's office. The uneasy feeling that she had was replaced by embarrassment. She walked through the office and could hardly look at the girls. She got in her office and was getting her things together. Natalie came in and asked is everything ok Sheila. Yeah

Natalie everything is going to be ok. Natalie gave her a hug and said I hope so. Natalie had an idea that Sheila was getting high but never said anything. Sheila looked at her with tears in her eyes and said it will. I will see you all tomorrow; I have to go take care of some business.

Sheila got to the clinic and took a number. She was sitting there and a million thoughts were running through her mind. She couldn't believe that she had gotten herself into this mess. She was sitting there looking around at the other people that were there. She thought that she was better than them. Some of them looked like people that she would never associate with. But in actuality they were exactly the people that she was associated with. On the inside she was just like them. She took her test and left.

On her way home her phone rang, it was her mom. Shit she said to herself. How am I going to tell my parents? What am I going to tell George? How are they going to look at me? After a bit her phone stopped ringing and she broke down crying. Guilt and shame was all over her. The more she thought about what she had been doing the more she cried. Sheila never planned for things to go this far, she was just trying to have a little fun. This little fun turned into something she had no intentions of being.

After she gained her composure, she picked up the phone and dialed her parent's number. Sheila had no idea what she was going to say. All of a sudden the words God help me came out. At that moment, a peace came over her. Sheila pushed the button and her dad answered the phone. Hi Dad. Hello baby, how are you? He had a sound of concern in his voice. She thought could he know no he couldn't. I'm not too good, is mom there? Yes she's here what's wrong? I need to talk to you all. Okay baby we're here.

Sheila pulled up to the house and her dad ran out to greet her. Sheila got out of the car and threw her arms around him and just broke down crying. Shhh baby what's wrong? All she could do was cry. Come on in the house. Her mom was standing at the door. She knew something was bad wrong. As Sheila and her dad approached the door her mom started crying and saying what's wrong baby what's wrong?

Sheila and her dad got in the house and her mom guided them over to the couch. She sat down and they sat down beside her with Sheila in the middle. Her mom wrapped her arms around her and they all cried together. Her dad asked what's wrong baby?

Sheila wiped her eyes and tried to get her composure. Well mom and dad with a nervous laugh, I've really messed up. What happened baby? I have been using drugs and I'm about to lose my job. Her mom said, "oh no baby" and broke down crying again. Her dad sat there quiet with his head down. He was trying to hold back his tears. He asked how long has this been going on? It's that Stephanie girl isn't it? No dad it's not her fault, I wanted it. You wanted it? Yes dad I wanted it. What do you know about something like that? Mom and dad I'm not the innocent little girl that you think I am. How do I know about something like that dad? I learned that in college also.

While I was in college I met this guy named Ralph. He was an attorney in Atlanta. We went out one night. It was him, my girls and one of his friends. After the club we went back to his friend's house for breakfast. It started out so innocent. We were just going to eat have a night cap and go home, then the drugs came out.

First it was some weed and then some cocaine. I had never done it before so I tried it. Then his friend got a test tube, water, and baking soda, and cooked some rocks. Her mom said oh no. We sat there and smoked it and I liked it instantly. Time went on and I continued to do it every now and then. I could stop on my own so I didn't think I had a problem.

When I graduated and moved home, I didn't even think about it. After I got my job and my apartment I wanted to celebrate. One thing lead to another and I ended up caught up. I started getting high more and more. I started missing work, half performing my job. My boss saw what was happening and told me if I didn't go to treatment and get straightened out I would lose my job.

I knew something was wrong said her father. When we didn't hear from you days at a time, I knew that wasn't like you. When we did see you, you looked tired. You know I know a lot of people in this town. I've heard that you and Stephanie were seen coming out of some bad places. I never did like you hanging with that girl. Dad don't blame her, it's not her fault, it's mine.

Her mom was in total shock. Imagine if she would have told them everything that was going on. Her mom had no idea all of the sex acts that she was performing. Sheila was just telling them half of the truth. This was going to be the thing that kept her sick and cause her almost complete destruction. The ability to be completely honest is the key to recovery.

So what are you going to do now Sheila? her mom asked. Well I have to go to treatment or I'm going to lose my job. Where are you going to go? I don't know. I just left from taking a drug test. When I go back to work in the morning, I have to see what Mr. Franklin has to say. Who is Mr. Franklin? That's my boss. He told me that he had been there before that's why he's giving me a break. Does George know? No mam, I haven't talked to him yet.

Well young lady, I hope you've learned your lesson. I know we didn't raise you like that. I have had some friends that got out there and got all messed up on that stuff. They lost their families, jobs, cars, I mean anything that ever meant anything to them was gone, and it didn't take long either. You know we love you and just want the best for you. Are you hungry, why don't you stay for dinner? I don't know, I have to talk to George. You both can come to dinner. Okay I'll see.

Sheila called George. Hey George. Hi Sheila, what are you doing? I'm over mom and dads. What did you do, get off work early? Yeah I had to take care of some business. What are you doing this evening? I don't have any plans, what's up. Mom and dad invited us over for dinner. What time? I guess you can come over when you get off work. I need to talk to you about something. What's wrong? I'll talk to you when you get here. Okay I have to go check on one of my properties and I'll be there. Okay.

Sheila went up to her old room and laid down on the bed. As she looked around the room, her mind started racing. One of her thoughts was how did she get here? It seemed not long ago she was in high school on her way to college. Somewhere something changed. It seemed like everything was crashing in on her. She thought about everything that she was doing. The getting high, the lesbian activity, then the guilt and shame started setting in. Sheila started crying all over again. Then the thought came into her mind how it would be nice to have a hit, just one.

Sheila laid there and started justifying in her mind why should I go get one. I'm getting ready to go into treatment anyway. What can I tell mom and dad? What time is it? Shit it's almost 4, George will be coming soon, I'll wait until later. After we eat I will have all the time I need. About that time Stephanie called.

Hello. Hey girl what you doing? I saw your car down to your mom and dads. Hey Stephanie, what's up? I just wanted to see if you wanted to get out and do something. I got twenty on something. Maybe later, we'll see. You need to see if you can get some more money. You know we're going to end up doing a lot more than that. Alright I'll see what I can do.

Sheila was lying there on her bed, mind still racing. She thought about the phone call that she just had. She started thinking about how good Stephanie makes her feel while they were getting high. She said to herself, George makes me feel good too but he probably won't want to do it. I don't want to ask him. If he brings it up then it's on. Then Mr. Franklin her boss called.

Hello. Hi Sheila, did you take care of that business? Hi Mr. Franklin, yes I did. Where are you Sheila? I'm over my mom and dads. What are you doing? I'm lying on my old bed right now. Good. While you are lying there I want you to try and remember how things were before you picked up. Picked up? Yes, you know started using drugs. I know your mind is cloudy right now. I know you're thinking about how one more would be nice but it could be your last. Sheila you show a lot of promise and I don't want to see you blow it, and you will if you don't stop now. I've been there before. Yes I've been right where you are. Ask God to help you and he will. I care about you Sheila. Do the right thing. Okay Mr. Franklin thanks for calling.

Wow, that was weird. How did he know what I was doing? He knew everything that I was thinking. Why did he call at this time? This call completely took the thought of using away. God sent a messenger at the right time, someone that had been there and could speak her language. This gave her a break for this moment; we'll see how long it lasts.

Sheila dropped off to sleep. She was tired and needed this rest. The only problem is it wasn't very restful. Sheila had a using dream only it wasn't so much fun. Oh it started out that way. It started out with her and Stephanie at a house getting high. Then they started freaking like they do. Only this time there were some guys standing around watching. It made her feel kind of nervous but they were supplying them with as much dope as they wanted. Then it turned ugly. The guys wanted to join in. Sheila resisted and they raped her and started beating her. At that point her dad and mom were at her bedside shaking her trying to wake her up.

This scared the mess out of her mom and dad. They didn't know what she was going through. Sheila, wake up baby they said, what's wrong. Oh hey mom and dad, I was having a bad dream. We know, we heard you screaming all the way downstairs. When we came up we saw you kicking and screaming like you were in the fight of your life. She jumped up and threw her arms around her mom and dad. She was shaking like a leaf. I'll be ok, it was just a dream. Babe are you sure? Yes I'm sure. Okay dinner will be ready in a bit. Is George coming? Yes mam, he has to take care of some business and then he'll be here. Okay.

Sheila got up and went in the bathroom and washed her face and brushed her teeth. She looked around and everything looked the same as when she left it. She started reminiscing about her childhood and how far she had come from there. She remembered how simple things were. Then another thought came in. My life isn't so bad. So what if I get high. I'll just go do this treatment thing and then I won't get high as much. They will teach me how to handle it and I will save my job.

Sheila got freshened up and bounced downstairs. Hi mom and dad. Hi baby they said. Are you feeling better? Yes I'm feeling better. Do you want a drink before dinner? Sure I'll take one. Her mom and dad were on pins and needles; they didn't know what to do. This was their baby, their only child, they had no idea what to do or expect.

Okay babe dinner is about ready. Do you want to call George and tell him? He'll be here in a few. At about that time he pulled up. Her dad said that boy has perfect timing. George came to the door and Sheila opened it for him. Hey babe come on in. You're right on time; dinner is just now getting ready. It smells good, what are we having? Meatloaf, mashed potatoes and gravy, corn, and muffins. Sounds good. Okay, everyone go get cleaned up and come to the table.

Everything looks good Mrs. Jones. Thank you George, I'm glad you could come. I wouldn't miss this for the world. I love a nice home cooked meal, especially when someone else is cooking it. Oh that's right, you cook a little too. Yes mam, nothing like this though. Ronald will you say grace please so we can eat? Sure dear.

George said this food is good Mrs. Jones. Thank you George. How have you been George, Sheila's dad asked. I have been great Mr. Jones, what about yourself? We don't get to see you much; I guess you and Sheila are off doing your own thing. Actually no, I don't get to see Sheila that much either. I would like to see her more but I guess we are both so busy. He just through a ton of heat off of himself and doesn't even know it. As they are eating the table is quiet for a bit. George is looking at Sheila and she can hardly make eye contact with him. He thought to himself; what the hell's wrong with her? He noticed that Sheila hadn't said hardly anything all night.

They finished eating and got up from the table. Sheila's dad asked George if he would like a drink. Sure Mr. Jones. Okay I'll get it for you. Would you like some desert said Mrs. Jones? No mam, I don't eat a lot of sweets. The thought went through his head. Why are they being so nice, and why is Sheila being so quiet? So he finished his drink and said, thanks for everything Mr. and Mrs. Jones. You're welcome George. We hope we can see you soon. You know we have church on Wednesday night. We may just see if we can make it. We would love to see you there. So what's up Sheila, what are you about to do? I was going to hang out with you for a bit if it's cool. Sure we can ride out if you like. Cool. Mom and dad I'm about to leave with George, I'll come back and get my car later. Okay bye you guys see you later.

Sheila and George left as her mom and dad watched from the door. Her dad said, that is a nice young man and he has no idea what our daughter is up to. I believe she is about to tell him. I hope it doesn't run him away. I hope it doesn't either. I believe that he would help her get straightened out. They had no idea that that was something that only her and God could do.

They pulled off and George asked what do you want to do? I thought you wanted to talk to me about something. I do, let's go down to Sawyer Point. Okay that's cool. What's up with you Sheila? I'll tell you George; let's just go down by the water. I need to be somewhere peaceful; I have so much going on in my head. George noticed a tear falling from her eye, he said oh boy what's really going on.? He had never seen her like this before. Sheila was really afraid of what this news would do to their relationship. George had told her what had happened with one girl that he used to be with.

So they get to Sawyer Point and park. They get out of the car and start walking down towards the water. Sheila reached out and grabbed his hand. This made George even more curious. He thought to himself is she pregnant, is it mine? All kinds of stuff was running through his mind.

They get to the water and sit on the wall overlooking the Ohio River. So what's up Sheila? Isn't the water beautiful George? Yeah it is now stop playing and tell me what's going on. But no George, isn't the water peaceful, I love this. So if you love it so much, why don't we come down here more? I don't know George maybe we will, that is if you still want me. Sheila stop stalling and tell me what's going on. He is getting a little agitated by now. Okay I'll tell you.

Alright George I'll tell you. I have been getting high too much. It was starting to affect my job and now I have to go to treatment. I knew something was wrong. You would always keep me away from you. You and Stephanie were always hanging out. So when did all of this come about? Today when I went to work, Mr. Franklin called me in his office and told me. He had had a couple of complaints and I have been late and absent a couple of times. He noticed a change in me and knew what it was. He told me that I had to go to treatment or lose my job. I went and took the drug test today. When he gets the results back I'll be going to treatment.

I could tell a change in you too. I thought it was another man at first, I almost wish it was. That would be easier to deal with. I could probably just walk away from you, but this could kill you. Sheila if you want me to, I will stand by you and help you get through it. George you would do that for me? Yes Sheila, I would. You have a lot of good qualities and I know without the drugs you would be a better person. Sheila grabbed him and held him tight and started crying and saying I'm sorry George. I never meant for this to turn out like this. I know you didn't, that's just what happens when you start messing around with that stuff.

After a while Sheila's train of thought shifted. She had started thinking about Stephanie's call. Then the thought came, I have to go get me one before I go to treatment. I know George isn't going to want to do it. Sheila, Sheila, are you listening to me? Yeah George I'm listening. You need to go to church with me Wednesday. There you go with that again. Sheila one day you're going to see that is where your strength comes from. If you want to get through this you're going to need more than my help, you're going to need God. At that point all she heard was blah, blah, blah, she really wasn't trying to hear it.

After a bit they left. On the way back to Sheila's parents' house Sheila asked George if he wanted to stop and get a drink. You know we have to go to work. I know, one drink won't hurt us, besides this may be our last night together for a while. When are you going in? I don't know, I'll find out tomorrow when I go to work. Okay we can stop and have one before we go in.

George drops Sheila at her car and follows her to Vito's. On the way there all Sheila was thinking about was getting high and having sex. She said to herself, I'm probably going to treatment tomorrow so I can have fun one more night. She was in a very dangerous place now. She was associating drugs and sex with having fun.

They get to the bar and go in. George acknowledges a couple of guys he knew as they go up to the bar. The bartender comes to them. What are you having tonight? George said two double Grey Gooses and cranberry. Cool, I'll be right back.

How are you feeling Sheila? She looked at him and said horny. No I mean about what you're going through. Oh I'm cool. It's going to be ok. I'll just go do what I have to do and come home and its back to normal. I hope not said George. I hope you see what this is doing to you, hell what it's doing to us. I was wondering why I don't see you much. You know I don't get down like that for real. I did it a couple of times with you but it just doesn't feel right in my spirit. I hope when you come back to me we can put this all behind us. I love you Sheila and I want the best for us. She gave him a look of disbelief and tears started to form in her eyes.

George I didn't know you felt like that about me. I thought you were just having fun. I didn't know you wanted to be all serious and stuff. Sheila I took you to church with me to meet my parents, I cooked for you; you think I would do that for just anyone? I told you about the issues I have with men. Yeah and I tried to show you that I'm not the one. It's still hard for me.

As they were sitting there having their drinks Flip walks in. Hey what up George and Sheila? This felt kind of awkward for Sheila because she knows that she just screwed him the other night. What's up Flip they said? Not a whole lot, just out taking care of some business before I go in. Cool, good seeing you. Alright, I'll holla. As he walked away, Sheila felt relieved. It made her feel kind of bad knowing what she had done.

Okay back to what we were talking about. Sheila I really do love you. I want us to be together but you have to put this demon behind you. When you do, you'll see how God will bless our relationship. See George how are you going to talk to me about God sitting in a bar having drinks? Sheila the Bible doesn't say don't drink. It says don't be drunk, there is a difference you know. I just want that woman that I first met. Okay George, I'll get better for you.

They were sitting there having their drinks and George said what's on your mind Sheila, you've gotten kind of quiet? Do you really want to know? Yeah I asked you didn't I? She turned to him and put her hand on his leg. She slid her hand up to his crotch and rubbed his penis. She looked in his eyes and leaned over and whispered in his ear, I want to fuck you tonight. George got hard instantly then he grabbed her hand and said, that would be nice but we have an early morning. George you're no fun. I can't be fun all the time. As they finished their drinks he said do you need me to follow you home? No I'm cool. They walked outside and kissed good bye.

Sheila pulled out onto the street and headed toward her apartment. She looked at the time and said, it's just eleven I got time to do one. She picked up her phone and called Flip since he was right there at the bar. Hey baby girl. Hey you good. Yeah what's up? I need you to bring me a G by my place. Okay give me a few, I'm waiting on someone else and I'll be right there.

Sheila thought to herself, I need some sex. She said if George won't do it for me I'll get Flip. Hell I can kill two birds with one stone. She went upstairs and took a shower and put on her nightgown. She started getting all of her tools together about that time her doorbell rang. Here I come she shouted down stairs. She came and opened the door and said come on in. Flip said damn girl you look good and smell good too.

Sheila said, "you want a lick? He laughed and said that sounds good but I got a couple of more stops to make. I brought that package by for you. How much is it? Give me fifty. She said all I got is forty. Okay let me have that. I guess I can do it for you this time, but don't make it a habit.

Flip left and Sheila took her package upstairs. She was feeling kind of rejected. She said fuck those niggas, I'll get myself off. She reached in the drawer and got out her toy and began to do her thing. It was about twelve thirty when she finished. She thought to herself damn it would be nice to have one more. It would be nice to have someone suck this off for me while I hit it. She grabbed her phone and called Flip he didn't answer. She called Stephanie she said she was in for the night. She said damn I guess I'll call Boo's black ass.

Hey Boo, what's up? Hey Sheila, what's good? I need to come by and see you. Okay, you know where I'm at. I have to stop by the ATM and I'll be right there. Cool. Sheila jumped up put on some clothes and grabbed her keys and raced out the door. She said to herself, it's just 11:30; I can be home by 1:30 and get some sleep. As she was on her way she was asking herself; should I do this? What the hell I'm out here now.

Sheila got to Boo's house and knocked on the door. His boy opened the door. What's up shorty? Come on in. I ain't your shorty, the name is Sheila. I could've called you a lot worse than that. Yeah and you could get fucked up in here too, where's Boo? You need to watch your mouth. She said man where is Boo. sounding impatient. He's in the bathroom; he'll be out in a second.

Boo comes out of the bathroom and says hi Sheila. What's up Boo? What can I get for you? Give me a gram. Is anyone in your back room? No, do you want to use it? Yeah I do. I don't want to ride with this, I just want to do it and go home. I have to get up and go to work tomorrow; I'm not trying to be up all night. Okay go on back there and I'll bring it to you. Do you want a drink? Sure Sheila said, " as she made her way to the back room. Sheila sat there for a second and started thinking, what the hell am I doing? I can't believe I'm thinking about letting him eat me, I don't even like him like that. Oh well what the hell I did it before.

Boo came in with a tray with some drinks on it and her piece. She said that looks like more than a gram. He said I know, I'm gonna sit in here and kick it with you for a few if you don't mind. It's your house. Yeah it is ain't it? Then he laughed. But if you wanted to be alone I would let you. No I'm cool; actually I could use the company right now. What's going on? It's a long story and I really don't feel like talking about it. I will tell you this. This is probably the last time you're going to see me for a while. Why is that? My job is making me go to treatment. I was wondering how long it was going to take. I figured you would either crash and burn or go to treatment or both. I'm glad your job is giving you another chance.

Sheila poured a drink and took a sip, boy this tastes good. It will be a long time before you're able to have another drink so you better enjoy yourself.

Sheila said, " yeah I plan to get it in before I go in. I know that I'm gonna be gone for at least thirty days.

She said let me have the pipe. Sheila took it and put a hit on it. She lit it and instantly started rubbing herself. Boo said damn girl you must be as hot as fire. Sheila blew the smoke out and said yes I am. You need to come and blow on it and put it out. Boo said you ain't said nothing but a word.

He came over and got down on his knees in front of her and pulled her pants down. She was still squirming from the first hit. She said damn this shit is good. Boo licked her pussy and said how was that. She said wait let me put a hit on here then do it. Boo said ok, put a nice one on there.

Boo took a big piece and put on there for her and said lay back and slide your ass out. Sheila laid back and slid out to the edge and Boo started licking. Damn that feels good she said. She put the pipe to her mouth and lit it. Instantly she started cumming. She gave the pipe to Boo and he took a hit and gave it back to her. He put his lips on her pussy and started sucking it while exhaling the smoke. As he sucked and licked her pussy she started squirting. She let out a scream and said I'm cumming and it won't stop. He rose up and stuck his dick in her. She said damn Boo that feels so big.

Sheila said, " ooh it feels so good. After a few strokes they came together.

Sheila and Boo sat there and finished the dope while they talked. He said Sheila when I first met you I never imagined you getting caught up like this. After I saw you coming around for a while I saw you about to slip. Why didn't you say something? I've been doing this long enough to know that you can't tell a person when they need to stop. That's something they have to figure out for themselves. I never figured that I would be having sex with you while getting high. I thought you were so much better than that. Sheila broke down crying and left.

Chapter Fifteen

The Journey Home

Sheila's first day in treatment was kind of tense because she had no idea what to expect. It's understandable why she would feel like that. This is the first time that she has ever lost her freedom. Even though it wasn't jail, she is still on lockdown. She is sleeping in a room full of women that she doesn't know and in a foreign place. This was going to take some getting used to.

Her first day in group, she was being standoffish. In her mind she shouldn't be there. Somehow she thought she was better than the other women. She did look a little better than the others, some looked very beat up. Although Sheila wasn't looking her best, she was still somewhat holding it together, but still she was in there for the same thing as everyone else.

When it came to the sharing portion of group Sheila didn't have a lot to say. She had this bougie attitude, because she didn't come off the streets. he couldn't identify with the stories of the other women. When they would share about jumping in and out of cars selling themselves, selling their kids clothes, or stealing, she would turn up her nose. Sheila didn't understand that. he just hadn't got there yet.

Her second day there was rough, she started having withdrawals. She had never felt anything like this before. When she was on the outside and she had a craving, she went and got some dope. This time she had to just tough it out. They gave her valium to calm her down a little, but that didn't continue long. They told her this was normal and not to worry, it would get better.

By her third day she started smoothing out a little bit. She still didn't get it, though; she was an addict just like the other girls. When she shared it was like the things she did was nothing. She didn't see how her sexual behavior was abnormal. She didn't see how it was becoming harder for her to enjoy sex without drugs. She didn't see that she really had a problem, in spite of the fact that her employer made her check into treatment.

Day three they let her make some phone calls. The first call she made was to her mom and dad and they were happy to hear from her. Her mom said that she was so worried about her. She assured them that she was fine. She told them when they could come to visit and they said they would be there.

Then she called George. Hello. Hey George. Sheila? Yeah this is me.

Hey baby, how are you? I'm good. Are you really? Yeah it's not bad.

I couldn't imagine being locked away in a place like that. I'll be home before you know it. I will be glad; I hope we can start fresh. I will be praying for you. Thanks George, you can visit me if you want. Okay, when? Visiting hours are six to eight on Thursday. You need to call my mom and dad to see when they're coming; I can only have two at a time. Okay Sheila, I can't wait to see you. I can't wait to see you also. I love you Sheila. I love you too George, I'll talk to you tomorrow.

This made Sheila feel good to know that she had people that loved her and was standing behind her. She thought everyone would turn their backs on her. Even though she saw that they wouldn't, she still couldn't be completely honest with them. She feared that they may not understand everything she was doing while getting high. George would never understand her sexual exploits with these other people.

That night, when Sheila went to bed, things got kind of ruff for her because her mind started wandering. She started thinking about how she really enjoyed getting high. She didn't understand why everyone had such a problem with it. It was her life and she should be able to enjoy it how she wants. She still hadn't made the connection that the drugs were causing problems in her life. She was still blaming it on everyone else.

As she laid there thinking about all of the experiences, the sex stood out the most. She remembered the first time Ralph gave her oral sex while getting high. She was thinking about Stephanie and all of the wild stuff they used to do. All she could think about was how explosive her orgasms were. The next thing you know she had her hands in her panties. She said damn I am so horny, I can't believe how wet I am. She rubbed her clit with her two middle fingers until she was about to explode. Then she slid them inside her vagina and it gripped them like it was a dick. She pulled them out and went back to her clit. Her body arched like it was going to break and then it slammed back to the bed. Her body went into convulsions as she reached her climax.

This sent Sheila into a tailspin. The cravings hit her so hard that she jumped out of the bed. Sheila was pacing the floor; she couldn't stop thinking about getting high. She put on her clothes and burst out of her door screaming, "I want to go home! I want to go home!" One of the aids grabbed her and talked to her. After a while she started calming down. The aid gave her a sedative and put her to bed.

The next morning she got up and went to breakfast. Some of the other girls were trying to warm up to her, but she wasn't having it. She was acting like she was so much better than they were. All she talked about was where she went to school, her job, and how much money she made.

Her counselor's name was Karla and she was a former street girl herself. She was starting to get fed up with Sheila's bullshit. Her counselor was a good student herself who once had a good job and a family, but drugs and the street life robbed her of all of that. She broke Sheila down right there:

Sheila let me tell you something. You are no better than anyone in here. All you talk about is the school you went to, the job you have, and how much money you make, you ain't shit. You're just another addict like the rest of us. Yeah I said us, I'm a recovering addict also and I see right through your bullshit. Yeah Sheila I'm just like you. I came from a good home, went to a good school, had a good job, and made great money, but look where I am now. That's what life is about, what you are doing right now? You need to be recognizing how and why you got here. If you don't, you'll be here over and over again if you're lucky.

If I'm lucky? Sheila said, " with a nasty attitude.

Yeah if you're lucky. The streets may kill your dumb ass.

At that point Sheila had had enough. She jumped out her seat and said I'm not a dumb ass. I graduated from Spelman at the top of my class. Karla said see that's exactly what I'm talking about. You got all of that education and don't know shit. Let me tell you what I know.

You grew up in a good family that gave you some good values. You graduated from a school in the hood so you were at the top of your class. That made you look pretty smart so you got a scholarship to Spelman. You got to Spelman and got turned out. Yeah I know you thought everything was your idea including the escapade you and your roommate had. Sheila's eyes popped wide open. Karla said yeah I know what goes on at those all girls' schools sometimes. That doesn't make you a lesbian but it opened your eyes to some things. You met some slick cat down there and he got you high for the first time and you liked it. He probably got you high, gave you some good sex, and then tried to pimp you out.

Sheila broke down crying. She was thinking in her mind, how could she know all of this? Karla said no wait it gets better. You graduate from school and come back home and get a good job. You probably already had it before you came home. You started making a lot of money, got your own place and then you wanted to celebrate. You remembered how sex and drugs made you feel so you sought it out. Stop, stop, Sheila cried. No wait it gets better.

You probably ran into one of your girlfriends that has been getting high. She is really jealous of you but your smart ass doesn't know that she is really trying to turn you out. She is jealous of everything that you have and she wants to see you lose it; in fact you and her have probably been getting freaky deaky. Sheila cried out again stop please. You've probably been screwing already to get high and your dumbass doesn't know it. Why do you think those dealers were giving you so much dope for your money?

Sheila couldn't take it anymore; she jumped up and ran out of the room. She was running down the hallway crying and screaming I want to go home. Karla ran after her and grabbed her and hugged her. She was screaming bitch get off of me. Karla said no Sheila I'm not and squeezed her tighter. You don't care about me Sheila said,

"Oh you're wrong about that Sheila, I do. I had to break you down like that so you could see that you're not unique. You really make a lot of these other girls feel real bad about themselves. I've been where you've been that's how I can see you so clearly. The only way that you're going to beat this is to get real with yourself. The sooner you stop lying to yourself and face your problem the sooner you will get better.

Sheila stopped crying and a calm came over her. She stood there in Karla's arms shaking like a leaf. Thank you Ms. Karla. I am so sorry for calling you a bitch. I know that you didn't mean it Sheila. You are afraid and hurt right now. I was you that's how I can see you. I not only lost a job, but I lost my husband and children with it. Karla and Sheila stood there and cried and hugged each other. Okay are you ready to come back to group now? Sheila you have so much to offer those girls if you don't alienate them. Just be yourself don't try to tell them anything because you are here just like them. Okay Ms. Karla.

Sheila got back to group and had a different attitude. She apologized to the group for being such a bitch. She sat in her seat and was willing to listen now. Karla had broken her down in front of the group. This made Sheila see that she was no better than anyone else.

It was now visiting hour and Sheila was feeling kind of anxious. She hoped her mom and dad were coming to visit her, but she wasn't sure if she wanted them to. She was embarrassed for being in treatment. She never thought in a million years that this is where she would end up.

The aid came and called everyone's name that had visitors. When they called Sheila's name her stomach sank. She said ok here we go and she moved to her place in line. When she saw her mom and dad she was a little nervous but happy just the same. They hugged each other and went to their seats.

They sat there and things felt kind of strange. It was quiet for a while, they just didn't know what to say to each other. Her mom and dad didn't know what to say because they never imagined their daughter using drugs let alone in treatment. Sheila was feeling some embarrassment because she never wanted them to find out.

Silence was finally broken, her mom said how are you feeling baby? I'm good. Her dad said, are you really, how can you be in a place like this. He was doing everything in his power to hide his displeasure. Dad I know you're disappointed in me, but I'm sorry I had to put you and mom through this. Sheila do you know how crazy it is out there as a tear started rolling down his cheek. You could have been killed out there. Dad I know, it really wasn't that bad. I was just having fun and got caught up. The only reason I'm here is because my boss found out. And how did he find out? He said my performance at work was changing, I think someone told on me. Well whatever happened he probably saved your life.

Sheila was in complete denial. She just didn't see where her life was headed. She had no clue that she had just been rescued. She thought this was just a break in the action. She was really looking forward to getting out and going back to business as usual.

They sat and talked for a little while more. Her dad expressed the thought that she should move back home. Her mom said yeah Sheila that's not such a bad idea.

Sheila said, "I don't think so, I can take care of myself. This is just a little bump in the road. Her dad said this is more than a little bump, this is life or death. I really want you to think about it. Okay dad I will.

Visiting hours were over and her parents went home. Sheila was left with feeling embarrassed that her parents had to come and see her in here. She was glad that they still loved her and had faith in her but it didn't make her feel any better. She went to her room and cried herself to sleep.

A few days have gone by and Sheila has been in treatment for about a week now. She was starting to feel a little better about herself. She was starting to loosen up and fit in with the group more. She noticed this guy named Thomas checking her out when she first got there. She didn't pay him much attention at first but now she was starting to warm up to him a little.

The next visiting day came and they were in group. George had told her that he was coming but she wasn't sure. The aid called her name and she got in line. She said oh snap he did come. All kinds of things started going through her mind. The main thing was fear. She was afraid of how he was going to see her, and if he still felt the same way about her. The fact that he came to see her in the first place was nowhere in her thoughts.

When they saw each other they embraced like they hadn't seen each other in months. George gave her a dozen roses along with a big kiss. It seemed like they held each other for hours, they just didn't want to let go. George even had a tear in his eye. He said I miss you so much Sheila. I miss you too George, thanks for the roses. You're welcome Sheila, I love you. I love you too George.

They went to their seats and once again they felt kind of tense. Neither one of them has ever been in this situation before. Finally they broke silence. How are you doing in here Sheila? I'm doing ok. It was a little tough at first, but it's smoothing out. I'm getting used to these people. They were hating on me at first. I can't wait until I can get out of here. You'll be out soon enough and you can go back to work. How are things going to be with us George? I hope they're going to be better.

The visiting hour was over. George left and Sheila went back to the unit. She sat up and watched TV with the other girls for a while and then went to bed. As she laid there her mind was just racing. She thought about her job, her mom and dad, her apartment, and then she thought about George. She thought about making love with him. This made her horny so she played with herself and went to sleep.

The next morning she woke up and went to breakfast. She was sitting at the table with the girls when Thomas caught her eye. Thomas winked at her. She said to herself no he didn't just wink at me. He did it again and she smiled.

They went to group and he made sure that he sat where he could talk to her. They got there a little early; the instructor hadn't got there yet. He said I've been watching you. She said you have. He said yeah, I think you're very beautiful. I understand that you just got caught up and your job sent you here. That happened to me before too. That went right over her head that this wasn't his first time in.

He went right to work on her, he was saying everything she wanted to hear. He was stroking her ego big time. He was validating her view that it wasn't her fault she was there, she was just misunderstood. He was saying things to make her laugh, oh he kept her smiling. He was setting her up all the time.

This went on for a couple of days, he was trying to break her resistance down. They had gotten real comfortable with each other. They were starting to say suggestive things to each other. This was starting make Sheila horny. He told her that he had a place that they could go. She said stop boy, where? Meet me down in the rest room at break.

Time came for break. They were on their way out of group and Thomas winked at her and she gave him the nod. They both made their way to the basement. He went one way and she went the other. This was against the rules and she knew it but she was so horny that she didn't care. Thomas didn't care because he was just doing what he did.

She got to the restroom, he had made it there before her. She opened the door and went in. She said damn you got here quick. He said I was in a hurry to be with you. They started kissing and pulling at each other's clothes. He pulled his pants down and sat on the toilet and Sheila pulled hers down and straddled him. She slid down on his dick and moaned, she was hot as hell. Thomas said shh, you have to be quiet. She went up and down a couple times and her legs started shaking. Thomas said damn this shit is tight.

Sheila said, " you like that don't you? Her body tensed and she said oh shit. Thomas said are you ready? She nodded yes and they both came together. She sat there trembling for a minute and said that was good. She got up and washed off a little and went her way.

This wasn't a good thing for more than one reason. First of all she has a man that loves and supports her. He had just came to visit her and brought her roses. The second thing is that this was going to cause her to defocus. When she was in treatment she needed to be trying to learn something instead of just resting.

The next day in group everything was going good. They had a guest speaker come in from the outside to do a sex education class. Some of the clients were making jokes saying we already know how to do it. One girl said yeah I know how to do it real good. They started laughing and Karla just shook her head. She said you just think you were doing it good you were just drug induced.

The speaker took the floor; she said my name is Mrs. Johnson from the City of Cincinnati Health Clinic. I am here to talk to you today about sex. I know you've all done it before and some of you probably think it feels real good. I say some of you because I know some of you just use it as a means to an end. More what I want talk about is what you run the risk of taking away with you. Some of you may be carrying diseases and not even know about it. What's worse some know and don't even say anything and have unprotected sex anyway.

Drug users and homosexuals are at the highest risk of contracting a disease. If you're a homosexual drug user you just increased your chances. In the heat of the moment or having sex for drugs you throw caution to the wind and have unprotected sex. Some of you even come to treatment and have sex in here. There is no way to protect yourself in here. How do you know that someone doesn't have something that you can't get rid of? When is the last time any of you have been tested for HIV or any other sexually transmitted diseases?

Mrs. Johnson stayed for about an hour. She told them a little about herself. She told them that she was in recovery; this made them feel a little more at ease. She talked about all kinds of diseases. She even told them that she was HIV positive. She has been living with it for twenty years and she is undetectable. She told them that meant that her treatments are working but she will still have to take her meds the rest of her life. This totally relaxed them and made them listen.

Mrs. Johnson left and Karla took back over the group. Karla said I know some of you think you can get away with having sex in here. Just remember that you don't know what each other has been doing out there or who they were doing it with. You will not get away with it. If you get caught you will be terminated from the program and be reported to your job or probation officer. If you don't get caught you may contract some kind of disease. One thing for sure you will probably end up relapsing because you're not taking this seriously.

This really made Sheila think. She had been having sex with George unprotected. She thought about how she had sex with Boo. He put his dick inside her without a condom. Then she thought about what she had just done with Thomas. What the hell is wrong with me, am I crazy?

The time was fast approaching for Sheila to get out. Sheila was looking better and feeling better. They were in group and Karla was giving the ones that were going home instructions. She told them if you really want to stay clean as soon as you get out find you a meeting to go to. If you do ninety meetings in ninety days you'll have a better chance at staying clean. Get you a sponsor so they can guide you through the steps. The twelve steps are your keys to recovery.

After group they were on their way to lunch and Thomas caught her attention. Sheila looked at him and shook her head no. He caught up with her and said what's wrong? She said didn't you hear anything that Mrs. Johnson said. Oh I've heard that speech plenty of times before, there's nothing wrong with me. How many times have you been in here Thomas? Four. Oh there is plenty wrong with you, bye Thomas. Oh you think you're too good for me now. You didn't say that in the bathroom.

The day came for her to get out and she was feeling kind of anxious. Karla pulled her to the side and said Sheila you're a pretty girl and you've got everything going for you, don't mess it up. I don't want to see you here again. Your job gave you a chance this time but they won't do it again. Okay Ms. Karla thanks for everything. You're welcome Sheila. As Sheila turned and walked away Karla just shook her head. She said to herself, that girl hasn't heard a word that I said.

The day Sheila got out George came and picked her up. He met her at the door with a hug and a kiss and some roses. Hello to you to George as she smiled. Where are mom and dad? I told them that I would come and get you. We're going over their house for dinner. Oh ok, I wonder what we're having. I don't know but my mom brought some yams. Your mother and father are going to be there too? Yes Sheila everyone cares about you and wants to welcome you home. Your parents must be so ashamed of me. No they're not, they just want the best for you. No they don't they're just coming to check me out to see if I'm good enough for their son. Sheila they know how much I love you and they just want to support you also. Unhum.

They get to the house and everyone rushes to give Sheila a hug. Her dad holds on to her and doesn't want to let her go. Her mom said Ron let the girl go so she can breathe. He said oh, oh, I'm sorry, I'm just glad my baby is home. Dad you act like I've been gone for years. I just missed you that's all. Are you ok? Yes dad I'm fine. Hello Bishop and Mrs. Daniels, how are you. We're fine Sheila; we just wanted to be here to welcome you home. We wanted to let you know that you have our support as well. You're a beautiful girl and we want to help you keep your life on track. Thank you all but really I'm fine and I'm going to be fine. Okay Sheila we're here to help if you need us. Her mom said, ok everyone let's eat. Bishop said yes this is my favorite time. George and Sheila looked at each other and smiled.

They sat down to the table to eat and Bishop offered up grace. It was kind of quiet at the table, it's like no one really knew what to say. They all had a bunch of questions but were afraid to ask. How do you ask someone how was treatment like they just came back from vacation? How do you ask someone what made you start using drugs in the first place? Those are subjects you let people bring up on their own, or wait until you are in a private setting. You don't just bust people out at the dinner table in front of everyone.

The food is great Josephine Bishop said. His wife said yes everything is delicious. Okay here we go. Did they treat you ok in there her mom asked. Yeah I guess, it's nothing like sleeping in your own bed though. I know said the Bishop, I can't wait to get home after going to speak somewhere. Do you travel a lot Sheila asked? Yes I do from time to time. You all should come with us sometime. That would be nice said her mom and dad. Sheila just sat there quiet; she wasn't really trying to have anything to do with that conversation. She didn't want them to start preaching to her.

Sheila you really ought to think about joining a church, hopefully ours said Bishop. Mrs. Daniels said yes we would love to have you. In fact we would love to have you all. Bishop said you know Sheila, Jesus can help you through anything you're going through. Oh yeah? Well where was he when Rene got killed? Where was he when Tonya got raped? I don't know why he allows things to happen to people Bishop said. What you should be looking at is why he didn't allow it to happen to you. It could have you know. I'm sure you heard a lot of stories in that place you were in. God is trying to tell you something Sheila, I hope you listen. I'll give it some thought Bishop, thank you.

Well thanks for having us over Ron and Josephine, the food was great. Anytime Bishop, it's always good seeing you and the misses. We hope to see you all in church soon. Yes sir, we'll be there. You too Sheila. Okay Bishop, you two have a good night. Dad let me walk you and mom to the car.

Son do you really love Sheila. Yes I do dad. Well if you really love her then stand by her. Don't preach to her or talk at her just be there for her. God is trying to tell her something but she is being defiant. He is going to do some great things through her but I believe that it's going to get worse before it gets better. She is going to need some soldiers around her. Her faith isn't strong enough to fight by herself. Okay dad, I've got her. Good night son, we love you. I love you all too. Good night mom and dad.

That was a nice little conversation you had with your folks. What were they telling you, to stay away from me? No Sheila quite the contrary. My parents really like you Sheila. My dad asked me if I really loved you. He told me if I did then I should stick by you and give you all of the support I can. My dad and mom don't judge people Sheila. That was nice of them having pity on the poor little crack head. Stop Sheila, they don't think about you like that. They know you're a good girl caught up in a bad situation. My dad sees big things from you. Really? Yeah really, you just have to see it for yourself.

I'm about to leave, do you want me to take you home? No, I think I'm going to stay here tonight. They told me to go to a meeting when I got out, but I'm tired and don't feel like it. Don't you think you may want to listen to them? George stop, I know what I need for me. I don't need you to start preaching at me. Let me do this ok. Alright Sheila, good night.

Sheila sat on the couch with her mom and dad. Her dad said I really like George and his folks. He comes from a good family. His folks really care about you Sheila. You have all of the support you need all you have to do is reach out for it. I heard you and George talking. If those people said you need to go to meetings I think that's what you need to do. Okay dad, maybe I'll find some this week end. I go back to work Monday. Okay babe we just want the best for you. Give me a hug I'm going to bed. I love you babe. I love you too dad.

Chapter Sixteen

Back to the World

Sheila's first few days in her apartment was kind of rough. She had all of her paraphernalia still there. She also had the toy that Stephanie had left. She threw her pipe away, but not the toy. She had no idea how much of a grip sex had on her and how it would play into her addiction. They told her in treatment that you only have to change one thing and that's everything.

Sheila did finally find a meeting to go to, she was very reluctant though. If it wasn't for her parents, George, and Mr. Franklin her boss asking her about it, she probably never would have. She didn't yet understand the recovery process. Just like in treatment she thought she was different from everyone else. What applied to them didn't apply to her. She hadn't got her head wrapped around the fact that she was an addict.

Sheila would hear other women's stories and cringe. In her mind she would say uhhh, how could she do that? She heard them talk about how they jumped in and out of cars selling themselves. How they sucked dicks in abandoned buildings to get that next hit. She would say to herself, I would never do that. The saying that everyone has a "yet" blew right past her, but she'll catch up to it in a few.

Her parents and George were keeping pretty close tabs on her. It was like they were monitoring her every move. Sheila blew up at George one day. She said damn it I'm a grown ass woman. I wish you all would stop treating me like a child. George hugged her and said Sheila I love you so much, I just don't ever want to lose you. I've already lost one to this addiction; I'm not going to let you go. Let's go out to dinner. Okay that sounds good.

Sheila and George get to their favorite spot, Pappadeaux. They go in and get seated and the waiter that usually takes care of them came out. They like his service so they always ask for his section when they go there. Hey George and Sheila. Hi Shawn. I haven't seen you two in a while. They said yeah, it's been a minute hasn't it? Can I start you off with some drinks?

Sheila said, " yeah I'll have the usual and George gave her a look. She said what, it's just one drink. Shawn looked at George and said what are you having. I guess I'll have the same in an agitated voice. Coming right up, as he turns and walks away.

See that's what I'm talking about, you all are treating me like I'm a child. If I want to have a drink I can have one. Sheila do you think you really should though? It's only one drink, it's not like I'm trying to get drunk. But Sheila they said that you shouldn't have even one drink. That's what they said for them, that ain't got nothing to do with me. Okay babe I don't want to argue. Good.

They got finished eating and left. When they got in the car Sheila said, " I'm sorry about that in there George. It's ok Sheila. No, I shouldn't have gone off like that, I just hadn't had a drink in a while and I really wanted one. What's going to happen when you really want some crack? That's different George; I'm not going to mess with that. In her mind at that moment she was done, but hold on.

They get to Sheila's and she asked will you come and stay with me for a while? Yeah I can come in for a little while; you know this is a work night. Yeah I know, I just don't want you to go right now. She ran her hand up his leg and kissed him. She grabbed his penis and it was as hard as cheap bubble gum. She said I can see someone else wants to stay also and they both laughed.

Once inside the house it was on, they just attacked each other. They started in the living room. They ripped each other's clothes off. George said I really missed you Sheila. I missed you too George. I don't ever want you to go away from me again. I won't I promise I won't.

He pushed her back on the couch and started eating her pussy. She said, oh George I really miss this, he said so do I. He was licking it real slow like his favorite ice cream cone. Sheila started getting wetter and wetter. George said damn baby you taste so good. I had almost forgotten how good you taste. Oooh George, you're eating that pussy. She started breathing heavier. She said I know you feel what you're doing to my pussy. Oh George damn I'm cumming. It's cumming oh shit it's cumming. She let out a scream and said what are you doing it won't stop. Her body flexed and started trembling. She said oh shit it won't stop. Okay I can't take it anymore give me that dick.

They got off the couch and went upstairs. She pushed George back on the bed and started sucking his dick. Oh damn baby that's good. You better not cum in my mouth George. You better stop then. Get up on this dick. Sheila jumped up on his dick and started riding it like a horse. George reached around and grabbed her ass while she was riding up and down. Damn this ass feels so good. You miss it don't you? You know I do.

He flipped her over and pulled her to the edge of the bed. He stood on the floor and spread her legs. He put his dick deep inside her. She said damn George, you're in this pussy. You like that baby? Yes George yes. Is this my pussy? Yes George yes. Oh shit I'm cumming again. At that time he turned her around and started hitting it doggie style. She screamed oh shit it's so good. I love it when you hit it like that. All of a sudden her pussy started gripping and popping. George said oh shit Sheila here it is. Are you ready for it. Here it comes. Come on baby give it to me. Ohhhh there it is and they crashed on the bed panting like to race horses.

George fell into a deep sleep. Sheila started having a craving. She said damn a hit would've gone good with that. She had become so accustomed to getting high and having sex it was natural to her. She didn't give it a second thought that getting high popped into her mind after having sex with her boyfriend. She had no clue that that could trigger her craving, plus she had a drink earlier. This isn't going to be good.

Sheila has been back to work now for a little while. Everything was going pretty smooth. She was getting back into the swing of things. Natalie was trying to find out where Sheila had been and Sheila kept evading her. Sheila told her that she just needed some time off to get her head together. Things were getting a little stressful with her and George and her mom had been ill. I guess it's hard to admit that you had been to treatment. You don't want everyone to know that you have a drug problem, although it runs a lot deeper than that.

Sheila was in her office one morning when she got a call from Mr. Franklin. Hello. Hello Sheila. Hi Mr. Franklin. Can you come up to my office for a sec? Sure I'll be there as soon as I finish these last few sentences of this report. Okay.

Sheila got up to Mr. Franklin's office and knocked on the door. Come in. Sheila went in to his office. Shut the door Sheila and have a seat. She shut the door and sat down. I just wanted to talk to you and see how you're doing. I'm doing good Mr. Franklin, how are you? Good thanks for asking, but it's not about me it's about you. Your work has improved. I feel like we have the old Sheila back. Thanks Mr. Franklin. I just want to keep it that way. If you need time to go to a meeting let me know, I am behind you 100%. Do you have a sponsor yet? No sir not yet. You need to get one and start working some steps. That's the key to staying on track. And remember one is too many and a thousand is never enough. Thank you Mr. Franklin, I will talk to you later.

Sheila got off work and was on her way to a meeting and Stephanie called her. Hey Sheila what you do'n. Hey Stephanie, what's up. Nothing I haven't talked to you since you came home. Yeah I know, I've been kind of busy. What are you doing this evening? I am on my way to a meeting then I will probably hook up with George. A meeting? What kind of meeting? Not one of those drug meetings, where people sit around and tell those sad ass stories. Yeah I guess. I tried that before, it didn't do nothing for me. Yeah well my boss thinks it will help me, girl I'm just trying to keep my job. Okay girl I'll holla at you later. Bye Stephanie.

Sheila got to the meeting. It was still a little early, there was a few people standing outside. She sat in the car and watched them for a bit. She thought what the hell am I doing here? I am nothing like these people. Then there was a tap on her window. She looked over and it was a girl that she was in treatment with. She unlocked the door and said get in have a seat. It's Sarah right? Yeah and your name is Sheila. You're looking good Sarah. So are you Sheila. It's amazing what thirty days of rest will do for you. Have you been here before? Yes I have. This is my third time trying to get clean. What happened the other two times? I guess I just didn't listen or I forgot what I'd heard. The bottom line is life got good for me again and I forgot that I was an addict. Okay it's time to go in, come on girl.

They get out and go in. Sarah said let's grab theses seats up front.

Sheila said, "I don't want to sit up there. Oh come on girl stop being afraid, they don't bite. They call this relapse row back here in the back. Why do they call it that? Because more times than not people are sitting back here doing other things, having conversations and not paying attention to the meeting.

Before the meeting they passed out the readings. Sarah grabbed two and gave Sheila one. Who's an addict? Sheila started reading it and the first few lines through her for a loop. It said Most of us don't have to think twice about this question. WE KNOW! Our whole life and thinking was centered in drugs in one form or another-the getting and using and finding ways and means to get more. We lived to use and used to live. Very simply, an addict is a man or woman whose life is controlled by drugs. We are people in the grip of a continuing and progressive illness whose ends are always the same; jails, institutions or death. Right away she discounted what she had read. She said to herself, my life isn't controlled by drugs. She totally missed the progressive part. She forgot about when she started using how hard it was to stop.

Sheila managed to sit through the whole meeting. She heard a lot of people sharing a lot of things and all she could do is say not me. Then one girl she heard share caught her attention. She talked about how she had it all at one time and it seemed overnight it all went away. She had a job, a nice house, a nice car, and a family that loved her. Her job had given her a chance to get clean and she through it back in their face. She shared about how she refused to believe in God until things got so bad that she had nowhere else to go. After the meeting Sheila was on her way to her mom and dad's house. Everything that she heard in the meeting was swimming around in her head. She said those people just had some bad luck. She discounted the fact that a room full of people not to mention millions worldwide ended up at the same place. They may not be at the same place physically but the pain was all the same.

While on her way to her mom and dad's, George called. Hey baby what you doing. Hey George, I'm just leaving a meeting. Good, how was it? It was ok I guess. I just don't see how going to those meetings is going to help me stay clean. I have a friend that has been going for ten years; it seems to be working for him. Well that's him. Okay Sheila just give it a try and see what happens. What are you doing George? Why are you getting an attitude with me? You know I don't like people telling me what to do. You need somebody to tell you something. Click. Sheila, Sheila, I can't believe she hung up on me.

Sheila gets to her mom and dad's and goes in the house. Hey baby her dad says, how are you? I'm good how are you? I'm cool. She gives him a hug and goes in the kitchen. Hi mom, what you doing and kisses her on the cheek. Hey baby, just my usual. Are you hungry? I have some leftovers. What did you all have for dinner? Chicken, greens, yams, and macaroni and cheese. You cooked all of that today? No honey that was left over from yesterday, it's just a little left. Okay I'll have some.

What have you been doing as her mom looks at her with a curious look. Not a lot just working. I went to a meeting today after work. You did? How was it? I don't understand it. It's just a bunch of people sitting around talking about their problems. What they had and how they lost it. Who they used to be and who they are now. Some people have been coming to those meetings for twenty plus years. Well honey if it's working for them it can probably work for you also. I don't know ma. Just give it a try. You sound like George. Speaking of George how is he? He's probably mad right now. I hung up on him on my way over here. Sheila!!

Sheila was leaving her mom and dad's. She said to herself that was wrong, I'd better call George and apologize. Hey George. Hi Sheila. George I apologize for hanging up on you earlier. You weren't even going to call me back either. No, for what, you hung up on me. Sheila I don't have time for games and power struggles. I was just playing with you and you got mad at me. I'm sorry George, how can I make it up to you. Where are you? I'm at home. What are you doing? Ironing a shirt for work. I'll be there in a minute. Okay.

On her way there her phone rang. Hello. Hey Sheila what's up? Who is this, Flip? Yeah baby it's me, where you been? I've been calling you for a month. You must have had your phone off because it kept going to voice mail. Yeah I went away for a while. Oh yeah where did you go? Just away, what's going on. I just thought about you. I got some real good stuff in and I wanted see if you wanted some. No not today Flip. I'll call you if I do.

That phone call shook her up. She wasn't even thinking about getting high. Now her stomach was flipping. All of a sudden she had to go to the bathroom. She got to Georges house and ran to the door. She was ringing the bell and knocking at the same time. George ran to the door and opened it. What's wrong, what's wrong? I got to use it bad. She gave him a peck on the cheek and blew past him straight to the bathroom. George stood at the door laughing.

When Sheila came out George was laid back on his bed watching TV. Did everything come out ok as he laughed? Oh you got jokes. She laid down and put her head on his chest and wrapped her arms around him. Are you ok Sheila? Yeah I'm good. Are you hungry? No I ate over mom and dads. George I'm sorry I hung up on you. I know you were just playing. I was just a little irritated. I just don't see the point in those meetings. You are new at this Sheila, just give it a chance. Okay George. I love you George. I love you too Sheila.

They laid there watching TV for a minute. Sheila started rubbing on his chest. What are you up to? You keep that up you're going to start something. That's the point. She worked her hand down his stomach and started rubbing his dick. She said somebody wants me to start something. Yeah we miss you. Is that right, well mommas home?

Sheila got up and took her clothes off. As she walked slowly around to his side of the bed, George couldn't keep his eyes off of her slender brown frame. Damn girl you're fine. Sheila got to his side of the bed and placed her fore finger on his lips and said shhh. She started kissing on his chest and slowly worked her way down to his pelvic area. At this time his soldier was standing at attention. She grabbed it with her hand and stroked it a couple times and said someone is very happy to see me. Sheila put it in her mouth and went to work. She was doing it so good that George grabbed the pillow and covered his face to keep from screaming. She went up and down a couple times and then stopped on his head. He said oh shit Sheila I'm going to cum. She kept going and finally it happened. He came so hard his toes curled. Sheila didn't stop until he begged her to.

George pushed her off and said oh you want to play like that huh. He grabbed her and threw her down on the bed. He started kissing her. He worked his way down to her ample firm breasts. He sucked and licked on one nipple then the other until her body started to squirm. He slowly worked his way down her stomach licking and nibbling. She was starting to pant. He made his way down to her pussy and started licking on her clit. He flicked it a couple times with his tongue then he licked in a circular motion around the opening of her vagina. He started sticking his tongue just inside licking her g spot. While he was working his tongue in and out he was rubbing her clit with the tip of his nose very gently. She got wetter and wetter. All at once she screamed I'm creaming George I'm creaming. Oh shit it won't stop. Her body started to shutter and then she stretched out as stiff as a board. Then she jerked away from him and balled up at the head of the bed shaking.

George stood up and pulled her to the edge of the bed.

Sheila said, " no George I can't cum any more. He said we'll just have to see about that. He slid her ass to the edge of the bed and opened her legs while he was standing at the side of the bed. He put his dick inside of her and put his hands on the bed.

Sheila said, " oh George you are so deep in this pussy. He started working it round and round in and out. He said damn girl this pussy is hot. It's all yours baby. Is it as he started hitting it harder she said fuck me George fuck me. Her pussy started spitting and popping. She said I'm going to cum George please come with me. Okay baby here I come, you ready. Yes George yes come on. Oh there it is baby there it is. He collapsed on top of her. They crawled up in the bed and fell asleep.

Sheila had a bad dream that woke her up at about four in the morn ing. She jumped up screaming. George jumped up and said what's wrong Sheila what's wrong? She said I had a dream that three guys were raping me and I couldn't get away. I got you babe. Come here and let me hold you. I got to get up George. I don't have any work clothes over here. We can fix it so you never have to leave again. What? Let's get married. Married? Me? I don't know George. I don't know if I'm ready for that yet. Well just think about it. I love you and I want to be with you. I've got to go George so I can get ready for work. I'll talk to you later.

On her way home she drove by Flip's place. She happened to notice a light on. She looked at her phone and said nah and kept going. She was thinking about George asking her to marry him. She wondered, if he knew who she really was would he still want to marry her. If he knew all of her dirty little secrets would he still want her?

The next morning Sheila got up and went to work. The first person she saw was Mr. Franklin walking into the building. Good morning Sheila he said. Good morning Mr. Franklin. You sure seem happy today. I'm happy most days Sheila; I don't have a lot to be sad about. How are you Sheila? I'm good. I must say you seem a lot better. Have you been going to meetings? Yes sir I have. Good. Do you have a sponsor yet? No sir I don't. Sheila you're going to need one to help guide you through the steps. Don't wait too long. If you need to talk you know where I'm at. Okay Mr. Franklin, thank you.

Sheila got to her office and put her things down. About that time Natalie walked in. How are you this morning boos lady? Sheila laughed and said don't call me that. That's what you are ain't it. Isn't it, you're so ghetto. What's up girl, you ok this morning? Yeah I'm fine. Do you have plans for lunch? No not right now. Do you want to do something? Sure, that sounds good. Get with me later and we'll figure out where we want to go.

As the day went on it was business as usual. Taking and verifying orders, taking care of customer problems, her normal thing. All of a sudden her phone rang. Hello. Hey Sheila. Oh what's up Stephanie? Not a lot, I hadn't heard from you in a while and I was just calling to check on you. Thanks for calling, how are you? I'm good same old same old. Boo has been asking about you. Yeah I had to drop off the scene for a while. Yeah I see. I haven't heard form you in over a month. I tried to call you and your phone was off. Yeah I went away for a little bit. Oh yeah where did you go? Just away. Oh ok. What are you doing when you get off. Not a lot. George and I are supposed to hook up. Okay call me when you get a chance.

Sheila hadn't talked to Stephanie since she got out of treatment. She knew that she had to steer clear of her. This phone call brought up some feelings of guilt and shame. She remembered all of the lesbian acts that she and Stephanie had engaged in. How they were getting high while they were doing it. This made her feel kind of antsy. It took a minute for the feeling to pass but it did.

Lunchtime came and Natalie came in and said, ok what do you have a taste for? I don't know, it's a nice day out lets walk over to the square and grab whatever. Okay that sounds good. I haven't had Chipotle in a while so that sounds pretty good. Yeah let's do that.

The girls left and got down to the street.

Sheila said, " this sun really feels good on my face. Natalie laughed and said you act like you've been locked away somewhere. Sheila snickered and said come on girl let's go.

They were making their way down towards the square. When they hit the corner of Fifth and Walnut Sheila heard someone calling her name. She turned to see who it was, it was Flip. Shit she said to herself. Why now? I don't want to see him.

Hey baby girl, what's happening? Hey Flip how are you? I'm good, How have you been? I've been ok. How are you Ms. Lady? I'm sorry I forgot your name. Natalie. Yeah that's it, how are you? I'm good. It's good to see you again. It's good to see you both. What are you doing down here Flip. I came down to take care of some business and get some lunch. I was headed to Chipotle where are you girls going. We were actually going to the same place. Cool come on I'll buy you girls lunch. Natalie said cool let's go. Sheila wasn't real cool with it but she said what the hell.

They get to Chipotle and order and get their seats. So what you been up to Sheila? Oh a little of this and that. I haven't seen you in a while. Yeah I went away for a minute. Oh yeah, where did you go, anywhere interesting? Just away she said in an irritated voice. I'm sorry, I was just making conversation. You're fine. What have you been up to Flip? Just waiting to graduate so I can get a better job. Do you have any leads? Yeah a few. Okay ladies it was good seeing you both but I gotta go. Okay Flip thanks for lunch. Ain't no thang. You two take care.

They get back to the office and her phone rings. Sheila speaking, may I help you? You sure can. Oh hey George. Hey baby what are you doing. I'm just getting back from lunch. Why didn't you call me on my cell phone? I thought I did. What's up? I was wondering if you wanted to go to church with me tonight. Okay that sounds good. Do you think your mom and dad would like to go? I don't know, I'll ask them.

Sheila got off work and was headed over to Georges to eat before they went to church when her phone rang. Hello. Hey girl what are you doing. What's up Stephanie? I'm on my way over George's to eat before we go to church. Go to church? Y'all are really doing the family thing now huh? Whatever, girl what's up. Not a lot, I was just thinking about you. Thinking about what? About tasting your sweetness. Girl you know I ain't into that anymore. I thought we could get us a piece and do it like we used to. You still have our friend don't you? Girl bye, I got to go.

That phone call sent Sheila's mind racing. She started remembering what they used to do. She started remembering how good it felt when Stephanie would get her off while they were getting high. Her stomach started flipping. The craving came back instantly. It crossed her mind to call Stephanie back but she fought through it.

They made it to church and went in and got their seats. The choir came up to sing Sheila was kind of fidgety. Her mom asked, are you ok dear? Yes mom, I'm fine. She really wasn't, she couldn't get Stephanie off of her mind. Even though she was sitting in church with the man that asked her to marry him. She couldn't get the drug induced pleasures that a woman gave her off of her mind.

Bishop Daniels got up to preach. His sermon was "It ain't over until God says it's over." He said God is calling us back to him. Whatever it takes to get your attention is what he will allow in your life. He said God gives us all free will. He wants us to come to him on our own. He gives us all a chance to get it together. He is going to show himself strong in our lives. Some are going to have to go to the depths of hell before they cry out for his help. God with his Grace and mercy will be right there. Jesus is waiting with outstretched hands. Won't you come? The doors of the church are opened.

After church they waited around for Bishop and Mrs. Daniels to come out. How are you Bishop and Mrs. Daniels? We are fine. How are you all doing? We are good. George how are you and Sheila? We are glad you all decided to come out. We are good dad George said. Sheila I would like to think that we are all family and anytime you need to talk day or night my door is always open. Thanks Bishop I will keep that in mind.

Chapter Seventeen

The Bitter End

A year has gone by now. Things were going good on the job. Sheila's relationship with George was strong. Things as a whole were going very well for Sheila. With all that was going good in her life there was still something missing. No matter how good things seemed to be she still couldn't find that happiness she was looking for. All of the secrets that she was keeping was eating her alive.

It was Sunday afternoon. Sheila and George had gone to church earlier along with her parents. They all met at George's parents' house for dinner. They were all sitting around talking and out it came.

Sheila said, "I just don't understand why people put all of that money in church. Bishop Daniels told her that that was one of the laws of God to pay tithes. That's what I don't understand. There are people that don't even believe in God and are doing better than some in church. A man said God said it and to my knowledge God has never spoke to me and told me anything. Oh he has Sheila. Either you didn't hear him or you just ignored him. There will come a time when you won't be able to ignore him. There is a calling on your life and you will answer one way or another.

George's mom brought out the food. Ron said Sister Daniels this looks and smells great. Thank you Ron I hope you all enjoy it. Josephine said I'm sure we will. They blessed the food and began to eat. George's dad was looking at Sheila with a bit of concern. He knew she was headed for some tough times and was worried about her, not only for her but for George. He knows how much George loves her and he doesn't want him to get hurt.

They had finished eating and everyone was about to leave. Bishop Daniels said Sheila let me speak with you for a minute as he pulls her to the side. Yes sir she said, what is it. Sheila you are a bright and beautiful girl. God has something for you to do. I know you don't understand a lot but don't stop asking questions. I want you to take this Bible and read it please read it. You are going to go through some things and you are going to have to hold on to this word with all of your might. Thank you Bishop I will.

As George and Sheila were pulling off, they waved to his parents. George asked, what did my dad said to you? Why nosey, that's between me and him. He told me he wants my body as she broke out laughing. George looked at her and laughed and said there is something wrong with you girl. No he gave me this Bible and told me to start reading it. He told me that God had something for me to do. What could God possibly want with me? I don't know Sheila but if dad said it, it's probably going to come to pass. God has used a lot worse people than you. The rest of the way home Sheila got quiet and looked out of the window.

They got to Sheila's apartment. Sheila asked are you going to come in George? Yeah I guess I can for a little bit. I have to go take care of a couple things before I go home and start getting ready for work tomorrow. Well don't put yourself out mister. No I have to go collect some rent. A couple of tenants owe me so I have to go by before it's too late. Well go get my money then as they both laughed.

Once in the house Sheila got her clothes off and got comfortable. She started thinking about what George's dad had said. Then she thought, what could God possibly want with me? I don't even know that there is a God. If there is a God why does he let all this stuff go on.

As Sheila was sitting there, her apartment was quiet. She was just sitting there alone in her thoughts. She started thinking about treatment and how she and Thomas had sex while she was in there. She thought about her and Stephanie having lesbian encounters. She thought, am I really gay? No I can't be. She thought about all of the times getting high. She had all of the things that she had done swimming around in her head with no one to talk to. The more she sat there and thought the more the guilt and shame started to come over her. She started having cravings. She said to herself I need a drink. What she had heard in her meetings went right out the window.

About that time her phone rang. Hello. Hey babe what are you doing? Hey mom. Nothing, just sitting here thinking. What are you thinking about? Just life mom. Oh everyone goes through struggles. Some are just more visible than others. Some people hide them very well but everyone goes through something. Do you need me to come over there? No mom, I'm ok. Okay babes, if you need me call me. Okay mom, I love you bye. Bye babe.

When Josephine got off of the phone she went in to the room where Ron was watching the game. She said honey I'm worried about Sheila. Oh yeah, what's wrong? I don't know she just seems kind of troubled. She's not coming by like she used to when she first got out of treatment. Josephine, she is just getting more relaxed now. I'm sure going to treatment was an experience for her. I just hope that she doesn't fall back into that mess.

Sheila's phone rang again. Hello. Hey girl what's up? Hey Stephanie, what's going on? Not a lot I was just thinking about you. What are you doing right now? I was thinking about going to get a drink, do you want to go? Sure. Sheila I thought you weren't doing that anymore. Girl we're just going to get a drink. I'll come and get you. Okay Sheila.

Sheila gets over to pick Stephanie up. Stephanie comes out to the car and opens the door. Hey girl what's up as she sits down? What up homie? I haven't seen you in a while. I know it seems like forever. Did you miss me? Oh you know I did. Where are we going? I don't know, let's go down town. Bet, where to. There is a couple of little bars in the west end that serve pretty good drinks. Okay let's do it. We can just hang out.

They get downtown and Sheila asked, is the Parktown still opened. Yeah that's my spot. I know the bartender, the bar maids and the owner. I know just about everyone that comes in there. Is that such a good thing Stephanie as she laughed? Girl bring yo ass.

They go inside and sit at the bar. The bartender comes up and says what's up Stephanie? Hey Chuck, how are you? I'm good. Who's your friend? Oh. Chuck this is Sheila, Sheila this is Chuck. They shook hands and Sheila said, " nice to meet you Chuck. Nice to meet you too Sheila. Damn you're fine. Sheila smiled and said thank you. Stephanie said slow down big boy, she's spoken for. Damn sorry about your luck.

What are you girls having?

Sheila said, " I'll have a double Cîroc and cranberry. Stephanie said I'll have the same. Chuck said that's a big girl drink. You sure you can handle that. Don't I look like a big girl? Yeah you do, but with Stephanie speaking for you I don't know. I can handle my own don't worry about me. Stephanie said you know that's what I drink all the time.

The drinks came and Sheila and Stephanie sat there drinking and talking. Stephanie asked what's up with you girl? I thought you were through. I have a drink every now and then. Stephanie said, you know according to the program you're not supposed to. Yeah well fuck the program. Ooh, listen to your potty mouth. Are you ok? Yeah, I've just got a lot on my mind. Do you need me to help you get it off? I don't think you can Stephanie. I used to help you get it off real good. Girl you are so nasty. I ain't thinking about you. Yeah I bet and they broke down laughing.

They sat there and had another drink. Sheila got kind of quiet. Stephanie got up to put some money in the jukebox. Chuck came over and asked Sheila if she was ok. Yeah I'm good. You look like you have a lot on your mind. I do. If you want to talk about it I'm a good listener. Thanks but I don't think you'd understand. I would probably understand more than you think. I 'm available after hours if you want to talk. Thanks but I'm ok and she smiled.

About that time she heard a loud commotion over by the door. Hey baby where you been. What up Steph, I been away for a little while. I just got home Friday. Are you ok? Yep, business as usual. Chuck just shook his head and said fool. He said Sheila that's bad news there.

Sheila said, " he and Stephanie seem to be close. Yeah that makes me wonder what you two could possibly have in common. Sheila just looked at him.

Stephanie brought her friend over. Hey Sheila I want you to meet someone. This is Frank, Frank this is Sheila. Hi Frank nice to meet you. You too baby girl. What you two ladies into tonight? We're just hanging out getting a few drinks. Sounds like a plan. Do you mind if I sit here with you two. Go ahead, there's plenty of room. Thanks. What's up Chuck? Give the ladies whatever they're drinking. Thanks Frank. Ain't no thang. There is nothing I like better than spending a nice Sunday evening with two pretty young ladies.

Chuck poured the drinks. When Frank went to pay for it, Sheila noticed that he pulled out a big roll of cash. She said to herself, I know what he does. He looked at her and smiled. He had gold all in his mouth. He even had a diamond in one.

Sheila said, " he must really be balling.

They sat there and had a few more drinks. They were laughing, talking and having a good old time. Sheila left home just to have a few drinks. She had no idea that this night was going to change her life forever. What started out so innocent would turn into a life and death experience.

The girls were starting to get pretty tipsy. Frank said what you two got going on for the rest of the night?

Sheila said, " it's getting late, I have to go to work in the morning and I'm already kind of tipsy. Aww girl it's early, it's only eight thirty. What about you Stephanie? I'm with my girl Frank. I rode with her, if she wants to go it's cool.

Stephanie slid around over to Sheila's other side and whispered in her ear. Come on girl let's go with him. He is hooked up. We can have big fun. I have to go to work in the morning Stephanie. Aww come on girl.

Sheila was pretty lit by now. She was starting to have crack cravings. It had been a year since she had smoked any so she told herself that she could handle it. That alcohol made her forget all about what they had told her in treatment. If the drugs don't get you, the lifestyle will. She was about to come face to face with the side of the lifestyle she knew nothing about. She had no clue that Frank was down on his luck and had resorted to robbery to get money now, but she will soon find out.

Frank had already marked Sheila. He could tell by the way she looked and carried herself that she had it going on. He was planning how to set her up for a robbery. But first he wanted to get both of them high and have sex with them. He knew how freaky Stephanie was so he figured Sheila was too since they were so tight.

They finished they're drinks. Frank said, are you girls ready to go.

Sheila said, " yeah, let's get this party started. Chuck was standing behind the bar looking in amazement. He thought to himself, what the hell is this girl getting herself into. He knew from talking to Sheila that she was nothing like these two.

They get to Sheila's car and Frank says, this is a nice whip. Thanks

Sheila said, "Where is your car Frank? I walked over here. I was just around the corner. Can I ride with you girls? Yeah I guess where are we going? We can go over to my spot and chill. I got some liquor, weed and cocaine; we can have a real party. With just us three huh

Sheila said, ". Frank said how many do we need.

They get to Frank's place. Come in girls and make yourselves at home. The liquor and weed is in the cabinet and I'll be right out with a little something else.

Sheila said to Stephanie, "girl what have you got me into. Girl relax it ain't gonna kill you. Besides he keeps some fire. Here roll a blunt while I pour some drinks.

Frank comes out of the back with a plate and a pipe. Sheila's stomach started bubbling instantly. I've got to use your bathroom Frank. Okay its right around there, first door on the right. When she came out Frank said are you ok?

Sheila said, "yeah I'm fine. Frank handed her the pipe and a piece. Sheila looked at Stephanie and said here we go. Sheila lit it and instantly her legs started shaking and she clinched them tight. She started squirming in her seat. She said shit this is good and she touched herself. Frank said damn that good huh and laughed. She gave it to Frank and he passed it to Stephanie and said I'm going to turn on some music. Go ahead and get you a piece Stephanie.

Frank went to turn on the music and he was thinking all the way, I'm going to freak these bitches. When he came back to the couch he asked how do you girls like that? They said that's some good shit. Sheila asked is that all you have? Yeah but I can get some more. She said good, that's not enough. How much can you get? I got you, I can get whatever you want. No I like to pay my own way. How much is a sixteenth? One hundred dollars, you can get an eight ball for one fifty. Do we have to go get it or will they deliver it. We can do it either way. I have to go to the atm so let's ride.

He makes a call to his boy and tells him that he will be by in a few. It's all set up let's do it. Sheila stopped at the atm and got some money out. Frank was watching her to see where she put her slip so he could see what she had in the bank. Just as he had hoped she was in such a hurry she laid it down on the console. He acted like he was pointing at something and knocked it off on the floor under his leg. Sheila never paid it any attention.

They get to the spot and Frank goes in and picks up the package. While he was in there he put the plan in motion. He told his guy that he had a couple of girls out in the car with money. He said that he wanted to get them high and rob them. He said he was going to fuck the hell out them first. Do you want in? Hell yeah. Come by my place in a couple hours and we'll do these bitches.

He goes back to the car and gets in. Okay let's go. I put your money with mine and got a quarter O. We can split it or we can just do it all if you want. I guess that's cool. I guess I'll be calling in tomorrow. I haven't taken a day off in a while, I'm about due.

You girls want to have some fun when we get back? What are you talking about Stephanie said. Frank said I feel like eating some pussy. Sheila and Stephanie looked at each other and laughed. Frank said, what are you two laughing about? We'll see. If this is as good as that other stuff you may get to eat more than you can handle.

They get back to Franks and go inside. He pulls out the dope and puts it on the plate. Go ahead Sheila get you a nice piece. She grabs the pipe and puts a big piece on it. When she lit it she instantly stuck her hand in her pants and started playing with herself. She said ooh shit this is good. Here Stephanie get you some. Frank said what you girls think, are you ready to have some fun.

Sheila said, " hell yeah.

Sheila was in full tilt now she was instantly caught up in the grip. She was right back where she left off and didn't even realize it. She was in for a very rude awakening. The warning that Georges father had given her was about to come true.

Sheila and Stephanie took their clothes off and started kissing each other. Frank was like damn this is going to be fun. Sheila sat down on the couch and said come here. You said you wanted to eat some pussy. Come and get this wet pussy. She laid back and put a piece on the pipe while he was licking her pussy. She said ooh that's it and lit it. Her body started shaking and she started cumming instantly. They got high and did each other for about two hours straight.

There was a knock at the door. Who is that

Sheila said, "? Frank said it's probably my cat. Okay I guess this party is over. Hold on baby he's probably got some more treats.

Sheila said, " we've got enough here. That's going to be gone soon Frank said. We're gonna keep this party going all night long.

Frank got up and let him in. This made Sheila kind of uncomfortable. This guy had a different kind of look about him. He had a real evil spirit about him. She got up and started putting her clothes on. He said hold on baby what you doing. I brought some candy for you. I got some here she said. Here I know what you like. Lay back and put this on there and I don't want you to pass it until you're finished.

This was bigger than any one piece she had ever done. She said ok and propped herself up. He got down in front of her as she lit it. He started sucking on her clit and fingering her. She said oh shit that's good. He said keep on, this is what you wanted. He kept sucking and licking until her whole body was shaking. She said damn I can't take it anymore.

Stephanie said shit it's my turn. He did the same thing to her. Frank slid over beside Sheila and pulled her over on top of him. She started riding his dick up and down and around and around. Frank said damn this pussy is hot. She said you like this pussy don't you George? Who's George? This shocked her and she jumped up and started freaking out. Oh shit what am I doing?

At that time Frank's boy grabbed her and bent her over the couch. She was saying no, no what are you doing? I'm giving you what you like as he stuck his penis inside her. No, no please don't. Frank said fuck her Joe. He and Stephanie continued getting high and doing what they were doing.

He finally stopped and Sheila said, " why did you do that? I asked you to stop. You raped me. Shut up bitch and come over here and suck my dick. I ain't sucking shit. In fact I'm ready to go. You ain't going nowhere. He pulled out a gun and said I said get over here and suck my dick.

He grabbed her by the hair and pulled her over to him. I said suck my dick bitch and if you bite me I 'm gonna blow your brains out. Stephanie said what are you doing? Shut up bitch you're next. She said mother fucker you're crazy. She rushed him and he hit her in the head with his gun and she fell and hit her head on the corner of the table.

Stephanie was lying there still. Sheila was crying and gagging as he stuck his penis deeper into her throat. Shut up bitch he said you're next. Frank shook her and said shit Joe I think she's dead. We've got to get rid of her body. Here find something to tie this bitch up with.

Sheila started to scream and Joe slapped her down and said shut up bitch before I put a bullet in your ass.

They tied Sheila up and gagged her. They took her car keys. They wrapped Stephanie up in a blanket and took her out to the car. Frank was driving he said man where are we going to take her? I don't know just find an abandoned building and dump her. You said my name in front of that other bitch, now were gonna have to kill her too. Look, her bank statement. She has over $15,000.00 in the bank and we're gonna get it all first.

They get rid of her body and make it back to Franks'. They started getting high again while Sheila was tied up. She was so scared. She had no idea what they were going to do to her. All kinds of things were running through her mind. The high had worn off and her senses were starting to come back. What started out as having fun turned into a nightmare.

The next day they still had her tied up. Joe took the sock out of her mouth and said if you scream bitch I'll kill you. I know you're thirsty so I'm gonna give you some water. Then you're gonna get dressed and go to the atm and get some money. And if you try anything funny I'm gonna put a bullet in your ass. By now the police had found Stephanie's body. They put it on the news that a female's body had been found in an abandoned building in Over The Rhine. No one had a clue that it was Stephanie, but they would soon find out.

At about nine o'clock, Stephanie's mom called Sheila's parents to ask for her number. She told them that Stephanie and Sheila left together and Stephanie wasn't answering her phone. She asked Sheila's mom if she had seen the news. Yes I did. You're talking about the girl's body that was found in the abandoned building. Yes and I am so worried, they have never done this before.

Sheila's mom gave her the number and then she tried to call Sheila herself. Sheila's phone just rang and rang and then it would go to voice mail. They tried for hours to reach the girls. Sheila's mom called her job and she wasn't there. She called George to see if he had heard from Sheila. Sheila's phone was blowing up by now.

Sheila's mom and dad were in a panic because this was so unlike Sheila. In the meantime Frank and Joe untied her and was taking her around to the ATMs withdrawing her money. They could only get five hundred a day out. They were determined to keep her until they got it all.

Sheila's mom and dad went and picked up Stephanie's mom and went to the police Station to file a missing persons report. The police said that it hadn't been twenty four hours yet so she had to wait until the morning. They asked could they see the girl that was in the morgue. After you file the report you can.

In the meantime, Frank and Joe were having big fun with Sheila. They were getting high and continuously raping her. They beat her and raped her and raped her and beat her. Then they got high some more and started over again. Their plan was to keep her for a couple more days and get all of her money,

By now everyone was looking for Sheila. They had dumped her car by now and set it on fire. The police found it and ran her tag. They traced it to Sheila's mom and dad's house. They showed up at the house. Everyone was at the house. George, his mom and dad, even Sheila's boss. He had been trying to call her because she didn't call in to work and that just wasn't like her. When he heard that no one could find her he became concerned.

Sheila's mom went to the door and she knew this couldn't be good. She feared the worst. She thought they were going to tell her that the girl they found was Sheila. When they told her they had found Sheila's car burned up she passed out. Her dad broke down in tears and said was my baby in it? No sir she wasn't. We are filing a missing persons report.

They went and got Stephanie's mom to take her to file the report. After she filed the report they let her go to the morgue to see if the girl they had found was one of the girls. Sheila's mom and dad feared that it could be Sheila. When they opened the drawer it was Stephanie. Stephanie's mom broke down right there. Sheila's mom and dad felt a little relieved, but where was their baby?

The next day came. Joe and Frank were out of their minds by now. They had been getting high for two days now. Frank said you know were gonna have to kill her. We can't let her go now that she knows our names. We have to get rid of her. We're gonna get some more money and fuck her some more first. Man, we can't take her out anywhere like this. Okay we'll just fuck her then.

By now Chuck had heard the news and seen the missing persons report and contacted the police. He told them that they had been in the bar Sunday night. He told them who they left with. They knew exactly where to go and find him.

It was around six o'clock Tuesday and they had just got finished raping her again. They were tired of her by now. Sheila started crying and calling on the name of the Lord. She said God if you are out there and you are who they say you are, I need you to come and save me right now Lord. I know I haven't been right but please father help me. She remembered she had heard when you pray, pray in the name of Jesus. She said Father in the name of Jesus please help.

Joe said Frank get the pillow and cover her face. Joe put the gun to the pillow.

Sheila said, " with her last thought Jesus please help me. Just then the police kicked the door in. They said drop it. Joe turned and they shot him dead. Down on your knees Frank! Frank threw up his hands and dropped to his knees saying don't shoot don't shoot. They ran over to Sheila and untied her. The one officer said we've got you. You're ok now we got you. She was holding on to the officer for dear life. She was shaking and crying thanking Jesus for saving her life.

They called the ambulance to come and get her and take her to the hospital. They called her parents and told them that they had her and was taking her to Christ Hospital. In the ambulance, all she could do is thank God all the way to the hospital. She knew that she could've been dead and if the police hadn't have got there when they did she would've been.

Her parents showed up at the hospital shortly after they had gotten Sheila there. They came into her room and she was unresponsive. They had her sedated by the time her mom and dad arrived. Her mom broke down and started crying. She was saying oh no look at my baby, look at my baby. Sheila had two black eyes, a busted lip, and her face was badly bruised from where they had beaten her. Her dad was trying to be strong but it was showing how bad he was hurting inside.

George and his parents got there a little while later. When George saw her he broke down beside her bed and started crying. His mom came over and rubbed his head saying baby she's going to be ok. Bishop Daniels hugged Sheila's mom and dad and instantly started praying. He told Sheila's mom and dad that she was going to be ok. I told her that God was trying to get her attention. As bad as this looks watch God get the glory. Sheila's dad said, man what the hell are you talking about? Look at my baby. Bishop said, Ron I know you're upset right now, but I promise everything's going to be alright. Just then a peace came over the room. Sheila opened her eyes and looked around the room. She said thank you Jesus and passed out again. Everyone in the room broke out in praise. They were all thanking and praising God. The nurses came into the room to see what all the noise was and the spirit fell on them too.

Chapter Eighteen

Redemption

Sheila came home from the hospital after about a week. She moved into her mom and dad's house because she was still kind of shaken. This ordeal really spooked her. Never in her wildest dreams could she imagine something like this happening. Then she remembered I did have a dream about this. This made her upset all over again.

Sheila's mom and dad wanted her to give up her apartment and move back in with them permanently.

Sheila said, " I'll be ok, I just don't want to be alone right now. Once I can get over this soreness and go back to work I'll be ok. I know God has me. He saved my life I know he'll protect me.

Ron asked, baby do you feel like talking about it? What happened? Okay dad I guess. Baby if you don't feel up to it you don't have to. Dad I can talk about it because truly God gets the glory. If it hadn't been for him hearing my cry I wouldn't be here right now.

This is what happened. Stephanie and I went out to get a couple drinks. I was sitting there talking to the bar tender and Stephanie got up to go to the jukebox. This guy came in that she knew and came and sat down with us, that was Frank. We sat and talked for a minute then we left with him to go over his house to party some more.

We got to his place and started getting high. We ran out of drugs and went to get some more. We got back to his place and started partying some more. She was thinking to herself, I can't tell them everything that we were doing; they wouldn't be able to handle it. She thought to herself, Lord give me strength.

Tears started coming to her eyes. Her mom said you can stop if you want to. No mom I'm good she said. As we were sitting there partying Joe came over. He was partying with us for a while and then it got crazy. That's when he raped me the first time. He pulled me by my hair and tried to make me suck his penis. Her mom and dad were cringing by now. He had pulled out a gun and said he would blow my brains out if I didn't. That's when Stephanie rushed him. He hit her in the head with the gun and she fell and hit her head on the table and died.

They tied me up and took her body to get rid of it. When they came back they took turns raping me until the sun came up. They took me to the atm to withdraw money out of my account. I heard my phone ringing but they wouldn't let me answer it. We got back to Frank's and they tied me up again and the raping started over.

They took me out again Tuesday morning before daylight. We came back and they tied me up again. They started beating me and slapping me. They busted my lip and blacked my eyes while they were raping me; it was so terrible she said as she started to cry.

I heard them talking about taking me out to get some more money. Frank told Joe that they couldn't take me out looking like I was looking. Joe said if we can't get any more money we might as well kill her. He said she knows our names so we can't let her go.

I started praying at that point. I didn't know what else to do. I begged them to let me go. They had me gagged so couldn't scream. I thought about everything that Georges father was saying and gave it a try. I started praying and praying. I didn't even know if I believed I just did it. They covered my face with a pillow. I felt them press the barrel of the gun to it. I saw my life flash before my eyes. My last thought was Jesus help me. The next thing I know I heard the door get kicked in and a gun shot. I thought I was shot at fist then I felt the pressure release off of the pillow. Then I heard them tell Frank to get down on his knees. They took the pillow off of my face and untied me, it was over. I know there is a God because he stepped in when I needed him most.

All of her disbelief was gone. Everything that George had been trying to tell her. Everything that George's dad had been telling had now come full circle. She was now ready to give it all up and live for Christ. But it would take much more than that for her to stay clean.

George called her later on that morning. Hey baby what's going on, how are you feeling? Hey George, I'm ok, a little sore though. That's understandable. Do you need anything; I'm coming over when I get off work. No I'm good but I really need to talk to you. Okay babe. You know I'm at mom and dads. No I didn't know that but I'm glad you are. Are you going to move back in there until we can get married? The phone got quiet. I'll talk to you later George. Okay babe, bye.

Her phone rang again. Hello. Hello Sheila, how are you? Hey Mr. Franklin, I'm ok. I am kind of sore but I'm getting better. How are you mentally Sheila? Fine I guess. Sheila I want you to take some time off work. This was a very traumatic experience and you need to take some time off. I don't know Mr. Franklin; I think I need something to keep my mind busy. Trust me your mind is going to busy enough. The sooner you deal with this the sooner you will get better. I want you to seriously get into recovery and start working a program, it will help you tremendously. Do you have a NA basic text? No I don't. That's the first thing you need. I will bring you one by this evening. Okay Mr. Franklin, thank you.

Later that day, George and his mom and dad came by. It's a good thing Josephine cooked a big meal because they were about to have a house full. They brought Sheila flowers, balloons, and cards. Everyone was wishing her well. She was so overjoyed she broke down in tears. She held onto George as tight as she could. They sat around laughing and talking like nothing had ever happened. No one wanted to bring it up but everyone had questions. In the midst of all of the laughs and smiles, they were all looking at her like what's really going on?

Josephine came out of the kitchen and said ok everyone let's eat. They all got up and went into the dining room and sat at the table.

Bishop will you do the honors and bless the food? Sure Ron I'd be glad to. Lord we come to you this day giving thanks for this gathering. We give thanks for you bringing our daughter back home to us safe and sound. Sheila and George looked up and smiled at each other when they heard that. Lord we thank you for this food we are about to receive and bless the hands that prepared it.

They were sitting there eating and the doorbell rang. Ron said I'll get it. He got up to go to the door. He could see a man's silhouette through the glass in the door. I wonder who this is he thought? He opened the door and said yes may I help you. Hi how are you? My name is Robert Franklin, I'm Sheila's supervisor. Oh come on in, thanks for coming by. Sheila your supervisor is here.

Sheila comes into the room. Hi Mr. Franklin. Hello Sheila, I'm not interrupting anything am I? No were just sitting down to dinner would you like some. No thank you, I was just stopping by to see how you were doing and bring you this book. Are you sure? We have plenty. Okay it smells so good. I am kind of hungry.

Sheila brings him in and introduces him to everyone. He says hello to everyone. Michael Daniels, what are you doing here? Hello Robert how have you been? I haven't seen you in a while. It has been a while. George is my son; he and Sheila are seeing each other. Oh Bishop, you and Mr. Franklin know each other Sheila said, "Yes we've served on a couple of boards together before. Oh I see. Well have a seat Mr. Franklin and dig in.

Bishop asked, Robert what brings you by? Sheila is one of my best employees and I had to come by and check on her. Thanks for coming by Josephine said. Mr. Franklin said I knew something was wrong when Sheila didn't call in for work. I asked the girls had they heard from her. Natalie told me that you had called looking for her. That's when I got really concerned. I started praying for you instantly and I see God answered my prayers. He answered everyone's prayers Bishop said.

It got quiet for a bit while everyone was eating. Mr. Franklin couldn't help but look at Sheila; she was looking kind of bad. It was going to take a while for those cuts and bruises to heel. Sheila noticed him looking at her and finally broke the silence.

So how are things at work Mr. Franklin? Work is work. You know we're coming into our busy season. I should be ready to come back in a couple weeks. No Sheila, I want you to take some time off to get yourself together. You may start to heel physically but the emotional scarring is going to take some work. Emotional scarring, what emotional scarring? You'll see. It just hasn't shown up yet. He's right honey, take your time. You can take as long as you want, we've got you.

Dinner was over and everyone was sitting around in the living room talking. Ron noticed the book that Mr. Franklin had brought in on the table. He picked it up and said; a basic text I haven't seen one of these in a while. Sheila asked, dad where would you have seen one of these? Sheila do you remember when I told you that I had a friend that's been clean for a while. Yes. Well that friend is me. No dad, get out. Yes it's true. That's why I was telling you about going to the meetings. I had to let you find your own way. It doesn't work when you try and force someone. I'm just sorry it had to come to this. Mr. Franklin said, I thought you looked familiar when I saw you but I couldn't place it, now I know.

You know that all sounds good Sheila said, ", but God has delivered me. Everyone looked at her and couldn't believe these words were coming out of her mouth. The Bishop said praise God. Sheila God has delivered you, but the meetings are a good place for you to learn more about yourself and spiritual principles. Don't they teach you that in church? Sheila there are people that have been in church all of their life and struggle with patience, tolerance, and acceptance, the most basic of the principals. Just try it; you may be surprised in what you'll learn.

Sheila said, " ok, I'll try it, but the way I feel right now, I never want to see another bar or drug again. It's more than just not getting high or drunk it's about helping someone else. What do I have to offer? That's what I'm saying. God will reveal that to you along the way.

It was getting late and everyone was leaving. Mr. Franklin said, you got a lot of good information tonight, you have a lot of support, I hope you take advantage of it. Thanks Mr. Franklin I will. Have a good night.

Sheila said, " George I need to talk to you for a minute. Okay babe, let me say goodbye to my mom and dad. Okay, I'll be right here.

Sheila was on such a spiritual high she wanted to just be honest about everything. She wanted to tell him about her and Stephanie, about the sex with other guys, the rape and everything. A voice inside her spoke to her and said that may not be such a good idea.

Sheila said, " to herself, no I'd better not do that right now.

George came back in the house after seeing his mom and dad off. What's up baby? He sat down on the couch beside Sheila and put his arms around her. George there is so much I want to tell you but I don't know where to start. Do you still love me George? Sheila are you kidding, of course I do. Even after you know I've been raped. Sheila that is something that someone took from you, it's not like you cheated on me with him. It's ok baby. I don't care what happened or what you did; I'm just glad you're home safe and not dead like Stephanie. When I went to that funeral I was so happy that it wasn't you laid out in that box. I know, I hate I had to miss it. It probably wouldn't have been a good idea for you to be there anyway. George, do you still want to marry me? Yes Sheila nothing has changed. I want to learn more about God. I want to go to church with you Wednesday night. Okay babe, are you sure, you may want to rest a little more. I'll be fine.

Sheila had this hunger inside of her to learn more about the Lord. She had only heard about the miracles he could perform, but when she witnessed them first hand, it put a different light on it. She had been rebellious to the idea of God before, but now she knows. Her life was all but over. She cried out to the Lord just in the nick of time and he showed up and answered her prayer.

George said, ok babe, we can go. Right now I'm going to go and let you get some rest. I'll be fine; do you have to leave right now? Yeah I have to get ready for work tomorrow. George you are always so responsible, I really need you in my life. You've got me babe, I'm not going anywhere. Sheila got up and walked him to the door. They hugged and they tried to kiss but the stitches in her lip were sore.

Sheila said, " I'll be glad when this crap heels. It will babe it's only been a week give it time.

Sheila sat and talked to her mom and dad for a bit before going to bed. She said dad why didn't you tell me that you were in recovery? Sheila it was just something that never came up. Then when I found out that you were having this problem I wanted to tell you but I'm not a good example for you. N/A teaches total abstinence from all drugs including alcohol and I drink occasionally. Well why haven't you relapsed? I have. I just don't do cocaine or smoke weed anymore and I'm ok with that. Sheila that doesn't work for everyone and it may not work for you. I suggest that you let it all go and see what happens for you. You have your whole life ahead of you and drugs will only stop you. Okay dad. Good night mom and dad. I love you. We love you too babe.

That was nice the way everyone showed up for Sheila Josephine said. Yeah George really loves that girl. His parents really care about her too. I can't believe her boss showed up. Yeah that was nice. Robert is like that though. I remember him from when I used to go to meetings. He is a real loving and caring guy. You know Josephine, this can either go real good for Sheila or it can go real bad. Yes I know Ron. Our baby has been traumatized and it hasn't really sank in yet. Josephine broke down crying and Ron put his arms around her to console her.

Sheila was upstairs getting ready for bed. She was in the bathroom looking in the mirror. She said to herself, man I am so ugly. I wonder if these scars are going to fully heal. How can George still love me looking like this? Sheila started crying and saying God please help me. Heal these scars that I have on my face. Help me to heal inside and out.

Sheila got in the bed. Her mind started racing thinking about her injuries, being raped, Stephanie being killed; she started crying all over again until she cried herself to sleep. This was not going to be a good night for Sheila. She is in a very bad space. Not knowing how these injuries are going to heal, how George is going to feel if they don't. She is going to bed with too much on her mind. She hasn't learned how to turn it over to Jesus just yet but she will.

Over in the night the dreams start coming, one after another. She kept seeing visions of her being raped and beaten. She saw Stephanie getting hit in the head and the pool of blood after she hit her head on the table. She heard Frank and Joe's voice saying that they were going to have to kill her. In her dream she was struggling trying to break free. She was trying to scream but no sound would come out in her dream. Then the pillow went over her face and she felt the barrel of the gun through the pillow. By now she was kicking and screaming. Her mom and dad jumped up out of bed and ran into her room and woke her up. Sheila was crying and screaming hysterically. Ron said baby, baby, its ok, you're home, you're home as a tear dropped from his eye. They got in the bed with her and held her until she went back to sleep.

There would be many more nights like this. This thing that happened to her is something that no one would ever imagine happening to them. Something like this can scar you for life. Let's see how she finally makes it through.

Wednesday came and Sheila was up moving around when her Phone rang. Hello. Hey girl what's happening? Who is this? This is Flip. Hey Flip how are you? I'm good. The question is how are you? Not too good right now. I can imagine. I saw you on the news, man that's fucked up. Excuse me Sheila said, ". Flip said that was fucked up what happened to you and your girl. Flip we're not going to be able to talk anymore. I just wanted to let you know that I got some good stuff in and I got you. No Flip Jesus has got me and I'm going to pray for you. Bye now and she hung up. Flip looked at his phone in disbelief.

He said yeah right she'll be back or so he thought. Sheila had already erased those numbers from her phone.

A few minutes later it rang again. Now who is this? She looked at her phone and it was an out of state number. Hello. Hey girl what's up? Tonya? Yep, yep, what's going on girl? Hey, I haven't heard from you in months. What's wrong with your fingers? I tried to call you but your number was disconnected. You know what, that's right I didn't call you and give you my new number, my bad. What are you into now Tonya? Girl I'm into Jesus. I had to get rid of all my old numbers and change mine also. Maybe that's what I should do also. I'm going to church to-night and I'm giving my life to the Lord also. Praise God. Girl when you do that be ready for a fight because the devil is going to come at you even harder.

Have you talked to any of the other girls? Not much. I guess ev-eryone is off doing their own thing. I've talked to Sharon and Lisa once I think since we graduated. Yeah me too. I think they both went back to school. You know they were on that doctor thing. I may go back to school later but not right now.

What's up with you Sheila? You say you're going to give your life to the Lord tonight, did something happen? Did something happen, girl you don't even want to know. Tell me Sheila. Girl I got held hos-tage, beaten, and raped. No Sheila. Yes, and my girl got killed. They were going to kill me too but God stepped in and saved my life. Praise God Sheila. I knew something was wrong, I could feel you in my spirit. Well how are you? I'll be ok. Do you need me to come and stay with you for a while? No, I'm at mom and dads. Okay Sheila if you need me just call me and I'll be there. Let me pray with you before we get off of the phone. They prayed together and got off the phone.

A peace came over Sheila that she had never felt before. She said to herself. Wow this feels better than any high I've ever had. I want more of this. Sheila went to her room and got on her knees and started praying. She said Lord this is new to me and I don't know what to say, but thank you Lord for saving my life. I don't know why you did it but I'm glad you did. Her mom and dad heard her praying and came and kneeled down beside her and started praying with her.

That evening came and George came to pick Sheila up. She was kind of ashamed about the way she looked, but she was going on anyway. As she was trying to hide her scars from George he reassured her that he loved her and her scars didn't matter. Her mom and dad were standing in the living room to see this display of affection. They hugged each other. Ron said Josephine, I believe everything is going to be alright. They saw how she wasn't ashamed to praise God with all of her visible scars so why should they be ashamed to praise him with the scars no one can see.

Bishop Daniels came up to preach and looked right at her and smiled. This really warmed her heart. He preached about Job and how he had lost everything and still praised God. He talked about how God told Satan that he could do what he wished with him but he couldn't kill him. He said God has some of you in his hands just like Job. If you've been through something and you wonder why he spared your life. You know you haven't done everything right and he loved you and saved you anyway. That's because he has a job for you to do. You may be saying to yourself, who me? Yes you. That's who God uses, that broken vessel. Won't you come and let him put you back together? The doors of the church are opened. Sheila jumped up and ran to the alter. She ran into Bishop's arms and started crying. Her mom and dad came down too. They gave their lives to the Lord also.

God took this bad situation and made it turn out for the good. He used Sheila with all the mess she had been through to lead her parents to Christ. She found out that it didn't matter how you looked, where you've been, or what you have, God can use you. When he has something for you to do, he will do what it takes to get your attention.

Sheila went on to do great things in the church. Her physical scars had healed, but it would take some time for the emotional scarring. She became a Sunday school teacher. She started an outreach program for women. She got a promotion on her job. Mr. Franklin retired and she took his place. She and George finally got married. She was finally starting to find her place in the sun. What she thought was success was merely a flash in the pan compared to where she was now.

When you give your life to the Lord, all things are possible. It doesn't matter what you've done or where you've been. It doesn't matter how bad you think you were, God can still use you. God can take someone that we think is completely worthless and make them his most valuable asset. We have to be broken before he can fix us. Wherever you are in your life I pray that you are saved and if you're not may you accept Christ as your savior right now. Don't think that just because you do, everything is going to be rosy; in most cases that's when the fight begins. Look for the sequel.